MW00814502
Mystery Muffin
&
Soda Pop Slooth:
The Legend of Mr. Creepy

Mystery Muffin & Soda Pop Slooth:

The Legend of Mr. Creepy

Chad A. Webster

Mystery Muffin & Soda Pop Slooth: The Legend of Mr. Creepy

Published by IngramElliott, Inc.
www.ingramelliott.com
9815 J Sam Furr Road, Suite 271, Huntersville NC 28078

This is a work of fiction. The names, characters, places, or events used in this book are the product of the author's imagination or used fictitiously. Any resemblance to actual people, alive or deceased, events or locales is completely coincidental.

Book design by Maureen Cutajar
Cover design by Jeanine Henning
Illustrations by Jaime Buckley and Hadleigh Charles

Publisher's Cataloging-In-Publication Data
(Prepared by The Donohue Group, Inc.)

Names: Webster, Chad A. | Charles, Hadleigh, illustrator.
Title: Mystery Muffin & Soda Pop Slooth. The legend of Mr. Creepy / Chad A. Webster ; [map by Hadleigh Charles].
Other Titles: Mystery Muffin and Soda Pop Slooth. The legend of Mr. Creepy | Legend of Mr. Creepy
Description: First edition, First international edition. | Huntersville, NC : IngramElliott, Inc., [2017] | Summary: "Whispering Hollow is a charming small town just outside of Charlotte, NC. Things take a creepy turn when a new neighbor moves into the town a few houses down from Mystery Muffin and her best friend, Soda Pop Slooth. It seems that a pack of wolves has also moved into the area. Rumors fly and the town comes to believe that the creepy old man may actually be a werewolf. Is the Legend of Mr. Creepy really true?"--Provided by publisher.
Identifiers: LCCN 2017935534 | ISBN 978-0-9981659-2-9 (hardback) | ISBN 0-9981659-2-1 (hardback) | ISBN 978-0-9981659-1-2 (paperback) | ISBN 0-9981659-1-3 (paperback) | ISBN 978-0-9981659-3-6 (ebook) | ISBN 0-9981659-3-X (ebook)
Subjects: LCSH: Werewolves--Juvenile fiction. | Neighbors--Juvenile fiction. | Child detectives--Juvenile fiction. | CYAC: Werewolves--Fiction. | Neighbors--Fiction. | Detectives--Fiction. | LCGFT: Detective and mystery fiction.
Classification: LCC PZ7.1.W43 Myl 2017 (print) | LCC PZ7.1.W43 (ebook) | DDC [Fic]--dc23

Published in the United States of America. Printed in the United States of America
First Edition: 2017, First International Edition: 2017

Acknowledgements

First of all, I need to acknowledge and thank my amazing wife. Her unwavering support and belief in me has been priceless. She's made me a better person, saw things in me that I didn't and always encouraged me to write and to finish this book. Her approval is everything to me – in my life and my writing.

I'd also like to thank my friends and co-workers: "The Great" Craig Vollman and Jason Peetz. From proofreading to grammar to story concepts, they were able to set aside my feelings and shoot it straight in a constructive manner. Craig went through a draft like a college professor and editor. Jason read one of my first drafts to his children. When he told me they wanted to read it nightly and wanted more, my heart melted and inspired me to finish.

Thank you to my editors, Lorelei, William and Andrea. Your input was invaluable.

I also want to acknowledge all those who have believed in me even when I kept my writing to myself.

Last but not least, thank you to IngramElliott for taking a chance on a first-time author stumbling through life disguised as a cop.

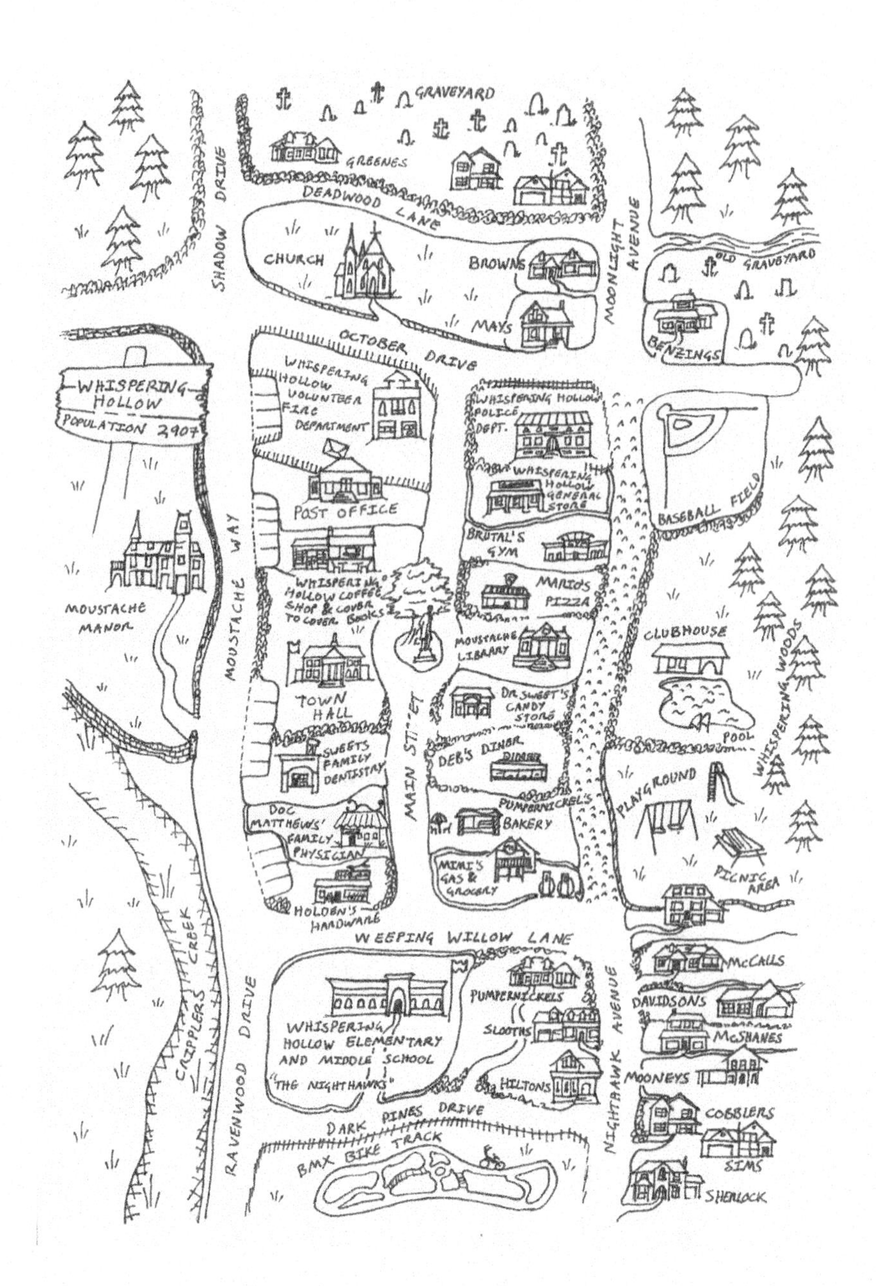

GRAVEYARD
GREENES
DEADWOOD LANE
SHADOW DRIVE
CHURCH
BROWNS
MAYS
MOONLIGHT AVENUE
OLD GRAVEYARD
BENZINGS
OCTOBER DRIVE
WHISPERING HOLLOW
POPULATION 2907
WHISPERING HOLLOW VOLUNTEER FIRE DEPARTMENT
WHISPERING HOLLOW POLICE DEPT.
POST OFFICE
WHISPERING HOLLOW GENERAL STORE
BASEBALL FIELD
BRUTAL'S GYM
MARIO'S PIZZA
WHISPERING HOLLOW COFFEE SHOP & COVER TO COVER BOOKS
MOUSTACHE MANOR
MOUSTACHE WAY
MOUSTACHE LIBRARY
CLUBHOUSE
TOWN HALL
DR. SWEET'S CANDY STORE
WHISPERING WOODS
POOL
MAIN STREET
SWEETS FAMILY DENTISTRY
DEB'S DINER
DINER
PLAYGROUND
DOC MATTHEWS' FAMILY PHYSICIAN
PUMPERNICKEL'S BAKERY
MIMI'S GAS & GROCERY
PICNIC AREA
HOLDEN'S HARDWARE
WEEPING WILLOW LANE
McCALLS
PUMPERNICKELS
DAVIDSONS
SLOOTHS
McSHANES
WHISPERING HOLLOW ELEMENTARY AND MIDDLE SCHOOL
"THE NIGHTHAWKS"
MOONEYS
HILTONS
CRIPPLERS CREEK
RAVENWOOD DRIVE
NIGHTHAWK AVENUE
DARK PINES DRIVE
COBBLERS
BMX BIKE TRACK
SIMS
SHERLOCK

1

She didn't think her heart could take it much longer. It was nearly pounding out of her chest with excitement. Even though the day was only half over, it felt like it had been a full day already. She stared out the window and dreamed of summer vacation as the bus slowed to a stop. It was the *last* stop—the last bus ride of the school year! The fifth grade was behind her. There were a few other kids on the bus talking and yelling, but she couldn't hear them. It was like she was alone, enjoying this precious moment. Some kids rode their bikes home or got picked up at school, but she wouldn't have it any other way. She loved the bus ride. It wasn't very long, hardly even worth it for the kids who lived in this side of the neighborhood, but there was just something about the last bus ride of the year. Of course, she loved school, but this was her favorite part of the year. Well, summer vacation and Christmas is a tie.

The bus chugged up the hill and turned onto her street, and she was already standing in the aisle next to the bus driver. Ms. Sweeney leaned forward and pulled the lever to open the bus doors. It seemed to take forever as she waited. She looked back to see if Soda Pop had gotten out of his seat and saw he was right behind her, sharing in this excitement!

"Have a good summer, Mystery! You too, Soda!" Ms. Sweeney said with a caring smile.

"Thank you, Ms. Sweeney," Mystery replied as she tied her long, light brown hair into a ponytail. "I will! You too!"

"Thanks!" Soda exclaimed.

Mystery stepped down to the edge of the bus. She looked down at her favorite sneakers that had gone from gleaming white to a dirty, worn off-white. She paused a moment before she got off the bus and took in the feeling with a big sigh. Her smile somehow managed to grow farther across her face, and her hazel eyes widened as her feet hit the hot road. School was over. It was summertime! Mystery could think of no greater freedom than summer vacation. The possibilities were already rolling through her head.

A few other kids spilled off the bus and onto Nighthawk Avenue as the sun beamed down happiness from the Whispering Hollow, North Carolina, blue sky. The full moon softly glowed, too, as if to express its significance during the day as well as the night. A few birds, happy and free, flew around overhead, watching the scene unfold. Giggling and hollering echoed as a few parents stepped out onto their porches and watched their excited children run safely home. One of Mystery's neighbors, Mr. Davidson, was on his riding mower in his front yard, steering with one hand and sipping on what was surely a cup of sweet tea with the other. He was likely getting the yard ready for the barbeque tomorrow. The smell of freshly cut grass filled the air. Mystery loved that smell and breathed it in. She waved at him, and he tipped his favorite hat at her with a smile behind his gray mustache and beard.

Mystery Muffin walked with her pink, sparkling unicorn backpack slung over her shoulder, happy as could be as Soda Pop walked up next to her. He was a little shorter than Mystery, a little less outgoing, but he was Mystery's best friend. Soda shrugged his backpack off his shoulder and set it on the ground. Mystery paused with him, just like she always did as soon as they got off the bus. Soda unzipped the backpack and dug out his well-worn—but not worn-out—Atlanta Braves baseball cap. He carefully and proudly positioned it on his head until he had it just right; then he slung his backpack back on.

"I can't wait for another exciting summer of fun and adventure, can you, Mystery?"

"It's going to be a great one, Soda. I just know it."

"For sure!"

Mystery Muffin wasn't her *real* name. Not that that mattered, since no one called her by her real name. Her nickname was appropriately given to her by the neighborhood kids who always came to her to solve a mystery of some kind. Muffin was what her father called her—she was his "little muffin." It had been a little embarrassing at first, but it grew on her and she had come to love it. Her friends, neighbors, family, and even the teachers at Whispering Hollow Elementary and Middle School all used her nickname. Both nicknames stuck, and thus Megan Mooney became Mystery Muffin.

Mystery looked down the road and saw her dad's police car was backed into their driveway.

"Yay! My dad was supposed to work today. I bet he took the day off so he could be here when I got home from the last day of school! Soda, are you going to come over and play later?"

"I hope so. We'll see what my mom says. But you know me. I'll convince her!"

Soda Pop walked farther down the road as Mystery picked up the pace. She couldn't wait to see her dad. A few houses down from her house, toward the dead end, Mystery saw a moving truck backed into the driveway. This seemed weird; the For Sale sign was still in the front yard. *Whoever bought it must have* just *bought it*, Mystery thought. She hoped it was a family with some kids her and Soda's age. Could they be that lucky? There were a few moving men in green uniforms walking back and forth from the truck to the house and back again, carrying boxes, furniture, appliances, and other household things. None of the stuff they were moving seemed to belong to children, but it was hard to tell from that far away; plus, they couldn't see inside the boxes.

There was one person who wasn't wearing the green uniform. He looked tall, old, and skinny. He was wearing a black top hat, a black suit with a white shirt, and shiny black shoes. Mystery caught herself staring at the man. As she stared longer, he removed his hat, and his nearly bald head slowly turned toward her, causing her pace to slow a little. Despite not being that close, she felt his eyes lock on to her stare and she stumbled. She regained her balance, and then froze on the side of the road.

"Mys, are you okay?"

She searched for her voice but couldn't find it. She just pointed at the man, with her hand down at her side by her hip, hoping not to make it obvious. Soda Pop felt an ice-cold chill walk up his spine, and he stopped in his tracks, too.

A creepy, clown-like smile stretched across the man's wrinkled face as he looked at the children. Goosebumps crawled over Mystery's skin like a thousand spiders.

The few puffy clouds in the sky drifted over the sun. The shade moved past the dead end and up the street over Mystery and Soda

Pop. It brought an odd, wintry breeze. Mystery and Soda Pop shivered as they subconsciously moved shoulder to shoulder.

Their friend Darren Pumpernickel, who got off the bus right behind them, also saw the creepy man and walked up behind them.

"That's the guy! That's the guy my dad was talking about, Soda!" Darren said, smacking Soda on the back; Soda hated that. "I've heard things about that guy—creepy things. You two should check him out. I hope he doesn't terrorize our neighborhood. See you later." Darren turned and ran home, leaving Mystery and Soda a little puzzled.

"Wonder what he meant by that?" Mystery asked as Darren slammed his front door.

"Who knows? You know how he is. He always thinks crazy things. But I don't like the sound of 'terrorize our neighborhood' very much."

"Well, it's going to be a *great* summer, Soda," Mystery said. "Just off the bus and we already have a mystery to solve."

"Yep, we need to find out who this Mr. Creepy is, what Darren's dad is talking about, and how he'd terrorize the neighborhood."

"Mystery and Soda are on the case!" Mystery exclaimed.

Mr. Creepy put his hat back on, and then suddenly turned and stomped to his house. He walked up the steps to the front door as Mystery and Soda gazed at him.

"Dang kids!" Mr. Creepy yelled.

He went inside the Johnsons' old house, his new home, in his new neighborhood, and slammed the door.

2

Mystery sprinted up to her house—the White House, as she called it. It was bright white with black shutters and columns on the front porch, kind of like the president's house in Washington, DC. When she busted in, her dad was waiting for her with outstretched arms inside the front door. He must have just gotten home because he was still wearing his police uniform. She untied her ponytail, shook out her hair, and flew into his arms. He picked her up and spun her around.

"I am so proud of you this year, Mystery! Straight As again!" he exclaimed, wondering how she had gotten so big.

Mystery's face turned rosy red with pride and happiness.

"Thanks, Daddy! I'm so glad you were here when I got home!"

Her dad put her down, and Mystery stepped back so she could look up at him.

"Well, I left work early so I could be here."

Mystery hugged him again.

Mystery ran down the hallway and into the kitchen, where she found her mom and Soda's mom, Mrs. Slooth, making Rice Krispies treats. Mystery was concerned that Soda was going home and his mom wasn't there.

"Are those for us?" she asked her mom.

"Of course they are, sweetie! We even put mini M&M's in there! Now go get—"

Mystery bolted out the front door and dashed down her driveway. Soda was sitting on his front porch with his head hung low. He looked about as blue-gray as his house. Mystery yelled to him, and his head snapped up.

"My mom's not home and she left the door locked. I already checked the back door. It's locked and the spare key wasn't there," Soda explained in a disappointed voice. "Plus, I need to let Sheena out to go to the bathroom."

Mystery could see Sheena in the skinny window by the front door. She was on her hind legs and pawing at the glass. Mystery swore she was smiling. Each of her excited breaths fogged up the window in front of her snout.

"Soda, your mom is over here at my house! Now, get over here! They're making us Rice Krispies treats . . . with mini M&M's!"

Soda's face lit up with excitement as he ran across the street and met Mystery halfway up her driveway. He was very relieved that he didn't have to wait for his mom to get home.

Soda had never known his dad, who had died when Soda was only two years old. There were a few vague memories floating around in Soda's head but nothing that left a solid impression. Or maybe he'd just imagined things about his dad, and they had become memories. Luckily, he had met Mystery and her dad. Soda looked up to Mr. Mooney, or Officer Mooney as a lot of people called him. Mr. Mooney was very happy to be a father figure to

Soda Pop. Soda was a happy-go-lucky kid and didn't mind at all that his best friend was a girl. He got picked on sometimes, especially at school, but he didn't get angry or yell back; it just rolled off him. He knew that's how Officer Mooney would deal with it.

Soda Pop had gotten his nickname from his father. All he ever wanted to drink was soda. No juice, no water, no Kool-Aid—nothing. While his mother was sort of ashamed that she let her son drink soda pop so much, she knew it made him happy. When he was two years old, she had set down her cup of Sprite, and he grabbed it and put it to his mouth. His father watched and let it happen. It started as a sip, but it ended with huge gulps. When she got back from the bathroom, it was completely gone. She had looked at Soda's dad, wondering why he hadn't stopped him; he had smiled and shrugged his shoulders.

"He's a soda monster. What a great nickname for him!" his dad had exclaimed.

Good ol' Soda Pop. In honor of her husband, Mrs. Slooth continued calling her son by his nickname. On his first day of school at Whispering Hollow, his teacher, Miss Madsen, had called all the students' names.

"Scott Slooth?"

"Here!" Soda waved his hand at Miss Madsen. "My name is Scott, but everyone calls me 'Soda' or 'Soda Pop.' Soda Pop Slooth."

And so it was, wherever he went.

Before running into the house, Mystery and Soda both paused a minute to look back at the dead end at the last house. The movers and the moving truck were gone. All that was left was an old car that was parked on the road in front of the house. It was long and all black, no chrome or anything. The shiny tires, the wheels, and even the windows were black—they were so black you couldn't see inside. Mystery thought the car had to be fifty years old. It was nothing like what people drove these days.

"What a creepy car," Mystery said.

"For sure. A creepy car for a creepy guy," Soda added. "I can't believe that guy moved into the Johnsons' old house. It's bad enough that Ronnie and Brandon are gone, but this makes it even worse."

Ronnie and Brandon Johnson were Mystery and Soda's good friends. Ronnie was in their grade while Brandon was a year behind them. Mr. Johnson had gotten a job transfer, and they had moved to New York a month before school ended. They hadn't really known how long the Johnsons would stay since they had moved five times in the last six years, but that hadn't stopped their friendships from blossoming. Ronnie and Brandon were Soda's sleepover buddies, and he wished they'd had one more night before they moved away. Soda felt a wave of sorrow wash over him, but he managed to shake it off.

The sun peeked back out from behind the clouds and pushed them aside with invisible arms.

Mystery wanted to get a closer look at that car. She waved Soda in that direction.

"Come on. Let's check it out."

"Mys, are you sure?" Soda asked with the utmost dread.

"Of course I am! Now, come on."

Despite his grumbling stomach, Soda slowly followed his best friend. He stopped for a moment to look back at Mystery's house and thought about those Rice Krispies treats. He could almost taste them, but they would have to wait. Summer adventure didn't happen at the kitchen table; it happened outside.

The two nonchalantly strolled up the street until they were at the second-to-last house on the block—Ms. Sims's house. Her car wasn't in the driveway, so they knew she wasn't home. It was always in the driveway; she had too much old junk inside her garage to fit her car in it. Well, *she* didn't think it was junk. In all reality, there could be some priceless antique or something hidden away in there.

They zipped up to the front of Ms. Sims's house and leaned against it like they were spies in hostile territory. They crept lower and slower, eventually stopping at the corner. Mystery just wanted a closer look at the car. No big deal. She peered around, all hunched over, trying to stay hidden. Mr. Creepy was nowhere to be seen; the coast was clear! Mystery looked back at Soda and gave him a thumbs-up; then she grabbed his hand and prepared to go. Just as she went to take her first step, an orange cat jumped around the corner of the house in front of them with what it surely thought was a tiger's roar. They both nearly yelped out loud.

"Ms. Sims and her cats! Jeez!" Mystery whispered as she caught her breath.

Mystery looked back at Soda. He put his eyes back in his head and took his hand away from his mouth, which was now in a smile. She smiled back.

Mystery snuck through the yard and up against Mr. Creepy's new house. The backyard had a privacy fence, and the gate was on the other side of the front door. There were two garage doors, both closed. They were about a foot back from the front of the house, and Mystery stood at the corner. Soda slid in right behind her. They were perfectly quiet and perfectly still. Mystery slowly and cautiously turned her head to get a better look at the front door. Both the glass storm door and the front door were closed. She mouthed *Come on* to Soda.

They ran down the driveway and out to the far side of the car, so as not to be seen if Mr. Creepy looked out front. They crouched down low with their backs against the driver's door. As Mystery slowly rose, she paused for a moment with her eyes to the sky. Now the full moon was shining almost as brightly in the Carolina blue sky as it would later that night. She nudged Soda and pointed up at it. He looked up and was also surprised at the moon's brightness—it sort of creeped him out for a moment and he wasn't sure why. Mystery pulled her eyes away from the moon and tried to look inside the old car. Yep, she was right. She couldn't see through the windows at all. It looked like they had been spray-painted black. She had heard her dad talk about how it was illegal to have really dark windows. She just might have to mention this to him, she thought, as she ducked back down and turned to face Soda.

"Mystery, let's go. We got a closer look. Now let's go eat some Rice Krispies treats, for crying out loud," Soda whispered.

Soda thought of the mini M&M's slightly melted in the treats, and his stomach rumbled some more. He knew they had to check this out, though. Once Mystery got started on something, there was *no* stopping her.

"Okay, okay. Let me just get a look at the license plate to see if it's North Carolina or from out of state."

Mystery slowly stepped to the rear of the car and memorized the license plate. She turned her head to check the front door again. It was still closed. Wait a minute, the storm door was closed, but the front door was wide open and there was a dark figure standing low to the ground. She spun back around behind the old car as fast as she could, but it was too late. She had been seen!

"Uh, oh," Mystery said to Soda with a look of serious concern in her eyes. Soda shook his head at her and wanted to say *I told you so* but didn't. His mom absolutely hated it when he said that.

They both waited for the door to open and Mr. Creepy to yell at them to get away from his creepy old car. Instead, they heard a long, deafening, creepy howl. It seemed to go on for half a minute or so. Ferocious barking followed, probably flinging foamy drool all over the glass storm door.

"Run!" Mystery screamed as they sprinted off to her house.

3

Mystery and Soda ran as fast as their legs would go! They didn't dare look back. The thought of what they might see was too much to risk. Up the street and into Mystery's driveway they flew. They stopped in front of her garage and crouched down behind her dad's police car to catch their breath. Soda slowly rose enough to look through the windows. He peered down the road, across the yards, and back again. Mystery leaned around the front bumper of her dad's police car and scanned the road toward Mr. Creepy's house. Neither of them saw anything. No one and nothing was after them.

"What *was* that?" Soda asked between breaths.

"It sounded like a dog—a mean, awful, horrible dog . . . or maybe a wolf?"

"A *wolf*?! You think Mr. Creepy has a pet wolf?"

"I don't know. It's just more of a howl than I've ever heard a dog make. Well, I've heard a beagle howl, but it didn't sound like that!"

"Did it come from inside the house?"

Mystery paused. "I think so. I mean, it sounded like it. I saw something in the doorway, but I couldn't tell what it was. It was just sort of a dark figure."

Soda gasped. "*A dark figure*?! What the heck do you mean?"

"I don't know. Kind of like a shadow, I guess."

"Like the shadow of Mr. Creepy standing in the doorway?"

"Not really. It seemed smaller . . . or shorter."

Soda tried to calm down for a moment and think rationally. His breathing was almost back to normal. The howl had been loud but didn't sound muffled enough to have come from inside. *Did it?*

"Come on," Mystery said calmly. "Let's go inside and get those Rice Krispies treats. And, of course, we don't mention this."

"For sure," Soda agreed.

They walked inside and into the kitchen where their parents were talking.

"Mom, you locked me out!" Soda said to her, making a fake pouty face.

"I'm sorry, Soda! I figured you'd come straight here," his mom explained as she hugged him.

He couldn't argue with that logic.

"Did you let Sheena out?" he asked.

"As soon as I got home."

"Okay, good. Thanks, Mom!"

"You're welcome, sweetie. Maybe you and Mystery can give her a walk later?"

"For sure!"

Mrs. Slooth—Sarah—wasn't much taller than Mystery, but she seemed much bigger when she was angry, which wasn't very often. She had big blue eyes and long blond hair, almost down to the middle of her back. Mystery thought she was a very pretty lady. She often wondered why Mrs. Slooth never got remarried.

"Well, it looks like we have a new neighbor. I didn't get a good look at the guy, though," Mrs. Slooth said and turned her attention back to Mystery's parents.

"It looked like it was just the one man. I didn't see anyone else. Unless they're coming later," Mrs. Mooney said.

"I caught a glimpse of him," Mr. Mooney said. "He seemed a little creepy to me."

Mystery and Soda looked at each other, wide-eyed. They both smirked.

"I think he has a dog," Soda said.

The three parents turned to Soda. Mystery looked at him in betrayed amazement. She said they *weren't* going to say anything. She didn't want to explain before they got a real chance to investigate.

"Oh, yeah?" Soda's mom asked as she was cutting up the pan of Rice Krispies treats into small squares.

"Yeah, Mys and I heard it barking earlier."

Mystery's jaw dropped and she glared at Soda. He shrugged his shoulders at her. He was just making conversation and didn't go into the details of them sneaking up to check it out, so he had kept the promise, technically.

"Speaking of dogs, did you see the Hiltons got a new dog?" Mr. Mooney said. "I saw it earlier. Big ol' German shepherd—beautiful dog. I think Jeff said she's a retired police dog."

Soda and Mystery looked at each other again. Could that have been what they heard—the Hiltons' dog barking from inside their big brown privacy fence?

"Police dog, huh? Well, then, y'all should get along," Mrs. Mooney said as she smiled at her husband.

"We should? Oh, you mean because he's former police?" When he said "police," it sounded like *PO-leese.*

"Actually, I meant since you're both dogs!"

Everyone laughed as Mrs. Mooney finished cutting up the treats and put them onto a serving plate on the counter. Mystery's dad grabbed one, and then two, then three, and then her mom playfully smacked his hand.

"I think that's enough, mister!" she said as she grabbed the plate and turned to the kids. Mystery and Soda grabbed two treats each and sat down at the kitchen table. The parents continued talking about boring "grown-up stuff."

"We need to see if he has a dog or not," Mystery said quietly without whispering. Her parents hated whispering.

"If you say so, Mys. Either he has one and it caught us snooping around or he doesn't and it was the Hiltons' dog barking at us. I don't see the big deal either way."

"Big deal? I didn't say it was a big deal. I just want to know! Remember what Darren said?"

"Okay, okay. We'll get to the bottom of it. Jeez!" Soda said as he took out a huge bite of Rice Krispies treat. His mouth was so full he could barely chew it right.

"You pig!"

Soda smiled at Mystery with marshmallow, mini M&M's, and Rice Krispies in his teeth. She smiled back and rolled her eyes. Then her face slowly got serious again.

"Besides"—Mystery leaned in close to Soda and looked around to make sure none of the parents were listening—"I want to know *what* that dark figure was . . ."

4

The parents joined the kids at the table, and they all enjoyed their treats. There were a few moments of silence as they all smiled at each other with mouths full of marshmallow goodness.

"So, you're okay to watch Soda tomorrow, Melissa? I wasn't planning to work on the first day of summer vacation, but Taylor called me from the coffee shop yesterday, asking if I could cover a few hours for Kelly. I told her I could and arranged for Rebecca to come over, but she had a family obligation she had forgotten about."

"Of course! I'm sure the kids will have a blast together!"

Soda and Mystery both cheered and pounded their fists on the table in excitement.

"Well, as long as you're sure. I wasn't planning on Rebecca canceling on me," Soda's mom explained.

"I know that. And as Rebecca gets older she's going to have more and more going on and might not be able to babysit as much. Plus, I think she's about to get her license. We love having Soda around, you know that," Mystery's mom said with a smile.

"Yeah, he's practically one of the family!" Mystery's dad said as he removed Soda's Braves hat just long enough to mess up his bushy dirty-blond hair. Mr. Mooney knew Soda's dad had given him that hat and knew how much Soda treasured it.

Soda blushed and smiled with embarrassment. Mystery pointed and laughed at him. It didn't bother him at all. He was very proud that Mr. Mooney had said that. After all, Mr. Mooney was the closest thing he had to a father.

"Besides, Mystery loves Soda being here! Don't you?" her dad said as he messed up her hair, too.

"*Daaaaad*!" Mystery's face turned red.

Now it was Soda's turn to point and laugh. This didn't bother Mystery either. Instead, she saw this as a perfect moment to ask her question.

"Well, since Soda will be staying here tomorrow, do you think we could both sleep out in the tree house tonight? I mean, it would be easier for everyone, ya know?" Mystery asked as she turned to look her father in the eyes.

The three parents looked at each other.

"I don't know, Mystery," Soda's mom started. "It's already a lot for me to ask—"

"Nonsense!" Mr. Mooney boomed. "It'll be a sleepover in the tree house!"

"*Yaaaay*!" yelled Soda and Mystery together as they darted out the back door toward the tree house.

"He just can't tell her no," Mystery's mom said to Mrs. Slooth.

"Oh, come on! I can so! I just . . . I just . . . oh, be quiet!" Mr. Mooney stuttered.

"See what I mean, Sarah? He's like putty in her hands."

A few minutes later, Mystery and Soda ran back into the house, yelling that they needed some things for the night. The parents had no idea what they were up to, and that's the way it had to be. Sometimes parents just didn't understand.

"Dad, can I borrow your binoculars, pretty please with a cherry on top?"

Mrs. Mooney looked at her husband and waited for him to say yes. He felt the look, but it didn't matter.

"Of course you can, sweetheart. Just don't break them. They're in the trunk of my police car, in the green bag."

"Thanks, Daddy! You're the best!" Mystery said as she ran to the front door, kissing her father's cheek on the way. She grabbed the keys off the little hook by the front closet.

He couldn't help but smile.

Soda ran with Mystery after he got the house key from his mom so he could get his things.

"Gee, Matthew, what do you think she needs binoculars for?" Mystery's mom hardly ever called her dad "Matthew." Mystery thought the only time her mother did was when he was in trouble or being silly.

"I'm sure it'll be fine. Besides, if she told us, we probably just wouldn't understand."

Mystery unlocked the police car's trunk, finding the green bag and the binocular case inside. She opened the case.

"Uh, oh."

"What?" Soda asked.

"They're not in here." She paused to think for a moment. "I must have left them in the tree house the last time we borrowed them."

"You're lucky your dad didn't come out to get them. Then we'd *never* get to use them again!"

"Or if he needed them at work and they weren't there! Yikes! I'll remember this time!"

Mystery slammed the trunk shut, and the two friends prepared to run across the street to the Slooths' house. Before they did, they stopped, looked, and listened. There was no one in the street, and there was no howling or barking. The coast was clear . . . for now.

5

Soda quickly unlocked his front door and was immediately jumped on by his four-legged best friend. Sheena licked his face and pushed him down onto the ground, knocking his hat off and continuing to kiss him. She wasn't a big dog, but she was strong and didn't know her own strength when she was excited. After all, she was a mutt: part German shepherd and part miniature sheltie. She had the coloring of the sheltie, but her face more resembled the German shepherd.

"Okay, okay, girl! I missed you, too! Jeez!" Soda laughed.

Mystery pointed and laughed at the two friends. Then Sheena crawled off Soda and jumped on her! She also fell down and was showered with loving doggie kisses.

"That's what you get!" Soda yelled, putting his hat back on.

They ran upstairs to his bedroom with Sheena close behind. Soda had Lego bricks all over the place—not messy or strewn about, but very organized; some were put together by directions while others were built from his own imagination. There were shelves on the wall with Lego dinosaurs and spaceships and police and fire stations, Lego monster trucks, and Lego race cars. Yep, Soda loved Legos. They were his mom's "go-to" present for him. He was never disappointed when he got some new ones. Soda's other prized possession was his Matchbox car collection. His dad had bought a car every month for him since he was born. Soda had all twenty-five of those cars on display in his room. He was very proud of them. On one shelf, he had a few of his favorite cars parked around a picture of his dad holding him when he was a newborn.

Soda went to his closet, as Sheena jumped onto his bed to watch. He grabbed his Batman sleeping bag and his overnight bag that had a travel toothbrush and toothpaste, nail clippers, a flashlight, and a few other odds and ends his mom had thrown in there—like an extra pair of clean underwear. How embarrassing. He put the bags on the floor by his door. He snatched his favorite Batman pillow from his bed and then rustled through his dresser for some clean pajamas and threw those things by the door, too. Batman was Soda's favorite superhero. He was the most realistic since he was only a man, not an alien or someone with superpowers. He had made himself what he was, and Soda admired that.

"Don't forget your walkie-talkie," Mystery reminded him.

"Oh, yeah, I can't forget—wait a minute! Are you planning something for *tonight*, Mys?" Soda asked, despite knowing the answer.

"Who, me?" Mystery asked as innocently as possible.

It didn't fool Soda at all. He gave her a *nice try* look as he grabbed his walkie-talkie off his nightstand. Mr. Mooney had given them the old, but nice, walkie-talkie set from the police station. They operated on an old frequency that the Charlotte police no longer used. Soda's had a white *S* painted on the speaker of his and, of course, Mystery's had an *M*.

They used the walkie-talkies whenever they could, and they would use them almost like a phone. Often, they would stay up at night, whispering back and forth to each other, or hold them while they watched TV together, but at their own houses. Mrs. Slooth would laugh at the sight of her son on the couch with his walkie-talkie as he and Mystery would discuss the details of the show they were watching during commercials.

Soda put his walkie-talkie into his overnight bag and grabbed his sleeping bag, pillow, and some clothes.

"Let's go!" he yelled excitedly as he ran out of his bedroom and down the stairs, jumping the last few steps.

Just before he ran out of the front door, he looked back, but he didn't see Mystery. He figured she'd be right behind him.

"You forgot something," she said from the top of the stairs.

"What? What did I forget?"

"This!"

She threw something down the stairs at him. He dropped what he had in his arms and caught it—his black cap with the silver Batman logo on it. Soda smiled. The only time he wore that hat was when it was time for something covert or sneaky. Yep, Mystery had a plan for them all right.

6

Soda set his stuff on the floor by the front door. He grabbed Sheena's leash off the little table by the door and attached it to her bright pink collar.

"Let's get this walk done, shall we?" he asked Mystery.

"Yes!"

Soda liked to walk down to the BMX track, or "The Track" as they called it, with Sheena to let her run around a little if no one was riding or racing. Today he was a little hesitant—he didn't know if he wanted to walk by Mr. Creepy's house after what had happened. But, it didn't matter. Sheena was already pulling him down the sidewalk in that direction. Mystery ran to keep up. Sheena ran like a race dog, pulling on the leash. Soda gave it two quick, firm tugs and she immediately stopped pulling.

"Good girl," he said as he patted the top of her head.

Sometimes he didn't even really need the leash. He only put it on her because there was a leash law and he didn't want any of the neighbors or kids to complain to the cops again. Half the time he just attached the leash and let her drag it along the ground next to her and would pick it up if someone, or another dog, happened by.

They walked down the sidewalk toward The Track and passed the Hiltons' house, a few houses down from Soda's. Both Mystery and Soda tried to look through any cracks in the fence to catch a glimpse of their new dog, but there was nothing. Sheena stayed on the sidewalk as they walked by and gave the air a little extra sniff. She knew there was a new dog on the block. Mystery was hoping the dog would've been outside so she could hear it barking at Sheena, to compare the bark to what they heard earlier, but no luck.

They walked past Dark Pines Drive and stopped in front of Mr. Creepy's house. Soda was holding his breath without realizing it, hoping there wouldn't be an issue. Both Soda and Mystery slowed a little and hesitantly walked step by cautious step. Sheena seemed content walking and smelling the grass on each side of the sidewalk, back and forth; she loved being outside. They walked farther and were almost past the creepy car when Sheena froze in her tracks.

"Uh oh," Mystery whispered.

"I *knew* this wasn't a good idea!" Soda said as he tightened his grip on her leash.

"Wait! I want to see what she does, Soda."

Reluctant but curious, Soda loosened the leash a little and watched Sheena sniff the air some more. She faced Mr. Creepy's house and then sat down. Both Mystery and Soda looked at the front door, but there was no one there—it was closed. Sheena sat there for about another thirty seconds or so, watching and sniffing.

"Okay, c'mon, girl," Soda finally said.

Sheena slowly stood back up, and the hair on the back of her neck furled up. Her gums pulled back, revealing bright-white razor-sharp German shepherd teeth. She let out a quiet, low growl that sounded like an angry motor. The growl was even, consistent, and didn't get louder or quieter. They had never seen her act like that before, *ever*. Soda pulled the leash just as Sheena took a vicious bite at the air in front of her. Her teeth crashed against each other and drool fell to the sidewalk. Then the growl was over. Sheena turned back in the direction they were going and started walking again, as if nothing had happened. Mystery and Soda stared at each other in disbelief.

Soda kept looking back at Mr. Creepy's house as they continued walking. There was nothing. No dog and no Mr. Creepy yelling at them. Even the house seemed indifferent to their presence. That *had* to be a good thing.

When they got to the dead end, they kept walking the other thirty or so feet to The Track, and fortunately no one was there. There were just the hills, berms, jumps, and dirt. The Track was kind of a weird *C* shape and had been constructed by the neighborhood kids over the years. What had started out as a few dirt jumps had turned into a competitive and enjoyable BMX race track. It was one thing that brought nearly all of the neighborhood kids together—well, that and baseball. Even the girls came out to The Track; some would watch, some would ride it, and others would race it. Mystery was one of the racer girls. Now that it was summer again, Soda figured the Saturday-morning races would resume. It was fun competing against the other kids in the neighborhood. Some kids even came from other neighborhoods to race in Whispering Hollow. It was a neat thing they had going on, and Soda couldn't wait—neither could Mystery.

Soda surveyed The Track and unhooked Sheena's leash to let her run wild. She went up and down some of the little hills and up to the top of the dune with the start-finish line. Then she went over to where The Track and Whispering Woods came together, and did her business. Soda had trained her well.

Soda stood at the start-finish line and ran his eyes over The Track. Mystery could tell he was running a race in his mind, and she knew he wished he had his bike with him.

From behind them came someone else who was looking forward to some BMX racing: Travis Greene. He was two years younger than Mystery and Soda, but that was fine—he was a good friend, nothing like his older brother, Trevor. Travis was very friendly and was liked by everyone at school. He probably would've had a million friends if it weren't for Trevor running them off. It was hard to be friends with someone whose big brother could come around at any moment and give you a wedgie or take your lunch money, or both.

"Hey, guys!" Travis exclaimed as he rode his bright neon-green Mongoose BMX bike, which nearly glowed, next to Soda.

A green bike for a Greene boy, Soda thought with a smile.

"Soda, you ready for some racing?" Travis asked.

"For sure!"

"I don't know if I'll be able to do many of the Saturday races this summer. I'm playing baseball finally, and there's a game almost every Saturday."

"Is Trevor playing, too?" Soda asked with a smirk, already knowing the answer.

"No, he stinks at baseball. He hates it. It's nice to be better than him at something. But don't tell him I said that. He'll pound me."

"Your secret's safe with us," Mystery assured him.

"Thanks, guys! Hey, did you see that new guy who moved in down the street from you? We've heard some creepy things about him. You guys should check it out! Oh, Soda, do you think you could help me with my swing this summer? I've seen you hit, ya know? Well, I hope you will!" Travis sped down the hill and was gone.

Mystery looked at Soda with a smile. "That was cute, wasn't it?"

"Oh, shut up. There was nothing cute about it. He must've seen me play in gym class or something. It was just one dude asking another dude to help him out on the diamond. That's all."

"Seemed cute to me. Besides, I'm sure you'll help him out. You'd be a great big brother."

Soda felt like grinning from ear to ear after that comment, but he managed to keep it down to a proud but embarrassed one instead.

After a few more minutes of Sheena's freedom, it was time to head back. Soda called her and she came galloping in a cloud of dust. They waved good-bye to Travis, who was on his second lap, and headed home. The walk back was less eventful than the way down. All Sheena did was sniff the air a little when they passed by Mr. Creepy's house. But when they were across from Ms. Sims's house, Mystery swore she saw a shadow duck in between the two houses. Her blood ran cold, but she didn't say anything.

7

"Why don't you put Sheena in my backyard?"

"You sure?"

"Of course!" Mystery said. She wanted to keep Sheena close.

Mystery walked to the left side of the house and opened the front gate for Sheena. Soda took her leash off, let her go, and shut the gate. They went to grab Soda's things from his house and then walked in the front door of the White House. As they did, Mystery took a peek down the block, at the dead end. Luckily, no shadows.

As was customary for the last day of school, and Friday nights, pizza was for dinner. Fortunately, there was never a debate about where to get the pizza from. The Mooneys only ordered pizza from Mario's. Mystery was so used to it that she didn't even like any of the pizza chains anymore. Nope, for them it was true Italian pizza—the thick stuff. Tonight, even Mrs. Slooth commented on how good it was and how she'd been craving it lately. Mario's had a great family atmosphere and it was run by an Italian family, the Ianuzzos, who just adored Mystery. They loved it when her dad and his police buddies ate lunch or dinner there. Sometimes, they let Soda and Mystery eat—and then allowed her dad to pay the next time he came in. Other times, the Ianuzzos didn't bother at all, and they would let the two friends eat for free. Of course, they wouldn't tell Mr. Mooney this. He'd be upset that his family was getting special treatment. He was a good, honest cop, and that's why the Ianuzzos kept it a secret.

The only debate was whether to have the pizza delivered or picked up. Mario's wasn't far away. In fact, it was just on the east side of Main Street—almost walking distance, really.

Mystery and Soda walked into the kitchen, and Soda plopped his things down by the back door.

"Okay, guys," Mr. Mooney started, "are we having the pizzas delivered or are we picking it up?"

"We'll pick it up!" Mystery exclaimed.

"Yeah!" Soda added.

"Okay, then. I'll order it and we'll head on up to grab it," Mr. Mooney said.

Mystery had a slightly disappointed look on her face.

"What is it, Mys?"

"Dad, can Soda and I ride our bikes to get it? *Pleeeeeease*? I still have the bungee cords and will secure it to my bike. I promise I won't ruin it."

Mr. Mooney looked at his wife and Soda's mom. They each shrugged at him. He couldn't help but think of the time she almost wrecked on her bike, which shook the pizza all over the place. When she had gotten home, the cheese and pepperoni had slid off to one side and stuck to the box.

"It's fine with me. Just ride safe, you two." He *couldn't* say no.

"Yay!" they both yelled.

Mr. Mooney ordered the pizzas as Mystery and Soda ran out to get their bikes. Bikes represented freedom to the two friends. Sometimes they would ride around the neighborhood for hours, enjoying the Carolina blue sky and the hot summer air in their faces.

Mystery grabbed her pink Huffy while Soda ran across the street to get his bike from his garage. Mystery used to have a basket on the front of her bike, but it wasn't used for holding dolls or Barbies or any other girlie thing you could think of. She put *useful* things in there. Things that would help her solve a mystery. But you couldn't put Mario's pizza in it! Last summer she asked her dad to take the basket off—she felt she was getting too old to have it. So, her dad installed a small wire shelf with a zippered bike bag behind her seat over the back tire. She now used the bike bag instead of the basket to transport her investigatory tools. She unzipped the black bag and made sure the bungee cords were still in there, took them out, and removed the bag. She set it on a shelf in the garage next to her dad's truck and wrapped the bungee cords around the frame of her bike, then rode across the street into Soda's driveway. Soda smiled as he pulled out of his garage on his shiny chrome Diamondback BMX bike and closed the garage.

"Let's go!" he bellowed.

They rode up Nighthawk Avenue, turned left onto Weeping Willow Lane, and then right onto Main Street. Main Street was, of course, the heart of Whispering Hollow. There was an old-time feel to the town, which catered to families. Whispering Hollow, a place where people lived to get away from big-city life, was about thirty minutes south of Charlotte. The small town was secluded enough to be peaceful, far enough away from Uptown Charlotte to see all the stars in the sky, but close enough to get to Uptown.

Both sides of Main Street had shops with covered porches. There was parking in the street and in the back of the shops. The area was referred to as The Main Street Shoppes. In the center of town was a circular "natural" area. There were beautiful seasonal flowers, plush bright green grass, and a few cozy benches. But the biggest part of the town center was a large deodar cedar tree. This tree was the oldest, widest, and second tallest in all of North Carolina. It was 102 years old and 130 feet tall, and next to it was a wooden sign that said Please Do Not Climb Tree. Beneath the historic tree was the monument of Sergeant Moustache, who was with the Confederate army during the Civil War. He had refused to allow the land to be decimated by what he called "an embarrassing and barbaric war." He was ashamed that a great country like the United States could be divided. The monument of the war sergeant was six feet tall and showed him in uniform with his right arm outstretched and his hand held up as if ordering traffic to stop. The statue was erected in 1865, the year that Whispering Hollow became a town, and to honor Sergeant Moustache, they left a small cedar tree undisturbed. The town center had become a bit of a tourist attraction, and the community – including the Moustache family – enjoyed the attention. The Moustaches had lived in Whispering Hollow for generations and built Moustache Manor on the west side of the town. It was one of the biggest mansions in the state and certainly the biggest Mystery and Soda had ever seen.

They rode past Mimi's Gas and Grocery, Pumpernickel's Bakery, and Deb's Diner. Soda was riding in a wave pattern—left to right, right to left—over and over. They rode by Dr. Sweets Candy Store and then the Moustache Library, and parked their bikes on the sidewalk in front of Mario's Pizza. Mrs. Ianuzzo saw them ride up and walked outside to greet them.

Beyond Mario's, on the east side, was Brutal's Gym and The Whispering Hollow General Store, and on the corner was the Whispering Hollow police station.

"Happy summer, you two! The pizza is almost ready, just a few more minutes. I'll grab you guys a drink while you wait. You can come inside or have a seat on the bench." Mrs. Ianuzzo was very happy to see the children.

"We'll just wait out here, Mrs. I.," Mystery responded.

Mrs. Ianuzzo went back inside for a few moments, then returned with a bottle of Stewart's Grape Soda, for Soda, and a bottle of Dr. Pepper for Mystery.

"Here you go. Enjoy! These are on the house, but I wouldn't mention that to your dad, Mys. I don't want him to be upset with me. I'll bring the pizzas out when they're ready."

"Thanks, Mrs. I.! Don't worry, I won't tell him."

Mystery and Soda sat on one of the wrought-iron benches with the red-and-white cushions and enjoyed their drinks. *Ahhh, the life.* However, their smiles slowly turned to dread as they heard some boys laughing up the way.

8

There was a laugh in particular that made them cringe. Both Mystery and Soda recognized it at once—it was Trevor Greene, Travis's big bully brother. Mr. Mooney told Mystery that Trevor's last name was very fitting for him. He said what made him a bully was that he was "green with envy" over everything and everyone. Trevor was a too-big-for-his-britches jerk whom no one liked, except maybe his band of buddies and maybe Travis on occasion. Trevor was in their grade but had been held back in kindergarten, and then again in first grade, making him two years older. Soda swore that Trevor had been shaving since he was six. He wasn't an extremely big kid, but he was bigger than average—and tough. Soda and Mystery heard that Trevor's dad was pretty physical with him on several occasions and that the police had been called out to their house a few times. They couldn't confirm this, but they had overheard Trevor talking about it before. Whether or not you could believe him was another story.

Trevor was accompanied by his gang: Linus, Brian, and Bryan. All four of them lived on the north side of the neighborhood, past

Main Street, and had been buddies, and bullies, since kindergarten. Travis and Travis's best friend, Kenny, were hanging out behind them. Mystery always thought that was strange since Travis was nothing like his big brother, other than the love of BMX, that is. The two younger ones weren't part of the gang, but they tagged along a lot of the time. They were riding their bikes in the middle of the street, passing Mario's. Someone drove by, honking their horn, and swerved out of the way so they didn't crash into Trevor. Mystery hoped the gang wouldn't see her and Soda. For a moment, it looked like they were going to ride right on by, but then Trevor jerked his bike around and skidded to a stop at the sidewalk in front of Mario's. He had his signature evil bully smile across his face.

Darn.

"Well, looky what we have here, boys. It's Little Miss 'My Dad's a Cop' Muffin and her boyfriend, Scooter."

Linus, Brian, and Bryan chuckled.

"His name is Soda," Mystery corrected. She was angrier than Soda.

"Awwwwww, isn't that cute? Your girlfriend is sticking up for you." Trevor sneered.

This was bad timing. They didn't need Trevor and his gang pushing them around. They might even take the pizza if Trevor so decided. Soda was afraid he'd take his Braves hat . . . again.

Earlier in the school year, Trevor and the Brians had cornered him in the hallway on the way out to the bus. Soda had been wearing his hat, and Trevor commented on how nice it was and how he wished *he* had a Braves hat. Soda told him to shut up, despite being scared with the three older boys surrounding him. Suddenly, each Brian grabbed an arm, and Trevor flipped the hat off Soda's head with one hand and caught it in the other. Soda saw Mr. Dean and yelled for him. The bullies immediately let him go, so Soda snatched his hat back and fled.

That experience was part of the reason he didn't put his hat on until after he got off the bus. Trevor didn't ride the bus anymore—the bus was for nerds. As this memory ran through his head, Soda pulled his hat down farther on his head without realizing it.

Trevor got off his bike and stalked toward them. Neither Mystery nor Soda said a word. Instead, they both searched deep down for their courage.

They didn't see Mrs. Ianuzzo peek out from behind the red-and-white curtains inside Mario's. They didn't see her look of disgust either. She opened the door and poked her head out.

"Okay, guys, pizzas are ready! C'mon in and get it."

"Thanks, Mrs. I.," Mystery said as they ducked inside.

"You're welcome, sweet muffin," Mrs. Ianuzzo said with a wink and a smile.

They waited inside Mario's, hoping that Trevor and his gang would leave. Soda kept carefully peeking, with one eye, out the curtain to see if they were gone, but they weren't. Soda and Mystery sat on the bench by the Please Wait to Be Seated sign near the cash register with their heads hung low. Each minute passed with the dread of what Trevor might do if they went out there.

"This isn't good, Mys. It doesn't look like they're going to leave any time soon."

Mystery was quiet for a moment; then her dreadful look became one of optimism and her head popped up.

"Soda, we're *not* going to let Trevor, Linus, and 'The Brians' ruin our day!" She pulled her hair back into a ponytail. "Let's go enjoy our pizza while it's still hot! I'll race you!"

As Mystery jumped off the bench, something or someone must have distracted Trevor because all four of them bolted across the street and into Cover-to-Cover Books.

"Why in the world would those knuckleheads go into the bookstore?" Soda asked in total bewilderment. "I think Linus is the only one who can read!" Soda laughed heartily at his own words.

"That *is* puzzling," Mystery added. "I wonder what–"

Then they saw it. It was Chief Andrews's police car.

Chief Stanley Andrews—often called just plain "Chief" by the locals)—was a former Charlotte police major who had retired after a great career and was then convinced to be the chief at Whispering Hollow by the mayor. He was a gigantic man. He stood at six feet six inches and weighed 280-plus pounds. He played football in high school and college, and had been drafted by the Atlanta Falcons, but he never signed the contract. He loved football, but serving the community was his true passion. Despite being in his late fifties, he was still in very good shape.

Chief Andrews was behind the wheel of his white Ford Crown Vic with the Whispering Hollow police badge painted on the door; the top part of the badge was red, the middle part white, and the bottom part blue. Under the badge were the words "Integrity, Pride, Service." His blue lights weren't on and neither was his siren, so he must have just been driving by. He had no idea he just prevented some trouble. He drove past the Whispering Hollow Volunteer Fire Department, the post office, and then Cover-to-Cover Books. He scanned each side of the street and likely saw Trevor and his gang's bikes, but didn't think anything about it. If he had seen them in the bookstore, he would've known something suspicious was going on. He drove by the town hall, Sweets Family Dentistry, and Doc Matthews' Office and then turned right onto Weeping Willow Lane, past Holden's Hardware.

Mystery and Soda walked outside with Mrs. Ianuzzo behind them, pizzas in hand.

"Let me help you, dear."

Mrs. Ianuzzo helped Mystery secure the pizzas to the back of her bike and waved good-bye as Mystery and Soda rode off; they hoped that was the last they had seen of Trevor for the day.

Normally Soda would've pedaled as hard as he could to beat Mystery home. This time he kept looking behind them, but there was no sign of Trevor or his gang. They pulled their bikes into the Mooneys' garage and brought the pizzas inside.

"We're back!" yelled Mystery as she carefully placed the pizzas on the kitchen table.

She opened the box really quick to inspect the pizzas—they were hardly disturbed. She had ridden very carefully. Her dad would be impressed for sure. She closed the box and they sat down at the table. Moments later the parents joined them.

Mr. Mooney blessed the food and opened a box.

"Nice to see the cheese and pepperoni are where they're supposed to be," he said with a smile. Mystery smiled back.

For the first few minutes after the pizza hit their plates, there was only the sound of *mmmm*s and *ahh*s and *yum*s coming from around the rectangular kitchen table.

Soda looked at the Mario's Pizza box that read "The Best Pizza Place in Whispering Hollow" and laughed.

"What are you giggling about, Soda?" Mystery asked him.

"I just love 'The Best Pizza Place in Whispering Hollow' . . . ya know, since it's the *only* pizza place in Whispering Hollow!"

"Ha! Well, they're not lying!" Mystery laughed, too.

"For sure!"

There were a few quiet moments as they ate, and Sheena watched from the deck with her mouth watering. Then the conversation took a turn.

"Hon, do you know anything about our new neighbor who moved in to the Johnsons' old place?" Mrs. Mooney asked her husband.

"Sorry, I don't know anything about that creepy-looking guy. It looked like it was just him. He did look sort of familiar, though . . . but I can't tell why . . . hmmm."

Mystery and Soda smiled at each other again. Mystery was glad they weren't the only ones who thought he was creepy.

"I was hoping we'd get some more kids for Mystery and Soda to play with," Mrs. Mooney said with disappointment.

"Well, I seriously doubt it. He looked too old to have kids their age. Grandkids, maybe."

"You're probably right, Dad," Mystery piped up. "But even if Mr. Creepy did have grandkids, I bet they'd be just as creepy!"

"Mystery Muffin! Stop it! You haven't even met him, and you're calling him that. That's disrespectful," her mom said with a hand on her hip.

"I'm sorry, Mom."

"Well, hon, she did say *Mister* Creepy."

Soda's mom turned away from the table to cover her smile.

"Yes, I heard that part, too, Matthew. Thank you for your input. And I saw that, Sarah! Don't encourage him."

Mr. Mooney smiled and winked at Mystery.

"Well, I'm sure he'll feel right at home soon enough," Mrs. Mooney said with high hopes.

"I don't know, Mrs. M.; this isn't a cemetery!" Soda laughed. Mystery joined in.

"Scott Adam!" Mrs. Slooth yelped in shock, nearly spitting pizza out of her mouth.

"Sorry, Mom."

"Well, if I was a creepy guy and I was looking for a place to lay low and saw Whispering Hollow on the map, I'd probably move here, too," Mr. Mooney surmised. "And there *is* the old cemetery near the church, if the house doesn't work out!"

They all looked at him.

"What?!"

"Oh, Dad, by the way," Mystery started, and felt Soda's eyes grow big without looking at him. "I did get his license plate number. Ya know, in case you want to run it? Just to be sure he's not some kind of killer on the loose."

Mystery searched her memory bank and wrote it on the refrigerator notepad.

"Okay, thanks," Mr. Mooney said, giving her a satisfied look.

Everyone had gotten their fill of thick Sicilian crust, homemade sauce, and mouthwatering pepperoni and was stuffed. Mystery could see that her mom was about to ask her a question. She knew she'd ask when and how she obtained the license-plate number from their new neighbor's vehicles, so she sprang into action. She grabbed her mom's plate and napkin for her.

"Here, Mom, let me get that for you!"

Soda followed suit, and they cleared off the table and loaded the dishwasher. The parents looked on, very proud, especially since they didn't have to ask them to do it.

"Thank you, kids, for cleaning up the table," Mrs. Mooney said after she finished her glass of Dr. Pepper.

"No problem, Mom!" Mystery said with a smile.

"You're welcome, Mrs. M.," Soda added. "Thanks for feeding me . . . again! I'm going to go put my stuff out in the tree house now!"

"I'll go grab my stuff, too!" Mystery yelled as she ran upstairs to her room.

Soda darted out the back door, holding his overnight gear, and onto the wooden deck that Mr. Mooney had built last summer. Just before he ran down the short flight of four stairs, his Batman hat fell out of his bag. He seemed to stop in midair to reach back, grab it, and continue on to the tree house. Little did Soda realize that Mr. Mooney saw his hat and knew what it meant. He smiled.

"What are you smiling about?" Mrs. Mooney asked him.

"Oh, you know, just happy to see how excited the kids are about summer vacation and the adventures that lie ahead," he answered.

Meanwhile, Mystery went up to her room and grabbed her pink-and-purple sleeping bag and her favorite fluffy pillow off the bottom bunk of her bunk beds. Mr. Mooney had bought the set of pink bunk beds for her despite knowing she didn't *really* need them. That was typical of him, though. Mystery just loved picking which bed she wanted to sleep on each night. She heard a car door shut and looked out her window, down into the driveway. Her dad was pulling out of the driveway in his truck—Silverstreak, he called it. She wondered where he was going right after dinner.

Mystery realized that when she'd grabbed her pillow off her bottom bunk bed, it had messed up her unicorn comforter. She felt compelled to fix it before running out to the tree house. While Soda had Lego bricks all over his room, Mystery had unicorns all over hers. She loved unicorns and constantly fantasized about riding one. On her nightstand, next to the lower bunk, was a digital unicorn alarm clock and a Lego unicorn that Soda had made for her. He'd followed some directions for a Lego horse, then modified it a little by using a Lego piece from a space set as the unicorn's horn—it was a "Soda original" for sure.

It was a sad day when Mystery found out unicorns were mythical creatures. A few years back, they were on their way to the zoo, and

Mystery made a comment about how she couldn't wait to pet the unicorns and how she wondered what their horns would feel like. Despite her father's delicate explanation, she was still devastated when he told her that unicorns were only real in her imagination. Mystery was very happy to keep them there. In her mind, they were the perfect animal, and they lived on forever.

Unicorns weren't the only prized possessions in her room. She loved to color pictures, especially ones from the police coloring book. There were police cars and police officers with children and police officers in police cars and all kinds of police stuff. She hung them up on the wall next to her closet very neatly. They were hung three wide and four down, all with double-sided tape and all the same distance apart, up and down; she had actually measured! In addition to the colored pictures, she hung some of her favorite photographs she'd taken.

She also had a teddy bear collection, with several of them lined up at the top of her bed like they were sleeping. There were all kinds and colors of teddy bears, all different sizes and varying degrees of softness. But there was one that she always took with her if she wasn't sleeping at home. His name was, no, not Teddy, but CB—short for Christmas Bear. She got CB for her second Christmas and was the last thing she grabbed, after her walkie-talkie, and she ran downstairs.

Her mom and Mrs. Slooth were still at the kitchen table, talking.

"Mom, where'd Dad go?"

"He went to the store to grab a few things. I would imagine you'll know what soon enough."

Mystery smiled on the way out to meet Soda at the tree house. Just as she shut the kitchen door, she heard something that made her jump a little—a spooky sound that seemed to echo throughout the entire neighborhood. It was a howl, a howl that filled the warm evening air with fright. It sounded like it was coming from Mr. Creepy's house.

9

"Mys, did you hear that?" Soda asked, despite knowing there was absolutely no way that she didn't hear it.

Mystery ran to the tree house, climbed the ladder, and poked her head up inside.

"It sounded like a wolf! Didn't it? It *had* to be a wolf."

She climbed in and closed the hatch. Soda already had his sleeping bag set up and was lying down with his hands behind his head and his feet crossed. Mystery threw CB and her other bedtime stuff on her bed. She knew she was a little bit too old to still sleep with a teddy bear, but it was a habit rather than a necessity. Of course, she wouldn't bring it to a slumber party with the girls, but she knew Soda didn't mind and would never tease her about it.

"A wolf? Do we even have wolves around here?" Soda asked as he sat up.

"Nope . . . but maybe now we do."

Soda knew what she meant. "You don't *really* think Mr. Creepy has a pet wolf, do you? And wouldn't it be illegal to have a wolf as a pet?"

"Well, I'm not jumping to conclusions. We need to do some investigating first. What I saw was too big to be a dog, I think."

"We're starting this summer off right!" Soda suddenly found his inner-Batman and was excited about what the night might bring.

Mystery opened the drawer under her tree-house bed and found her dad's binoculars. *Whew*. She made a mental note to return them to his trunk when she was done this time. She pulled up the shade and peered out at Mr. Creepy's house.

Mystery focused the binoculars into the creepy backyard and spied around. It took a few seconds as the trees and the backyard went in and out of focus. There was no sign of a dog or wolf.

"Yep, we'll figure this out, for sure." She pulled the shade back down, not satisfied with the view the binoculars provided.

"For sure," Soda said as he plopped his head back down on his pillow and peered up at the tree-house ceiling.

Mr. Mooney and their next-door neighbor's son, Kris McShane, had built the tree house together. Kris was like a big brother to Mystery and Soda, and he loved to build and fix things. He had taken special pride in helping build the tree house. He looked forward to adding on to it each summer when he wasn't working on his Trans Am—Kris loved that car. Despite being too old to play in the tree house, Kris made it big enough so he could still get inside, to make it better for Mystery and Soda. From the outside, it looked like a mini log cabin in a tree. Inside there were three beds with wooden drawers underneath, a small living area with a coffee table made from a tree stump, a lookout tower, a mini table and chairs, and a mini fridge. There was a medium-sized dark-green area rug under the tree-stump table that gave the room a cozy feeling. The rest of the floor was all wood. Kris installed screens on all the windows along with the shades on the inside. There were dark-green mini shutters on the outside of the windows. All the wood was a dark stained oak that had been pressure and weather treated.

There were two ways up: the ladder and the rope. To get down you could use the ladder or the fire pole that Kris added last summer. It was just outside the front door. Of course, the fire pole was the preferred way to exit the tree house. The lookout tower had a periscope in it. Kris had wanted to build the tower much higher, but Mr. Mooney said he'd have to find a safer way to look around. So, he made his own periscope using PVC pipe. It went up past the trees and could see over the Mooneys' house and deep into Whispering Woods behind them.

After running electricity to the tree house for the mini fridge, Kris added a small ceiling fan and an old lamp from his bedroom. It was a grand tree house and a perfect headquarters for the kids.

Mystery put the binoculars back into the drawer, climbed up the short ladder into the lookout tower, and peered into the periscope. She maneuvered it up and down and back and forth until she had a good view of Mr. Creepy's backyard.

"See anything yet, Mys?"

Mystery looked around a little more and tried to focus on the back door. It was hard to get a good angle since Mr. Creepy's house was a bit closer to the street than theirs.

"Nope. Nothing. You know what that means, right?"

"Yep. A covert operation," Soda said with an excited smile.

"Exactly right, Soda!" Mystery hopped down from the lookout tower. "Time to bust out your Batman hat. I hope you have your covert clothes, too?"

"Of course I do. They're still in there from last time."

"Great. We'll wait until dark and get started."

10

Mr. Mooney walked out of Mimi's Gas and Grocery with everything they needed for s'mores, put it all in the front passenger seat, and pulled around to the first pump. Just as he put the nozzle in Silverstreak, he heard a man's voice from behind him. It almost startled him—*almost.*

"I see you got yourself a new neighbor there, huh, Matt?"

He turned around and saw Paul Pumpernickel, Darren's father and owner of Pumpernickel's Bakery, standing there in his white baker's uniform. Paul had taken the bakery's trash out as Mr. Mooney pulled up to the pumps. Everyone in Whispering Hollow knew who drove Silverstreak. Mr. Mooney was a regular customer at Pumpernickel's Bakery, which was located next door to Mimi's.

"Oh, hey, Paul. Yes, looks like it. I haven't met him yet. He *does* look familiar, but I can't place him."

"Maybe that's because you don't recognize him anymore. It's been several years, after all. He's Tom Sherlock's brother."

"Sherlock's brother? The Sherlocks who used to live in the Johnsons' house?"

"Yep, that's the one," Paul Pumpernickel said as he clapped his hands in a cloud of flour. The flour all over him made his dark brown hair and mustache appear gray. "After the Sherlocks passed away, the Johnsons rented the house from the Sherlock family. Now I guess the brother decided to move in."

"Oh, so that's why he seems familiar. I didn't get a real good look at him, but now that I think about it, he does resemble Tom Sherlock—but maybe just a little creepier."

"Well, here are a couple other creepy things. I heard that his behavior can be a little erratic . . . maybe hairy is the better word. It has something to do with the moon, and that he's not particularly fond of silver, if you catch my drift."

Mr. Mooney understood. He was just bewildered.

"There's also a rumor that he died a few years ago. Well, I guess technically it's not that he died, but he was killed"—he paused and looked around—"by a wolf." The last three words struck Mr. Mooney like a bolt of lightning.

11

Mr. Mooney returned home and walked out onto the deck, with a smile and the brown paper bag in his hands. "Mystery! Soda! C'mon down!"

They busted out of the tree-house front door, slid down the fire pole, and sprinted to meet Mr. Mooney. He reached inside the bag and pulled out graham crackers, marshmallows, and Hershey's chocolate bars.

"S'mores!" yelled Mystery and Soda in unison.

Mr. Mooney knew the kids had already had Rice Krispies treats when they got home from school, but he loved making s'mores with them. The weather was warm, but not too warm to make use of the fire pit.

"Can you guys get some wood and newspaper so we can get started?"

"Sure!" they both yelled.

Mr. Mooney opened the packaging and started getting everything ready. Soda ran to the back corner of the deck, grabbed a few pieces of stacked wood, and brought them to the fire pit. Mystery ran inside the house to get newspaper.

"Mom, Dad bought us stuff for s'mores! I need newspaper to get the fire going! Are you coming out with us? Huh, Mom?"

"Yes, sweetie, Soda's mom and I will be joining you. There's newspaper in the recycle bin out in the garage."

Mystery was already out the door to the garage before her mom finished her sentence. She grabbed a bunch of newspaper and bolted back through the house, out the back door, down the deck stairs, and out to the corner of the yard where her dad had dug out the fire pit. Her dad was proud of his fire pit. It wasn't just a hole in the ground. It had another hole a few feet from it that connected to the main hole underground. Mr. Mooney said this helped get more oxygen to the fire. He also installed some piping in the ground so the rain water would drain. Around the main hole were several large rocks they collected from Whispering Woods. They provided a barrier from the flame, and they looked nice as well. Mrs. Mooney wanted to paint the rocks, but Mr. Mooney kindly told her this was his area and there was no need for painted rocks at the pit. There was a small grate-like screen over the smaller hole that helped oxygenate the fire. Mr. Mooney put it there after he stepped in the hole and hurt his ankle the day after he made the fire pit. Nope. That wouldn't happen again.

Mrs. Mooney and Mrs. Slooth set up the outdoor chairs around the fire pit while Mr. Mooney showed the kids how to start the fire. He used the newspaper and a tic-tac-toe pattern with the kindling to get the fire going. Then he made an almost round wooden tepee around the wooden tic-tac-toe board. He lit the newspaper with the lighter from his grill on the deck. The paper burned and started the kindling on fire, which slowly spread to the wooden tepee. In a few minutes, they had a nice medium-sized fire—the perfect size for roasting marshmallows and making s'mores!

Mystery and Soda loved the backyard. The plush green grass, the deck with the hot tub, the fire pit, the tree house, all surrounded by a nice tall privacy fence with a gate on the side and one on the back that opened into Whispering Woods. It wasn't a huge backyard, but it was just right for the Mooneys. Mystery's parents had always taught her that bigger or more wasn't always better. It wasn't about comparing what you have to what others had, but instead working hard for and appreciating what you *did* have.

The Mooneys and the Slooths, including Sheena, sat around the fire and roasted marshmallows as darkness settled in. Mr. Mooney, Mystery, and Soda all had their marshmallows stuck on tree branches they had set aside for just this sort of thing, while the moms used metal s'mores sticks from Mimi's Gas and Grocery. They weren't hardcore campers like the others. They each smashed the marshmallows and chocolate between the graham crackers and enjoyed their dessert. Mystery got her marshmallow just hot enough to melt the chocolate while Soda burned his black on the outside.

After they were done eating, it was time to do what they usually did in the summer when they would sleep in the tree house. It was lightning-bug time! They used a big Mason jar with a special top that had a bunch of airholes punched in it, so the lightning bugs could breathe. The parents sat around the fire pit, watching Mystery and Soda run around the yard while trying to catch as many lightning bugs as they could. Sheena chased around with them, too, as they laughed, yelled, and nearly fell over each other. It was a challenge capturing the next lightning bug without allowing the others to escape. Mystery started turning the jar upside down while Soda would release the bug up into it. This technique seemed to work the best so they kept at it. When they were done, they had about six lightning bugs inside. Perfect.

Mystery and Soda collapsed, out of breath, with their giggles still fresh in their hearts. It had only been a few minutes, but it had gotten much darker. Several quiet minutes passed with only the sounds of nature. Every now and then they heard a sharp, electric *peent* call from a nighthawk high atop a tree in Whispering Woods. The nighthawks were all over in Whispering Woods, which earned their street its name and the school its mascot. When Mystery had first seen one, she'd thought it was an owl, but her dad explained that the white bands on the underside of their wings were a dead giveaway that it was a nighthawk.

"Did it just get very, very dark or is it just me?" Mrs. Slooth asked hesitantly.

No one answered. More silence.

A few dark clouds moved out, and the backyard was lit up with moonbeams from the giant full moon overhead. Almost on cue, from somewhere in the summer night, came another howl that pierced the silence like a sharp blade. Sheena stopped rolling around on her back in the grass and sprang to her feet. Surprisingly, she didn't make a peep.

The woodland insects were now silent as well.

12

"Jeez! That sounded like a wolf! Did that sound like a wolf to you, Matt?" Mrs. Mooney asked.

"Do we even have wolves around these parts?" Mrs. Slooth asked, in fear and confusion.

Mystery added up the howls; so far there'd been three.

"Well, North Carolina *does* have wolves," Mr. Mooney explained. "They're mainly in the mountains and the coast, but I've heard that hurricanes have pushed them farther west. So, I'm sure they could be dwelling out there deep in Whispering Woods."

"That didn't sound like it was very deep, did it?" Mystery asked her dad. She looked at Soda with her eyes popping out of her head.

Soda looked toward Mr. Creepy's house.

"No, it did not. But sounds can travel funny at night . . . and through trees. I'll make sure the back gate is secure, just to be safe."

Mr. Mooney finished chewing his s'more and walked to the back gate with Sheena behind him. It was about ten feet beyond the tree house and the gate was latched.

"We're good, everyone. Everything is fine," Mr. Mooney reassured.

Everyone enjoyed another s'more or two, except for Soda—he had three more.

The moon and stars continued to light the nighttime sky above them, and eventually the crickets began to refill the air with their insect songs. Everyone cleaned up and put the chairs back onto the deck.

"Well, it's getting late," Mrs. Slooth said with a sigh. "I'm going to head home and get some sleep. Soda, do you have everything you need?" she asked, giving him a kiss.

"For sure, Mom!"

"Okay, then. Let me know if you guys need anything," Mrs. Slooth said to the Mooneys, and she headed home. "Come on, Sheena!" Sheena followed her out the front fence gate.

Soda wished there was a way for Sheena to climb up into the tree house. Even though Mr. Mooney said they were safe and the gate was latched, he'd feel a little better having her nearby. She slept at the foot of his bed every night. It was a comfortable habit for both of them. Tonight, though, Soda would have to go it alone while Sheena kept his mom company. He didn't have a CB like Mystery did.

"All right, guys, how about you two go inside and brush your teeth, and then you can come back out to the tree house for the night?" Mrs. Mooney suggested.

They flew inside and did just that. Mystery's parents had finished cleaning up the backyard when the kids came busting back out the door.

"G'night, Mom. G'night, Daddy!" she told them each with a kiss.

Mystery's parents told them good night, and Mr. Mooney gave Soda a high five as they ran out to the tree house. When they were out of earshot, Mrs. Mooney turned to her husband as her smile straightened into a look of concern.

"I didn't like that howl at all. Not one bit, Matt. Do you really think wolves are moving in closer to Whispering Hollow?"

"C'mon, let's go inside."

Mr. Mooney opened the door for his wife, followed her into the kitchen, and shut the back door. He locked it.

"Don't forget to leave the door unlocked, in case the kids need to come inside," Mrs. Mooney said as she cleaned the kitchen up—even though it was almost totally clean.

"I know," he said as he quietly unlocked the door. "Hon, I'm not really concerned about wolves. We've never seen one before now, and that howl could've come from anywhere. We can be *aware* but there's no reason to be paranoid. There is one thing I *am* concerned about," he said as he plopped onto the couch and turned on the TV.

"What would that be, hon?" Mrs. Mooney asked as she loaded a few dishes into the dishwasher.

"Well . . . it's about our new neighbor."

Mr. Mooney grabbed the phone and called the Charlie-1 Team Office, his office, of the Charlotte Police. The night-shift sergeant answered the call.

"Charlotte Police, Charlie-1 Office, Sergeant Smith here."

"Hey, Sarge, it's Mooney. Can you do me a favor? I need you to check someone out for me."

Mr. Mooney gave him the info, thanked him, and hung up.

"Sarge is going to look into it and give me a call back in a bit."

"Okay, good."

Mr. Mooney returned his attention to the TV while his wife turned her nervous energy to feverishly cleaning the kitchen counters. He was thankful she wasn't messy when she was anxious. But now, *he* actually felt a little nervous about what Sergeant Smith might find out about their neighbor.

13

Mystery and Soda climbed up to the tree house in excitement. Mystery set the Mason jar—their lightning-bug night-light—on the table. It was fascinating to watch them fly around, lighting up at different times and giving off just enough light to overcome the darkness but not enough to keep them awake. They settled into their beds and got comfortable. Soda would watch the lightning bugs until it put him to sleep, but first things first.

"All right, so what's the plan?" Soda asked in anticipation.

"First thing—" she started.

"What?"

"I forgot my camera."

"Oh, nice going, Mys!"

"Oh, shut your mouth, Soda Pop!" She laughed. "I'll go grab it. I think it's up in my room."

Mystery went out the front door, slid down the tree-house fire pole, and dashed for the back door as quickly and quietly as she could. When her hand hit the knob, she wondered if her dad forgot to leave it unlocked. She carefully twisted it and it turned; she slowly opened the back door, trying to keep it from creaking. She was lucky. That door always seemed to squeak. It was only open a few inches when her mom walked from the kitchen into the family room. Mystery closed her eyes tight, hoping it would make her less visible. Her parents didn't like eavesdropping, but she didn't mean to, at least not this time.

"Thanks for calling me back so quickly, Sarge. I appreciate it." Mr. Mooney paused. "Nope, that's all I need." Sarge said something else. "Yes, sir, I agree. People have a lot of nerve telling these kinds of things to the police . . . Okay, thanks again." He hung up the phone.

"Well, Matthew, what's the story?"

Mystery opened the door a little more and crawled inside. She didn't want to explain why she needed her camera at this hour.

"Hmm? Tell me. What's the story with our creepy neighbor?" her mom demanded.

Mystery froze and listened. Her dad explained what Sergeant Smith had discovered and what Mr. Pumpernickel had told him about Mr. Creepy. She couldn't believe her ears. She hardly moved or breathed during their conversation.

She slunk past the kitchen table, saw both her parents were still in the family room, and snuck down the hallway past the bathroom. She was very careful not to bump any of her photo collages her mom had framed and hung on the hallway wall. Then she crept upstairs to her room. Her camera was in her nightstand drawer, which she slowly opened and closed without making a sound.

Mystery tiptoed back to the kitchen where she crawled to the back door, pushed it open, closed it ever so gently, and dashed back to the tree house, nearly tripping down the short flight of wooden deck stairs.

"Soda! Soda!" Mystery whispered loudly, trying to contain the information she had just heard. She felt like a can of soda that had been shaken up and was going to explode all over the place when opened.

"What? What is it?" Soda asked as Mystery plopped down into her bed and tried to catch her breath.

Soda sat up in bed with a quizzical look on his face. Her excitement piqued his interest, and he wondered what in the world could've happened that was so exciting while she'd merely gone to grab her camera.

"You're not going to believe this. I just heard my parents talking—"

"Mys, were you eavesdropping again? You *know* your parents hate that."

"I didn't mean to. Not this time."

"If you say so."

"Yes, yes I do say so. Now, would you listen to me?!"

"Okay, I'm listening." Soda faced Mystery, crossed his legs, and gave her his full attention. "Go."

14

Kris's old lamp cast a cozy glow as Mystery prepared to relay what she'd heard her parents discussing. Outside, the previously moonlit night had grown even darker. The warm reddish-orange glow from the fire pit was gone, too, except for a few embers here and there. More clouds marched in, blanketing the moon as if they wanted all the moonlight for themselves. The stars continued to shine, but no one in Whispering Hollow could see them. This was not the weather that had been forecast—it was supposed to be a warm, clear night. But sometimes the weather reports were way off. Maybe this was one of those times . . . or maybe not.

"So, I had to sneak in to get my camera, ya know, so they wouldn't get suspicious, and they were talking in the family room."

"Uh-huh."

"I heard my dad get off the phone with a sergeant from work. Then my mom asked him about Mr. Creepy. He told her that his name is Sylvester Sherlock and that—"

"Wow! Really? His name is Sylvester? That's crazy, Mys!" Soda said with a smirk.

"Oh, stop it! Dad also said that years ago, in Virginia, he was attacked by a wolf. A few hours later when his neighbor found him, his heart wasn't beating. It was a brutal attack that happened in his backyard and left him a bloody, mangled heap of a man. His neighbor ran inside to call 9-1-1, and when the ambulance got there, Mr. Creepy was gone."

"Gone? Whattaya mean *gone*?" Soda said, flabbergasted. "Are you telling me that Darren Pumpernickel might be *right* about Mr. Creepy?"

"I mean he wasn't there! He was gone, vanished. There was a week-long search for him, or his body, and he wasn't found. To make things even weirder, the same neighbor who found Mr. Creepy saw him stroll out of the woods and walk inside his house like nothing ever happened. Apparently, he wasn't limping and didn't have any cuts or bites or anything."

Soda tried to digest the story Mystery had just fed him.

"Well? What do you think?" Mystery asked him.

"I'm not sure. I mean, doesn't that sound a little far-fetched? Was the neighbor on drugs or something? And what did he tell police when he returned?"

"I wondered the same thing. So did my mom. Dad said that Mr. Creepy told them that he and his wife had been out of town, taking care of her parents for a week. Apparently, they took a cab to the airport so that was why his creepy car was in the driveway. I guess since he didn't commit a crime and he wasn't dead, the police didn't really push the issue."

Soda lay back down. He was usually pretty skeptical of things, and this story about Mr. Creepy was no different. Neither he nor

Mystery liked to jump to conclusions, but this sounded like something you'd see on TV or in the movies, not in real life. But then again, this *was* Whispering Hollow.

"I dunno, Mys. Sounds made up," Soda said.

"Maybe a little, but that's all the more reason we've got to investigate and get to the bottom of this mystery."

"You're right!"

"I know! So, as soon as my parents' bedroom light goes out, we make our move."

Soda was excited but didn't want to do anything too rash, though.

"Aren't you concerned about that howl at all? What if there really *are* wolves out there?"

Mystery crawled into her bed and got cozy.

"We'll stay close to the backyards—and bring our flashlights and walkie-talkies in case we get separated."

"I don't know. Maybe we should just get up really early, at sunrise, and go then. It'll be easier to see Mr. Creepy's house anyway."

"C'mon, Soda, quit it. We'll be fine!"

Soda knew there was no reason to argue, so he grabbed a bottle of water—one for him and one for Mystery—out of the mini fridge and then turned off the old lamp. Both of them snuggled up in their sleeping bags and waited for the Mooneys' bedroom light to go off. Now the darkness also engulfed the inside of the tree house. The only source of light was from the intermittent flashing from the lightning bugs.

"Oh, I almost forgot," Mystery said.

"What?"

"My dad said that there was another rumor about Mr. Creepy, but no one really believed it."

"Well, what is it?"

"Dad also said that, according to the police report from Virginia, some witnesses thought Mr. Creepy was a werewolf. Mr. Pumpernickel told my dad the same thing."

15

Inside the Mooney house, Mr. Mooney calmed his wife down a little by telling her how people always lied to the police and that he'd go meet Mr. Sherlock tomorrow to make sure he was just a creepy old guy who had moved in down the street, and nothing more.

"Let's go up to the bed, hon. I'm exhausted," Mrs. Mooney moaned as she slammed shut the book she was reading. "I just hope I can stop thinking about all this so I can actually sleep."

Mr. Mooney flipped off the local news and hopped up off the couch. He followed his wife out of the family room and turned toward the back door to lock it. Mrs. Mooney didn't even have to look back at him.

"Leave the back door unlocked, Matthew."

"How did you know what—? Oh, never mind."

They went upstairs to their bedroom to get ready for bed.

From the tree-house window, Mystery saw her parents' bedroom light come on. She told Soda it wouldn't be long now. She was nervously excited. A few minutes later, their light went off. It was time. Mystery knew that her parents slept with a loud box fan on to drown out any noises that might wake them, so there was no need to wait for them to fall asleep. Besides, she was getting pretty tired herself despite her curiosity and excitement.

"Soda, let's go," Mystery whispered.

Soda didn't move. He had his Braves hat over his face. She whispered his name a few more times with no response. Then she nearly yelled his name.

"*What*??" he exclaimed as he bolted upright, nearly jumping out of his sleeping bag. His hat flew off and landed at his feet.

"It's time," she said, whispering again.

"Oh, okay. I musta fallen asleep for a minute," he said through a yawn.

They changed into their "covert" clothing while inside their sleeping bags, and then put their shoes back on. Soda swapped his Braves hat for his black Batman hat while Mystery pulled her hair back into a ponytail. Mystery grabbed her backpack, put the binoculars inside it, and zipped it back up. They each grabbed a flashlight from their bed drawers, and their walkie-talkies. Mystery quietly opened the tree-house front door, letting in the damp night air. Mystery slid down the pole, then Soda, each being careful to land on the ground as quietly as possible.

Mystery started for the back fence gate when Soda stopped her.

"Wait. I think we should bring Sheena. There's a chance my mom left the back door unlocked. I can zip over there and get her right quick. She'll help protect us if we need it. I know it."

Mystery pondered this for a moment. The only issue would be if Sheena barked and gave them away. She figured the reward outweighed the risk in this case. If there really was a wolf out there, Sheena would know right away. Just like she'd known the Hiltons had a new dog. Just like she knew there was something weird at Mr. Creepy's. Mystery nodded at Soda.

"Let's get her," Mystery said with conviction.

"Okay, but I'll have to be very careful. She's probably at the foot of my mom's bed—if Mom's in bed already, that is."

They carefully went to the front fence gate and opened it as delicately as possible. There was a slight creak as it opened and the bottom of the gate scraped some grass, but it wasn't loud enough to draw anyone's attention. They snuck across the Mooneys' front yard silhouetted by the front porch light. It provided the only light since the moon and stars were still hidden by cloud cover. The few streetlights were burned out between there and the dead end. Mystery wondered if they had been out the previous night.

"Mys, the streetlights aren't on down there," Soda said apprehensively, looking toward Mr. Creepy's house.

"It'll be okay; we'll have our flashlights. Besides, there aren't any streetlights in Whispering Woods anyways."

Soda nodded in agreement as they scurried across the street and around to the Slooths' back door. Soda looked up and saw his mother's bedroom light was off. He looked through the back-door window and saw the dim light over the kitchen sink was on; he gave Mystery a thumbs-up. His mom only turned this one on when she went upstairs for the night. He figured they were good to go—*if* the back door was unlocked.

The two crept onto the concrete patio and around the patio furniture, and then stood at the back door on the welcome mat, hoping the door would be open. Soda reached his hand up to the knob and quietly wrapped his fingers around it, trying not to make a noise that would make Sheena bark. Soda slowly turned the knob, but it didn't move. Mystery looked at him with disappointment. He closed his eyes and hung his head. So much for *that* idea. Soda wondered if they should continue with the investigation without Sheena or call it off for now.

Soda opened his eyes and looked down at the mat. Maybe his mom put the key back under it in case he had to run home for some reason! He stepped off the mat, motioning for Mystery to do the same, and pulled up the top right corner. Bingo! The key was there. They both smiled.

Soda held his breath, unlocked the door, and slowly slipped inside. Mystery wondered how he was going to get Sheena to quietly come downstairs if she was, indeed, up on his mom's bed. She didn't have to wait long to find out. She watched from the doorway as Soda walked over to the kitchen sink, opened the cabinet underneath, and pulled out a bag of dog treats—Beggin' Strips, Sheena's favorite. He purposely made noise opening the package.

Upstairs, Mrs. Slooth had fallen asleep nearly sitting straight up with the eleven o'clock news on the TV. Soda had seen her in this position many times. Sheena was at the foot of the bed, all stretched out and utilizing every bit of bed space. She was fading in and out of doggy dreams when she heard the Beggin' Strips bag rustle. She sprang off the bed and scurried downstairs quickly and without a sound.

"Good girl," Soda whispered as he petted her head and handed her a Beggin' Strip. She devoured it.

Soda waited a few moments to make sure his mom wasn't coming and then walked to the front foyer to get the leash off the little table, just in case he needed it. When he returned to the kitchen, Sheena was nestled up against Mystery, getting some love.

"Let's go," he whispered as they slipped out the back door. He locked the door and returned the key under the mat. "Sheena, sit!"

Sheena sat still so Soda could clip the leash on her collar.

"Here we go," Mystery said.

16

Mystery and Soda returned through the Mooneys' backyard and slipped out the back fence gate as quietly as they could. Sheena led the way with Soda right behind. As Mystery turned around to close the gate, she saw her parents' bathroom light go on! Her eyes grew as wide as baseballs and her heart skipped a beat. Soda turned back and saw it, too. If they had to, *they* could just run back up into the tree house and Mystery's parents wouldn't know anything was up. That would be easy. But what would they do with Sheena? Mystery waited to close the gate to make sure they didn't have to abort the mission. A few seconds later, the light went off. They weren't in the clear yet, though. One of her parents could go downstairs, open the back door, and yell out to them or something. It was unlikely, but they were still careful. After a few more moments that felt twice as long as they truly were, Mystery closed the gate. The gate used to swing inward and stay open if it wasn't latched, but Kris McShane had fixed it last summer. Now it would appear secured from inside the yard, but they'd still be able to open it from the woods.

"Okay, we're clear," Mystery whispered.

They stealthily walked, with their flashlights ready, through the edge of Whispering Woods toward Mr. Creepy's backyard, trying to be as light-footed as an elf. Sheena was very excited to be a part of the mission and was running ahead and back. Soda gave the leash two tugs and she settled down; she got in line with him and Mystery. They didn't want to use their flashlights unless it was absolutely necessary, but it was just too dark. The moon and stars were still hidden behind the clouds, so they *had* to turn them on.

The Mooneys' other neighbors, the Cobblers, had their house pitch-black. Dan and Denise usually went to bed early, so they didn't have to worry about them. They quickly passed their house with no issue.

As they passed Dark Pines Lane, Soda saw the streetlights were still out. They went behind Ms. Sims's house slowly but surely. Soda hoped that none of her cats would jump out on them like earlier. That would surely send Sheena into a barking fit, and Ms. Sims would definitely hear it. She was a light sleeper and was always afraid that someone was messing with her cats. She'd yelled at Soda before when Sheena had gotten too close to a cat that walked out to the sidewalk one time. Like Soda could control what her cat did, or the fact that dogs and cats didn't typically get along. They didn't need that hassle right now.

Things were going fine as they crept onward, pushing back tree branches and bushes. Soda couldn't help but think of the howling, however having Sheena with them put him at ease. At this point, the excitement overpowered his nervousness.

The trees were sparse at the edge of the woods. It wasn't until about ten to twelve feet in that it got really thick and difficult to navigate. This was especially true in the dark, but luckily, they didn't need to go that deep. It was good to know that if they needed to "disappear" they could just turn off their flashlights, go deeper, and freeze. Many of the people who lived along the wood line had had the brush cut back to give them a little more backyard space.

They tiptoed closer and closer until they were behind Mr. Creepy's fence. The biggest issue they had was the spider web Soda walked into. Luckily, the spider ran to the top of the web and held on for dear life rather than descending onto his head and biting him. Mystery hated spiders, so she was glad that she was a step behind Soda and Sheena when he hit the web. Soda hated spiders, too, but not as much as he hated rodents. Rodents really gave him the heebie-jeebies.

Mystery put her flashlight away and pulled out the binoculars. She tried her best to look through the slats in the fence, but it was hard to get a good view. She wasn't able to really see anything. Mr. Creepy had the back-porch light on, and there were a several lights on inside his house. Soda told Sheena to sit and they watched Mystery. She moved the binoculars around, trying to see something, *anything*. If it was light out, she wouldn't even need them, but it wasn't. It was dark—very dark. Just as she started to get frustrated, she stifled a sigh and remembered a piece of a slat was missing farther down the fence. Mr. Johnson never fixed it! How could she have forgotten that? She motioned for Soda to follow her and walked a little farther until she found it. The bottom half of the slat was completely missing. She squatted down and took a good, hard, long look. It was uncomfortable, so she got down on her stomach. The binoculars were too strong so she put them away and grabbed her Nikon—her precious camera. That was much better. At first, there wasn't any movement inside the house; then Mystery thought she saw something at the big back window. Through the sheer curtain, it was hard to tell what the shape was, other than a shadow, but whatever it was, it was moving around.

"Do you see something, Mys?"

"I think so. But I can't tell what it is."

"Why does one guy have so many lights on in his house at this hour?" Soda wondered.

"I'm not sure. Maybe he's a night owl?"

"Maybe. Or scared of the dark?"

"I doubt that," Mystery said skeptically as she looked around some more. "I think most grown-ups aren't afraid of the dark . . . especially creepy ones."

Mr. Creepy's backyard was basically empty. The concrete patio had nothing on it except one outdoor chair; there was no table, no umbrella, no grill—nothing. The Johnsons had a play set next to the patio, but it was gone. They hadn't taken it with them, though. Mystery figured that Mr. Creepy had the movers take it. The backyard was now empty and barren—not just of things, but of life and fun times.

Mystery tried to peer through the windows of the two-story house. It seemed that every light was on downstairs and maybe just the hallway light upstairs. It was hard to tell for sure since the upstairs blinds were all shut.

Mystery looked back to the big bay living room window, when the back-porch light went off! She took her eyes away from her camera when Sheena began to growl a little. Mystery snapped a few pictures when she looked back. The camera quietly beeped, but the flash was still on! It lit up the night like a strobe light. Hopefully, Mr. Creepy hadn't seen it!

"What the heck was that?" Soda asked.

"I forgot to turn the flash off!" Mystery said as she fumbled around, trying to quickly turn it off.

Sheena's growl got louder and deeper. Barking was sure to follow.

"What's the matter, girl?" Soda asked, hoping to distract her enough to prevent any barking.

Sheena stood there like a statue in the summer night. She was either terrified or ready to attack; Soda didn't know which, and it frightened him. Mystery looked back at Sheena and accidentally snapped a few pictures at Mr. Creepy's big window. She took a few more pics of the backyard and then set the camera down. The broken slat was wide enough for her to push her face partway through, so she surveyed the far corners of the yard. Soda petted Sheena, trying to calm her down. It wasn't working.

"What's wrong with her?" Mystery asked.

"I'm not sure. I hope she doesn't sense a wolf out there."

"We need to figure it out before she gives us away!"

Sheena's growl became a snarl. Mystery and Soda went from cautious to scared. They frantically looked around, trying to figure out what was upsetting Sheena while hoping it wasn't a wolf. Mystery suddenly realized that no one knew where they were and if they got attacked and needed medical attention . . . well, it would be bad—really bad. They didn't see anything, though. Some leaves were lightly rustling in the summer breeze, but that wouldn't upset Sheena, and she was still focused on Mr. Creepy's house. Mystery poked her camera back through the missing slat and looked around the yard again. She didn't see anything so she set her camera down and looked some more—nothing but darkness. The clouds moved out and moonbeams filled the dark air. It was like someone had turned on Mother Nature's night-light. That's when they heard it. It was coming from the other side of Mr. Creepy's fence!

17

Something was echoing, or answering, Sheena's growl. Out of the corner of her eye, Mystery saw a shadow. Or at least she thought she did. Fear pulsed through her veins, turning her blood to ice. She carefully backed away from the broken slat in Mr. Creepy's fence. Slowly, the fierce German shepherd part of Sheena overtook the miniature sheltie part of her. She was no longer Soda's best friend; she was now his bodyguard. Her growl became louder and more ferocious. Mystery's gaze met Soda's eyes. The other growl rose to the occasion. The whites of Soda's eyes reflected moonlight and fear. Soda saw the same in his friend. Sheena upped the ante and her growl grew more fierce. Again, whatever was on the other side of the fence answered the challenge. Soda could feel the slack tightening on Sheena's leash. She was starting to pull away from him. He started to panic.

"Let's get outta here!" he yelled in a whisper.

Soda pulled Sheena's leash. Mystery didn't hesitate at all. He and Mystery ran for their lives. Soda suddenly jerked to a stop, nearly falling over. The leash was taut in his hand—Sheena hadn't moved. He pulled the leash with both hands and all his might.

"C'mon, girl! Let's go!" He gave another big tug.

Sheena took a few steps forward, pulling Soda with her. He turned and saw Mystery was a few feet away now. Sheena managed a couple more steps before Soda fell to the ground. Overhead, the clouds reclaimed the sky once again. Mystery didn't hear Soda behind her, so she stopped to look back for him. He was on the ground, eyes wide and holding on to the leash for dear life. Despite his best effort to hold on, the leash slipped out of Soda's hand. Sheena disappeared into the darkness. Soda jumped to his feet and started to chase her, when the growls became vicious barking and snarling. There may or may not have been a howl mixed in there. It was too hard to tell.

"No, Soda, don't," Mystery pleaded as she ran back to him and grabbed his hand.

Soda looked Mystery in her eyes and, sadly, realized she was right.

"Okay."

They scurried along the wood line back to the Mooneys' house. They ran so fast they nearly tripped on the woodland floor of Whispering Woods. The snarling and barking continued and maybe they heard a man's voice, or a grunt or something, but they couldn't tell. Soda felt his Batman hat nearly come off his head. He pulled it back down onto his head tightly. At this point, they weren't very concerned about being stealthy; they just wanted to be safe.

18

Mystery and Soda finally made it to the Mooneys' back fence, full of fear and out of breath. Soda pushed open the gate, let Mystery run into her yard, followed her, and then slammed the gate shut. Soda and Mystery leaned both their arms against it, putting all their weight into it. Soda secured the latch. They slowly took their arms away, afraid something would bust through.

Soda was glad to be safe, but his mind immediately turned to Sheena.

"I've got to go back, Mys. I can't leave her out there. I don't even know what the heck happened. Did you see anything? What was snarling? How did it get out of the fence?"

Mystery was afraid for Sheena; she was afraid for her and Soda, too.

"I heard the snarling, too. But, all I saw was a shadow. I couldn't make out what was casting the shadow, though. I thought it was . . ."

"Thought it was what? A wolf?" Soda questioned.

"I can't say. I think it may have been a tail . . . maybe from a wolf or a dog."

"Well, I kinda figured that, Mys. At least, I didn't see the movers unload a lion or tiger. But, that's almost what the growl sounded like. Either way, I need to go make sure Sheena is okay. Are you coming with me?"

Mystery listened for any more snarling, growling, or howling for a few moments. The night was now still and quiet. She didn't know if that was a good thing or not.

"Yes, of course I'm coming with you," she replied.

"C'mon," Soda said with a big swallow as he undid the gate latch. He slowly pulled the gate open.

"*Where do you think you're going*?!" Mrs. Slooth's voice boomed, not caring how loud she was.

Both Soda and Mystery jumped and nearly fell to the ground. Neither of them wanted to answer. They looked at each other, waiting for the other to say something, and realized the gate was wide open.

"Mom, how did . . . Why are you—?"

"I woke up and realized Sheena was gone. I searched all over, and when I opened the front door, I heard all the snarling and barking. It scared the crap out of me! You'd better have a good explanation for going out into Whispering Woods in the middle of the night. Where's Sheena? And what are you wearing?" Her voice quieted somewhat. "I mean, what in the world—?"

Mrs. Slooth turned her attention to the open gate. Her big, furious eyes returned to their normal size as her anger became concern. Soda and Mystery stared at her in fear, so they didn't see right away. Mrs. Slooth dropped to her knees and reached her arms out.

"Come here, girl. It's okay."

Sheena slowly emerged from the darkness of Whispering Woods. Her head was hung low and she was limping a little on her front left leg—it was bleeding a little, too. There was also blood smeared on her fur, though the blood didn't appear to be hers. Soda and Mystery dropped to the ground, too. All three of them carefully stroked Sheena's fur and told her it was going to be okay.

"Mom, I think she saved us. Is she gonna be all right?"

"I . . . I think so." Mrs. Slooth hesitated as she examined Sheena. "Her leg is hurt and she's bleeding from her mouth and gums, but I don't see any major damage to her leg. We'll have to take her to the vet to be sure, though."

"Okay, Mom."

"You guys said you think she saved you? Saved you from what?"

Soda and Mystery looked at each other.

"Well, Mrs. Slooth, we're not really sure."

The Mooneys' back door opened, and Mr. and Mrs. Mooney hurried out to the deck. They hadn't turned on a single light—not that Soda or Mystery would've noticed anyway.

Mr. Mooney folded his arms against his bare chest. "What is going on out here?" He wasn't surprised at all to see the children wearing their "covert" clothes.

"It looks like Sheena got into it with someone's dog," Mrs. Slooth said.

"Would that someone be our new neighbor, Mystery?" Mr. Mooney inquired.

19

Mystery innocently explained how they were merely checking things out when Sheena was attacked by a dog or maybe a wolf.

"You guys are lucky that you didn't get hurt!" Mrs. Mooney scolded. "Why would you two even go out into Whispering Woods after the howling we heard? I can't believe you guys went sneaking around like that!"

Mr. Mooney gave her a look that said he was surprised that she was surprised.

What had started out as a simple investigation had turned into a whole lot more. Now that they'd had time to think about it, they realized how lucky they'd been that they hadn't gotten attacked or hurt by whatever Sheena had tussled with.

"I think maybe they need to spend the rest of the night in the house," Mrs. Mooney suggested.

Mr. Mooney thought about it. He knew they were scared and wouldn't dare venture out again.

"How about this?" he started. "You can stay out here tonight on one condition . . ."

The children listened intently as he explained it. When he finished, they nodded their heads.

Mystery and Soda were glad they didn't have to go inside, but neither of them was looking forward to what they'd have to do—but, there was no avoiding it. Mystery knew her dad would make them do it no matter what, so it was best to accept it.

Mrs. Slooth helped Sheena home. She was sure Sheena would have to go to the animal hospital, or at least the vet, in the morning.

Mystery and Soda climbed back in their tree-house beds and into their sleeping bags. They changed back into their pajamas, and Mystery let her hair down again. Soda changed out his Batman hat for his Braves hat.

"I can't believe I got Sheena hurt," Soda said with a yawn to Mystery through the darkness.

Even the lightning bugs were exhausted.

"Soda, we didn't know anything like that would happen. It's my fault, too, though," Mystery contradicted. "But she saved us. My head was basically in Mr. Creepy's backyard when it all happened. I could've had my face bitten off or something."

It had all happened so fast, and now it was really sinking in. Soda watched the Mason jar, hoping the lightning bugs would light up. As they waited to fall asleep, they both imagined what could have happened if Sheena hadn't been there. The worry managed to keep them awake for a few minutes, but that was it. Then they fell asleep.

They'd been asleep for a few hours when suddenly they both woke up, jumping out of their sleeping bags. It was another howl. But this time it was louder. It didn't sound like it came from deep within Whispering Woods or even from Mr. Creepy's house. This time it sounded closer . . . like it was at the Mooneys' back fence.

Mystery jumped up and grabbed the periscope while Soda went to the back window and flung the shade up. Mystery frantically turned the periscope toward Whispering Woods. She turned it back and forth but was only able to see tree limbs and tree shadows moving in the moonlight breeze; beyond that was darkness. Soda stared at the fence gate with wide eyes.

"Mys, do you see anything?" he whispered.

"No." She looked around a little more but still couldn't get a look at anything. "Do you?"

"Nothing."

Mystery pulled her eyes away from the periscope and sat next to Soda by the back window. They each looked around for a few more seconds until their eyes froze, locked onto the fence gate. Not because they could see something— it was just too dark—but because they *heard* something. At first, neither of them could tell what it was; then, suddenly, it hit them both at the same time. It started out quiet and short, but grew louder and longer—it was scratching. Something was *scratching* at the gate. Mystery and Soda looked at each other in the lightning-bug-lit tree house. The bugs were all flying around and lighting up over and over. They could feel the tension, too. The scratching *had* to be whatever had fought with Sheena, and it sounded like it was trying to claw down the wooden gate. Mystery thought a dog wouldn't be acting like this, though the behavior would probably be strange for a wolf, too.

It continued to scratch, whatever *it* was. The scratching turned to banging—loud banging. They couldn't see anything through the fence, though. It was like *it* was smashing into the gate, perhaps head first, backing up a little, then running and crashing into it again. This happened six or seven times. Each time the gate shook more and more. Mystery stared at the latch and it appeared to be loosening. She blinked her eyes, trying to focus better, hoping she was imagining it. There was another crash, and then another. The latch shook and slipped a little. Another crash.

"Soda," Mystery said, "do you see the latch? It looks like it's coming undone."

"I see it! I see it!"

Crash! The latch slipped some more.

"Soda?"

Soda didn't answer. Instead, he went out the front tree-house door, slid down the fire pole, and ran to the gate.

Crash!

He reached his arms out to the gate.

"Soda! Soda!" Mystery nearly yelled.

The latch was practically undone. One more solid hit and the gate would fly open, letting *it* into the backyard!

Soda was in an all-out sprint. His legs were burning while his pounding heart pumped fear and panic through his veins.

Crash!

The latch slipped and came undone.

20

The gate was still and all was quiet. It stayed that way for a moment. Then Mystery saw the gate swinging open. It wasn't slow motion like in the movies; it *literally was* slowly opening. The fear of what was going to bust through was sickening; Mystery's stomach rolled. The thought of Soda getting hurt was unthinkable, but it couldn't be avoided. It was nearly impossible, but she somehow managed to pull herself away from the window. She had to go help Soda. She had to do *something*. Despite all the fear, there was a moment when she wondered how all that banging hadn't woken her parents up. The one time that she actually wanted her dad to wake up, he didn't. They were on their own for this.

Mystery darted out the open front door, since Soda hadn't closed it in his haste, and slid down the pole. The ride down seemed to take forever instead of the split second it normally took. She touched down and raced toward Soda and the back gate, but it was too late.

Through the darkness, she saw the gate was closed. There was no sign of Soda. Mystery thought she was going to throw up. She closed her eyes, trying to make her pupils bigger so she could see better in the dark. Another quick scan of the gate area yielded the same results. Had it taken him? Or eaten him? Both? Before she could think of any other horrible fate that may have become of her friend, and before she could scream his name with all her might, Soda sat up like a zombie from the ground in front of the fence gate.

"*Soda*?!"

He turned to Mystery, startled at how scared—yet relieved—her voice was.

"Yeah?"

"*Yeah*?? I thought you were gone! Or taken! Or eaten! Or . . . I don't know what!"

Soda got to his knees and then stood up as Mystery ran over to him. Without even thinking about it, she gave him the biggest hug she could muster. He returned the hug and she squeezed him tighter. After a few seconds, he thought the hug was over, but she still held on. He put his arms back around her so she wouldn't feel weird. After a few more moments, she realized she was still hanging on to him and finally let go.

"I pushed the gate closed and held my arms out so it wouldn't move; then I latched it. After that, the scratching and banging stopped. I don't know why or where *it* went. I fell down in relief and lay there for a minute, waiting for my heart to stop trying to beat itself out of my chest. I almost bit my dang tongue off when I hit the gate." He kind of smiled when he said this and stuck his tongue out to see if it was bleeding.

There was another howl that sounded like it came from deep within Whispering Woods. Not a long one, but a howl nonetheless.

"Let's get back in the tree house. We should be safe now," Mystery said, almost trying to convince herself as much as Soda.

"Yeah, safe and sound."

They went back up into the tree house as Mystery's heart had nearly returned to a normal beat. Soda shut the hatch while Mystery pulled the front door closed. The lightning bugs flew around in their jar, intermittently lighting up at a normal rate now as if completely oblivious to what had nearly happened to their captors.

Mystery and Soda snuggled back into their sleeping bags, perhaps a little deeper than last time. They both lay there with their eyes open and staring at the ceiling in silence. Then, at the same time, they called out to each other.

"Go ahead, Soda."

"No, you go ahead. What were you gonna say?"

"I think you said my name first, so you say whatever it is you were going to say first . . . since you spoke first and all," Mystery rationalized.

"Ladies first, Mys. I'm a gentleman, ya know? For sure."

Mystery paused for a moment, preparing a comeback, then stopped.

"I'm glad you're okay. That was totally cool how fast you got down to the gate and latched it. Now what were you going to say?"

"I was just gonna say thanks for running down after me, ya know, to help me."

"Well, we're a team, aren't we?"

"For sure!"

They both smiled, unaware of the other's smile.

"Oh, Soda, we *definitely* have to go talk to Darren tomorrow. We need to know what he's heard."

"Good idea." Soda yawned. His adrenaline dump was over and the aftereffects were exhausting.

It was silent again for a few more minutes. Then the silence became the sound of sleep—deep breathing and almost snoring. The excitement had worn them out. They hardly budged for almost two hours. It was a great, restful sleep. Then the scratching started again. But this time, somehow, it was at the tree-house front door.

21

Soda's eyes popped open while the rest of him remained still. His Braves hat was pulled over most of his face, but he could see the front door out of the corner of his eyes. He couldn't believe his ears. At first, he thought maybe he was hearing things. Then he heard it again. It was possible there was a slight breeze and there was a branch rubbing against the back side of the tree house. He listened closely. It wasn't coming from the back wall or from the ceiling. No, it was definitely coming from the front door. He whispered to Mystery, but she didn't hear him. Fear kept him from saying her name any louder. So, he just lay there, motionless. The scratching continued. As it did, it got louder with each scrape. He pictured a giant, bloody paw on the door and frothy red slobber dangling from sharp, jagged canine fangs. The urge to get up and hold the doorknob from turning came over him. The realization that a dog, or wolf, could not turn a doorknob kept him still, but it didn't take his fear away. The scraping and scratching was louder now. It was probably safe to call out to Mystery now. Soda opened his mouth, but it was too dry to whisper. He licked his lips, but there was no moisture there, like sandpaper. He tried to quietly clear his throat—it did no good. How was Mystery still asleep with all the scratching? He couldn't believe it!

The scratching came before the crashing at the fence gate, so he thought the sharp bangs would start any second at the door. That would surely wake Mystery. Soda wanted to pull the sleeping bag up over his entire head; however, he was either too weak or the sleeping bag was too heavy. Seconds ticked by while he waited for the crashing into the door to start.

More scratches. More scrapes. Soda wondered how in the world it got up to the front door. It would've had to climb *up* the fire pole somehow. That didn't seem likely, but there was no other way he could think of.

It was quiet again. He closed his eyes in anticipation of the first crash. Soda held his breath. No crash. Instead, the doorknob jiggled and then wiggled. He asked himself how this could be happening. On top of it, Mystery was *still* sound asleep.

It didn't matter if he was frozen in fear. If he wanted him and Mystery to be safe, he absolutely *had* to thaw out his fear and keep that doorknob from turning all the way to keep *it* outside. Wait, maybe the door was locked? Could it be? They usually locked it at night. Did they tonight, though? He couldn't remember. Regardless, he wished they had one of those chain locks on it. Then he wouldn't have to get out of his sleeping bag at all.

Please let it be locked please let it be locked please let it be locked, he thought.

He watched as the doorknob wiggled more and more. The wiggles became small turns. The small turns became bigger ones until the doorknob was turned far enough to open it. Soda's eyes opened so wide it hurt. He wondered who would get attacked first. He wondered how it was going to feel to have teeth bury into his flesh. He wondered how loud he'd scream and yell in pain and agony. He wondered why in the world he still couldn't move.

The door opened inward about an inch or so. There was a deep, long growl as the door opened another inch. A deafening howl filled the tree house with terror. Soda glanced at Mystery—still asleep. It seemed impossible after that since Soda's ears were ringing. The door opened a little farther and Soda saw *it*! It was a wolf—a wolf standing on its two back feet. It slammed the door the rest of the way open. He could only see the wolf's bottom half—even Soda had to duck a little to go through the doorway. It had to be about six feet tall. The wolf pulled its right paw away from the doorknob, like a hand, and crouched down onto all fours. It was huge with glowing red eyes looking directly at Soda. Its fur was puffy black and matted down with blood in a few places. Just like Soda had pictured, its teeth were bright white, as sharp as a shark's, and dripping with reddish foam.

The wolf took a few steps into the tree house, turned toward Mystery, and then rotated back to Soda—back and forth. This *had* to be the creature that had fought with Sheena. He wanted to make it pay for hurting her, except he still couldn't move. What would he do, even if he *could* move? He didn't have a weapon or anything. How would he stand a chance against this . . . this monster?

Soda was afraid the wolf would attack Mystery. Okay, it was time to warn her, really warn her. He couldn't move his arms or legs, and his sleeping bag felt like a cocoon prison, but he was able to clear his throat. He was ready to scream at the top of his lungs. No, he was ready to scream his lungs *out*! Soda's mouth slowly opened. The wolf took a step toward Mystery, licking its chops. Bloody foam dripped onto the floor. He tried to scream like Mystery's life depended on it, and maybe it did, but his tongue fell out of his mouth and down his chin. The only sound that came out was a grunt. He reached down for his tongue, to put it back in his mouth, and realized his teeth were gone. He was confused and scared. He popped his tongue back in his mouth. It felt weird and disgusting since it wasn't attached. He spat it into his hand and looked at it in awe. The wolf turned its attention to him and lunged with a grunt and a growl. Soda could've sworn it had a creepy smile on its face for a split second. Its mouth was wide open and about to clamp down on his entire head. Soda closed his eyes just before the teeth were about to tear him to pieces while his best friend was asleep near him. He somehow managed, without his tongue or teeth, to scream *nooooooooooooooo*!

22

He woke up from the awful nightmare, covered in sweat and breathing like he had just run a marathon.

The scream startled Mystery awake. She looked over at him in the dim, lightning-bug-lit room. He was still half frozen in fear with his sleeping bag up over his nose and only his eyes visible from under his hat.

"Um, Soda," Mystery said, her heart pounding, "are you all right?"

His scream had truly frightened her. She reached up and turned on the lamp, causing both of them to squint.

Soda wanted to sit up. He hoped his arms would cooperate, but he was afraid they wouldn't work. Luckily, they did. He sluggishly sat up and looked over at the front door, which was still closed and locked, safe and secure, and then he scanned the rest of the tree house. It was just the two of them—no one else and no*thing* else. He listened . . . There was only silence—no scraping or scratching at the door, no howling. The lightning bugs were silently flying around in their jar, and the mini fridge was quietly humming. He cautiously reached up to his mouth to feel for his tongue and teeth. Everything was where it was supposed to be. He stuck his tongue out far enough to see—yep, still there. Mystery watched with a very puzzled expression.

"What are you doing?" she asked. Her heart had slowed some.

"Oh, I . . ." He didn't really know what to say. "I had an awful dream, a nightmare really."

"Well, I kind of figured that. What was it about? Do you remember?"

Soda didn't know if he wanted to tell her the truth or not. He was embarrassed and was still shaken a bit. Plus, he'd never dreamed about his tongue and teeth being gone.

"It was crazy—scary really. I dreamed I heard the same scraping and scratching we heard at the gate, but this time it was at the front door." Soda pointed to it. "Somehow it opened the door and I saw it standing there. I know it was what attacked Sheena; I just know it. But it wasn't on all four legs. It was standing there like a man would stand, like a creepy man. Then it dropped to all fours and came at me with its mouth wide open, about to rip my head off. Then I woke up."

It felt weird saying all of this out loud, although it made him feel a little better.

"Like a werewolf, huh? Why did you touch your tongue? And your teeth?"

"Oh, I tried to wake you up, but when I went to yell, my tongue fell out and my teeth were suddenly gone." He smiled an uncomfortable smile.

"That sounds awful, Soda. Are you going to be okay? Do you want to go inside the house?"

He felt better with each passing moment. He thought about the creepy smile he saw on the monster's face.

"I'll be fine," he said as he readjusted his Braves hat and lay back down to sleep. He hoped his voice hadn't cracked as much as he thought it did. If so, he hoped Mystery hadn't heard it.

"If you say so."

She didn't say anything about his voice. It must not have been as bad as he thought. Good. He moved his arms and legs around again just to be sure he could. This helped a little more.

"Yeah, I'm good."

"Okay, well, good night, again," Mystery said. She flipped off the lamp and turned onto her side, toward the tree-house wall.

"G'night."

Before Soda closed his eyes, he wondered if the creature would return if he fell back to sleep. When it had nearly bitten his head off in the dream, he could have sworn he could feel the warmth of its breath on his face. He shivered as goose bumps covered his skin. It would be okay. He told himself it would be okay—he was almost certain; nevertheless, he couldn't keep his eyes off the door. He stared at it, hoping nothing would happen. He was too afraid to close his eyes. He kept them open as long as he could until finally they fell shut. He popped them open and blinked a few times to keep them from getting too dry. For a few minutes, he did no more than take some quick blinks. Sleep, slowly determined, settled in and overtook Soda. His eyes closed and remained closed. Luckily for him, there were no visions of a wolf or werewolf or getting his head bitten off. It was a dreamless sleep.

It had been one heck of a day. Neither of them was looking forward to what Mr. Mooney was going to have them do in the morning. He didn't have to work, so at least they didn't have to wait until he got home to do it. That would've made for a very long day.

Mystery and Soda both slept until morning. Neither of them thought about what was waiting for them on Mystery's camera. If only they had known.

23

Mystery and Soda woke up without saying a word. Mystery grabbed the lightning-bug jar and went out the front door. She took the top off and all the lightning bugs flew out—they all survived the night.

Soda took a few big breaths in through his nose, out through his mouth. The delicious aroma of smoked meat already filled the air.

"Ahhh, smells like Mr. Davidson is already busy grilling for the Bob-B-Q."

"Smells delicious!" Mystery said with a couple of sniffs of her own.

Then they went into the house through the unlocked back door.

Despite the commotion the children had caused, Mr. Mooney still got up early, showered, and made everyone breakfast: pancakes, bacon, sausage, and scrambled eggs. All four of them looked exhausted. Soda looked like he could fall back to sleep while sitting up at the table. Mystery's and Soda's hair was all messed up even though you couldn't see most of Soda's since he still had on his Braves hat. Mrs. Mooney had put her hair up in a bun while Mr.

Mooney was wearing a funny chef's hat that Mystery had made him for Father's Day last year. She had used fabric paint to write "DADDY" on the front of it. He looked pretty silly wearing it, but he didn't care and Mystery loved that he wore it whenever he cooked or grilled.

"I hope you two will be respectful later," Mr. Mooney said as he flipped over a few more pancakes.

The kids nodded.

"I should make something for you to take," Mrs. Mooney said as she got up from the table, still in her nightgown.

"Hon, can we get through breakfast first? Then you can make something, you crazy lady," Mr. Mooney said with a smile.

"Oh, fine!" Mrs. Mooney smiled back and sat back down.

"Daddy, we were planning on going to Crippler's Creek today to see if we can catch some frogs. Can we still go afterward?"

"It's fine with me, as long as you guys handle this."

"For sure!" Soda said.

"We will, Dad, we will."

Mr. Mooney put the last few pancakes on a platter, dumped the eggs onto a plate from the frying pan, and brought everything over to the kitchen table where Mrs. Mooney and the children patiently waited.

Mrs. Mooney's cell phone rang on the counter, and she picked it up.

"It's Sarah," she said. Soda picked his head up and looked over at Mrs. Mooney as she answered the phone. "Hey, Sarah . . . Oh, that's no problem . . . Uh-huh, yeah . . . That's fine . . . I'll tell him . . . Okay, bye-bye," she said, and then hung up. "Sarah's not coming over for breakfast. She doesn't want to leave Sheena. I'm supposed to ask you, Soda, if you are going to the vet with her in a little while."

"Yeah, I'll be goin' with her," Soda said, feeling miserable about what had happened to her.

"Don't worry, Soda, I'll go, too. Is that okay?" Mystery asked as she turned to her mom. Her mom turned to her dad.

"Yes, I think you *should* go since you're partly responsible for what happened. We'll handle business when you guys get back."

"Deal!" Mystery exclaimed with a nod.

Mystery set out the plates while Soda put out the silverware. Mr. Mooney removed his baker's hat, blessed the food, and said how thankful he was for his family. They all dug into the deliciously greasy breakfast.

There were a few moments of uncomfortable silence until Mrs. Mooney piped up.

"So, what were you two doing out there last night?"

Mystery hesitated for a moment as the temptation to make something up to stay out of trouble ran through her mind. She knew it was best to just be honest, especially since she knew they hadn't done anything more than check things out. So, that's what she told her mom.

"You need to think things through before you do them. That's all I'm gonna say about it, ya hear?"

They both nodded their heads since their mouths were stuffed with food.

After they finished eating, Mystery and Soda started to clear the table when Mrs. Mooney waved a hand at them.

"I'll get it, you two. Y'all need to get ready for the vet," she said.

Mystery ran upstairs to her room to get dressed. She put on her Whispering Hollow Nighthawks T-shirt and some shorts, quickly brushed her hair and her teeth, and ran back downstairs.

"Let's go, Soda!" Mystery said, and gave each of her parents a quick kiss.

They ran over to the Slooths' house and went inside the front door. What they saw was not good, not good at all. Mrs. Slooth sat on the bottom of the stairs with Sheena on the floor in front of her.

"Mom, what's wrong?" Soda asked. He thought he could see tears in her eyes.

"She won't walk. She hasn't moved all night. This is where she slept. She must really be hurt—worse than I thought."

"What are we gonna do if she won't even walk? How are we gonna get her to the vet?" Soda was very worried.

"I know! I'll go get my dad! He can put her in Silverstreak and drive us!"

"Oh, Mystery, I don't know—"

Mystery ran out the door before Mrs. Slooth could finish. Soda lay down on the floor next to Sheena and petted her head and face. She looked pitiful but wasn't whining.

A few minutes later they heard two car doors close from their driveway. Mystery and Mr. Mooney came in the front door. Mr. Mooney was wearing his Boston Red Sox hat. It was always exciting when the Red Sox played the Braves and it was on TV. He and Soda hoped that someday they could go to Atlanta to see a live game.

"Alrighty, let's do this," Mr. Mooney said while clapping his hands.

"Oh, Matt, you don't have to do this."

"Nonsense. Now let's load her up. Soda, can you get the door for me?"

Soda opened the front door. Mr. Mooney scooped Sheena off the floor and gently put her in the back of Silverstreak. He had thrown a few blankets in the bed of the truck for her to lie on.

"Let's go. Hop in," he said.

Mrs. Slooth opened the front passenger door to get in and saw Mrs. Mooney in the middle backseat.

"Hi there!" Mrs. Mooney smiled. "Looks like we're *all* going!"

During the drive, Soda and Mystery kept checking on Sheena as they drove; she was fine. When they got to the vet, Mr. Mooney dropped the tailgate, picked up Sheena, and carried her inside. Shortly after, Sheena went back for X-rays. The five of them waited for about twenty minutes until the vet came out to tell them what was wrong with her. He didn't look hopeful.

24

The Slooths and the Mooneys huddled together as they waited for the vet to break the news.

"Well, folks, I've examined Sheena and read her X-rays. Her left front leg has a hairline fracture and we're going to put a cast on it."

There was a collective sigh of relief that it wasn't any worse. Mrs. Slooth felt bad that she hadn't just taken Sheena to the emergency vet last night.

"Now this *was* a dog attack, right?" the vet asked.

The parents turned their heads to the children. Soda nodded his head.

"Why do you ask?" Mr. Mooney asked.

"Well, it's just that Sheena has an odd bite mark on her neck."

"Odd? How so?" Mrs. Slooth asked.

"The teeth pattern seems strange," the vet started. He saw the concerned looks on Mystery's and Soda's faces. "But it's probably just because the other dog probably shook its head back and forth.

At first, I thought maybe the attack was from a wolf, not that there's a big difference between a dog's teeth and a wolf's teeth."

They all looked at each other.

"We did hear some howling last night in Whispering Woods," Mr. Mooney stated. Then he turned to the children. "Did you guys actually see the other animal?"

"Not really," Soda said.

"All I saw was the shadow of a tail. But, it looked like a dog's tail. It was in Mr. Creepy's backyard."

Before the discussion went any further, the vet stopped them.

"Either way, I've cleaned the wound and given her some antibiotics that you'll need to give her twice per day for the next seven days to prevent an infection. I'd keep her inside as much as possible to help keep the wound clean. Just give us a few minutes to get the medicine ready, and we'll get y'all out of here."

They all thanked him, and Mr. Mooney shook his hand. Ten minutes later, Sheena came hobbling out in a cast, but she looked much better. The vet assistant gave Mrs. Slooth the antibiotics while Mr. Mooney boosted Sheena into Silverstreak, and they headed home.

"Mom, can I go to Crippler's Creek with Mys after we get Sheena all settled? We wanna catch some frogs," Soda asked as they pulled into the Slooths' driveway.

"It's okay with me as long as you two stay together. Remember why it's called *Crippler's* Creek, okay?"

"I don't want to rain on your parade, but we need to go handle something before you go," Mr. Mooney said in his "dad" voice.

Darn. They were kind of hoping he would have forgotten.

25

Mr. Mooney brought Sheena into the Slooths' house and set her in the doggie bed in the living room just to the left of the front door. She curled up and was almost instantly asleep.

Mr. Mooney walked back outside to Silverstreak. He turned to Mystery.

"Let's go get this done, shall we?"

"I guess so."

"You can go now, Soda," Mrs. Slooth said. "I'm sure she'll sleep most of the day. Just make sure you check on her and let me know if anything is wrong with her, okay? I have to get ready for work now before I'm late."

"Okay, Mom, I will."

Mrs. Slooth gave her son a kiss and went upstairs to put on her Whispering Hollow Coffee Shop outfit.

Mr. Mooney drove his truck across the street to their house with Mrs. Mooney.

Soda and Mystery each gave Sheena a few strokes on her head and back before they walked over and met in the Mooney kitchen.

"Hon, I'm going to make some brownies right quick before you go, okay?" Mrs. Mooney asked.

"Brownies, really?" He saw the look in her eyes. "Okay, fine." This was not a battle worth fighting and he knew it.

When the brownies were ready, Mrs. Mooney cut them and stacked them nicely onto a paper plate.

"Hang on. I have an idea," Mystery said as she looked through a kitchen cabinet. "Aha! This will work perfectly," she said as she pulled out a silver platter. There was a glimmer in her eye.

Mr. Mooney and Soda knew exactly why Mystery chose the silver platter, and they were anxious to see what would happen.

Mrs. Mooney smiled and loaded up the silver platter with brownies.

"Now make sure you don't drop this," Mrs. Mooney warned her husband. "And you'll need to make sure I get this back."

He looked at her with a smirk. "I'm not you, hon. And I will."

Mr. Mooney, Mystery, and Soda all walked to Mr. Creepy's house. Mr. Mooney carried the brownies, and Mystery and Soda carried their heads hung low. They were not looking forward to this—not one bit. Mr. Mooney explained that he'd introduce himself, offer the brownies, and then tell Mr. Creepy that the children had something to say. Even though they had backup with them this time, both Mystery and Soda were still nervous. Soda kind of hoped Mr. Creepy wasn't home or wouldn't answer the door. He realized that would just temporarily delay the inevitable. It was going to happen now or later. Mystery, on the other hand, was anxious to see what, if anything, would happen with the silver platter.

They walked down the sidewalk along Nighthawk Avenue, past the Cobblers' house, and were in front of Ms. Sims's house. There were about a dozen cats on her front porch, and they all stopped at the same time and glared at the three humans walking by. It was a little eerie.

Mr. Mooney realized he still was carrying his backup gun concealed on his right hip. He almost always had it on him when he wasn't working. He never knew when a bad guy might recognize him as an officer and give him or his family a hard time. It was just a safety precaution. After what he'd heard about this guy, it was probably better he had it. He didn't want to turn around and go put it away, so he kept on walking. Besides, he'd rather have it and not need it than need it and not have it.

Mr. Creepy's car was parked in the driveway. Mr. Mooney noticed how dark the windows were as they went by.

The three of them walked up to the front door. Well, Mr. Mooney walked, the children reluctantly trudged. Mystery's and Soda's mouths were like a desert.

"Showtime," Mr. Mooney said, and rang the doorbell.

It didn't ring, though. It was broken . . . or Mr. Creepy had disconnected it. Mr. Mooney opened the storm door and knocked on the front door. There was no response. He knocked again.

"Who is it, and what do you want?!" came a loud, cranky old voice from behind the door.

Mystery and Soda jumped a little. Mr. Mooney was a little surprised as well.

Mr. Mooney started to answer. "It's your neighbor—"

The door flew open. "Well?! Why are you bothering me?" Mr. Creepy demanded.

Mystery and Soda looked at the angry old face, but something else caught their attention. Their gaze slowly went down to Mr.

Creepy's right shoulder, down his arm, and to his hand. Mystery and Soda looked at each other in amazement and wonder. It was covered in a bloody bandage!

26

They finally got to see Mr. Creepy up close. He wasn't exactly ugly, but he wasn't good-looking either. He was . . . *creepy* looking. Mystery and Soda couldn't stop staring at his bloody bandage. He had such an annoyed look on his face, like they interrupted the most important moment of his life. His head was bald and shiny, his brow was furled into a gray scowl, and his eyes were an empty dark color—almost black. A light gray beard sprouted from his cheeks and he had a mustache, but no hair on his chin. His skin was pale white with some pink blotches here and there. It looked like he was wearing the same black suit without the top hat. From a distance the suit appeared brand new; however, up close it looked almost as old as he was. The sleeves of his suit jacket were tattered but intact. His white shirt was a worn, off-white color that reminded Mystery of her sneakers. She looked at his non-injured hand and saw his wedding ring—gold, not silver. He had the door open only far enough for them to see his body and nothing else beyond that. It was like he didn't want them to see inside.

It was surprising that a dog hadn't barked when they'd knocked, especially since Mr. Mooney had knocked hard, twice.

"Hi there, Mr. Sherlock, I'm Matt Mooney. I live a few houses up the road here. This is my daughter, Mystery—well, Megan—and for all practical purposes, the son I never had, Soda—I mean, Scott."

Mr. Mooney reached out for his hand, but Mr. Creepy left him to shake the air. Mr. Mooney didn't know if this was because he didn't care to or if it was because his right hand was all bandaged up. He held his hand there for another awkward moment—but then pulled it back and offered the plate of brownies. Mr. Creepy looked at him in the face, with his empty eyes, and then at the brownies. Mystery wondered if he would take them or slam the door in their faces. At first, he didn't do anything. He looked up from the brownies and stood there in silence. Mr. Mooney slowly turned his right side away from Mr. Creepy, hoping to make the bulge of his gun under his shirt less visible, and looked back at him. The children couldn't hold Mr. Creepy's gaze, so they glanced away. They could feel anger and hate shooting out of his eyes like evil laser beams.

"How on earth did you know my name?" he snarled.

"I'm sorry. I'm a police officer in Charlotte and I—"

"Good for you, *officer*! Checking up on me, eh? You cops are always messing with people!" He closed the door a little more on himself as if Mr. Mooney were trying to peer inside or force his way in.

Mr. Mooney was a little surprised at Mr. Creepy's rudeness.

"Well, sir, we just wanted to welcome you to the neighborhood and to bring you some brownies my wife made for you. Also, these two have something to say to you."

Mr. Creepy turned his attention to the children without saying a word. They felt like they were on a spotlighted stage in front of hundreds of snarling monsters waiting to boo them and then devour them. At first, they stared back with their mouths partway open and their eyes wide. Mr. Mooney saw their apprehension. It was like they were in a trance of some kind. Finally, he nudged Mystery, which snapped her out of the trance.

She blinked and shook her head a little. She took in a breath and spoke quickly, as if she were competing in a word race. "Yes, sir, we just wanted to apologize for all the commotion last night. Soda's dog, Sheena, and I guess your dog, got into a fight last night. We were out in the woods behind your house and shouldn't have been and we're very sorry and we hope your dog is okay," she said all in one breath and turned to Soda.

"Ummmmm . . . yeah, what she said. We're sorry, sir, very sorry," Soda managed to say.

Mr. Creepy folded his arms like he couldn't decide if he wanted to step out onto the porch or go back into his house. They waited for him to speak . . . and waited and waited . . . for him to say something . . . anything, but he did not. Instead, Mr. Mooney spoke up.

"I assure you it won't happen again, Mr. Sherlock. Is your dog okay?"

"Goliath is fine. He's . . . well, he's . . . shall we say, resting right now. You dang kids had better stay clear of him from now on! If you hadn't been snooping around, none of this would've happened. Goliath was just protecting the house."

Mystery and Soda both nodded like they were being scolded by the school principal.

"Like I said, it won't happen again," Mr. Mooney reassured.

"Well, I should hope not!" Mr. Creepy snapped, looking Mr. Mooney right in the eyes.

"Okay, so welcome to the neighborhood."

Mr. Creepy again said nothing and started to close the door.

"Mr. Sherlock, may I ask what happened to your hand there?" Mystery motioned to the bloody bandage.

"Thanks to your snooping around," he snarled and pointed at her and Soda with a long wrinkly pointer finger, back and forth at each of them, "I had to break up the dog fight, and Goliath accidentally bit *me* instead of your mutt!" He stepped back and slammed the door, leaving Mr. Mooney holding the silver platter of brownies.

Mr. Mooney looked down at the children and removed the plastic wrap from the brownies.

"Brownie?" he asked.

"Why not?" Mystery said as she smiled and snatched one from the plate.

Soda carefully looked for the biggest one, and then grabbed it.

"Good job, guys," Mr. Mooney said as he walked down the steps. He popped an entire brownie into his mouth, nearly dropping the platter. "At least we got some brownies out of it," he added with his mouth nearly full.

Mystery and Soda were glad that was finally done. Mr. Mooney was also relieved. But, it wasn't over.

Before they got to the bottom step, something slammed into the front door from inside the house! It was followed by vicious, loud barking and the sound of fingernails scratching and scraping at the door, as if it wanted to claw through the barrier and attack them. Mr. Mooney almost dropped the rest of the brownies.

27

The barking continued as they hurried down Mr. Creepy's driveway. It was just barking, no howling.

"I guess Goliath is done resting." The barking continued. "Boy, that thing sounds rabid," Mr. Mooney said.

"He'd better hope not," Mystery said, motioning to Mr. Creepy's house with her thumb, "for his sake."

"Sheena's, too," Soda added with a worried look.

"Don't worry, buddy, she's okay," Mr. Mooney said as he patted Soda on his Braves hat.

Soda smiled.

When they got back to their house, Mystery reached for the front door and paused. She wanted to ask her dad what he thought about Mr. Creepy refusing the brownies . . . or the silver platter. Just as she opened her mouth, she changed her mind.

"So, Dad, now can we go to Crippler's Creek? Pleeeeeease?"

"Absolutely."

"Yay! Let's get our bikes!" Soda yelled.

They each got their bikes out of their garages and met on the sidewalk in front of the Mooneys' house.

"Oh, I'd better grab my camera in case we see something cool!" Mystery said.

She set her bike down carefully, ran to the backyard to get her backpack from the tree house, and put her camera inside. Then she ran back to her bike and hopped on.

"Got it?" Soda asked.

"Yep, let's go!"

"Be careful out there, okay, my little muffin?"

"Daaaaaaad! I will. Jeez!" Mystery said as embarrassment colored her face pink.

Mr. Mooney smiled as Mystery pulled her hair back into a pony-tail and Soda turned his Braves hat backward.

"Wait, Soda," Mystery said. "We need to go talk to Darren first."

"Oh, yeah, let's go."

"Dad, we're going to go see Darren first, then go to Crippler's Creek, okay?"

"Okay," Mr. Mooney said. Then he thought, *I bet I know why they want to talk to him.*

The Pumpernickels lived at the corner of Weeping Willow Lane and Nighthawk Avenue. Soda rang the doorbell and Darren answered the door.

"Hey, y'all, what's happenin'?"

"You tell *us*, Darren," Soda demanded.

"About what?" Darren asked as his black hair fell over his forehead.

"About Mr. Creepy, of course!" Soda nearly yelled.

"Darren, can you meet us over at Crippler's Creek?" Mystery asked.

"Sure, just gimme a few minutes and I'll be there right quick."

"Hurry!" Soda yelled as they got back on their bikes.

They took off as fast as they could to Crippler's Creek. It would've been faster to go straight across Weeping Willow Lane, but they decided to take the long way. A long bike ride beat a short one any day.

Crippler's Creek wasn't a bad place. It ran from behind Moustache Manor and out to Highway 74. There was a point where it opened up into a small pond near the corner of Weeping Willow Lane and Ravenwood Drive—kind of behind Holden's Hardware. It was only a foot and a half or two deep, but it had a bunch of tadpoles, frogs, toads, and snakes all around. They were mostly garter snakes, but every now and then there'd be a copperhead. The pond was surrounded by trees, a bunch of weeds, and some wildflowers. You wouldn't even know it was there if not for the worn-down path from the dead end of Weeping Willow Lane. Up to and away from the pond, the creek flowed over rocks—large jagged rocks about the size of softballs.

The story about the creek was local folklore and retold each Halloween. A long time ago, before the town was very developed, a young boy named Jack was playing at the creek by himself. Back then the creek didn't have a name; it was just a creek. Jack went out to play without telling his parents where he was going. He stopped by his best friend's house, but he wasn't allowed outside until after dinner, so Jack went out alone to the creek. He played around in the pond, trying to catch frogs, but there weren't many out on that particular day. After being there for about twenty minutes, he was ready to leave. It just wasn't as fun by himself. As he stepped out of the pond onto the rocky area, he slipped. Jack tried to catch his balance but couldn't, and he fell. His head slammed in between a few jagged rocks and busted open, his blood mixing with the pond water as he drifted into unconsciousness. He lay there, sprawled out under the hot summer sun, with his feet on the edge of the creek and his head on a pillow of rocks. A little while later, he awoke and tried to get up, but he couldn't move. He tried and tried to sit up; however, his body wouldn't listen to what his brain was telling it to do. Jack was crippled and scared to death. He couldn't even scream for help. Eventually the help came, but it was too late. Jack had been dead for days before his body was discovered. Thus, the creek became known as "Crippler's Creek." Rumor was his parents had been embarrassed and held a private funeral for him, rather than burying him at the graveyard. Jack was buried somewhere out near the pond without a gravestone—just a rock with a *J* carved into it.

Mystery and Soda raced down Dark Pines Lane. They were neck and neck until they turned onto Ravenwood Drive, when Soda took the inside track and pulled ahead of Mystery. She tried with all her might to get her pedals moving faster, but she just couldn't catch up to him. They passed the driveway to Whispering Hollow Elementary and Middle School on their right and came to Weeping Willow Lane. Again, Soda took the inside track as they turned left. He led the way to the dead end and jumped onto the path leading to Crippler's Creek.

"Woo-hoo!" he yelled.

"Nice job, Soda," Mystery said politely.

"Thanks. I'm ready to do some racin' on The Track!"

Little did he know he'd get his wish sooner than he expected.

They rode up to the edge of the creek and squatted down, checking for frogs. It hadn't rained in a few days and the water level wasn't as high as it normally was, so they walked farther up toward the pond. Even though it was only about fifty yards off the roadway, it felt like they were in the middle of nowhere. They scanned the pond and creek for a few minutes. The only activity was a few tadpoles swimming around near the edge, dreaming of the day they could hop out and explore life beyond the pond as a full-grown frog. Soda was fascinated at how tadpoles transformed into frogs. It wasn't a very common thing in nature, other than the caterpillar turning into a butterfly—which was one of Mystery's favorite animals.

A minute later, Darren arrived on his bike.

"Well?" Mystery said, before Darren could stop his bike and get off.

"Well, what?"

"Don't you think it's time to talk about some things? About some *creepy* things you've heard?"

"I thought you guys already heard. My dad saw your dad yesterday and told him. Why? Did you guys find something?" Neither of them answered. "You did, didn't ya? Tell me what ya found out." Darren was intrigued and hopped off his bike.

Even though Mystery knew they were alone, she still looked around to be sure.

"Okay, so we went investigating last night."

Mystery went over everything that happened, including the howling and the attack on Sheena.

"Guys, I'm tellin' ya, he's a werewolf," Darren said.

Mystery stared at him.

"C'mon, do you really think he broke up a dog fight? No way! He was in wolf form and *he* fought with Sheena. That's why he had the bandage on his hand."

Soda thought about it for a moment. "Well, that's what we thought when we first saw the bandage."

Darren continued. "Plus, he wouldn't take the brownies because of the silver platter! And wasn't it a full moon last night?!"

"Darren, that's just werewolf stuff from the movies," Mystery rationalized.

"If so, then why did you try the silver platter?"

Mystery and Soda were speechless.

The sun was overhead and beating down on them. Mystery walked over to her bike and grabbed her backpack. After some searching, she pulled out a small tube of sunscreen, which they quickly used all over their necks, faces, arms, and legs. Mystery put the sunscreen back into the backpack and took out her camera.

"Still don't believe me? Then how did Mr. Creepy's dog get outta his fenced-in backyard? Did it just open the gate?" Darren asked, knowing there was no way that was possible.

"I don't know of many dogs that can open gates. Actually, I don't remember the Johnsons' gate being that easy to open either," Soda remembered. "Ronnie kept saying that his dad was going to fix it, but he never got around to it. A werewolf could maybe open a gate."

"And another thing—have you guys actually seen Mr. Creepy and his dog? Together? At the same time?"

No, they *hadn't*.

Mystery and Soda had thought all the same things Darren said, but it sounded more real, more possible, to hear someone else say it.

"It's still not proof," Mystery stated, although she couldn't help but wonder.

A few mallard ducks landed on the pond and swam around, eating water bugs. Mystery aimed her Nikon camera at them and snapped a few shots. When she was done, she looked at the small screen to see how they came out. She scrolled through the three she had just taken, when she came to a few that she had forgotten about. They were the shots from Mr. Creepy's house! Soda saw the surprised look on her face.

"What is it, Mys?"

"I don't believe it. I think there's some evidence to support this *legend* that Mr. Creepy could be a werewolf. Take a look at these," she said and handed him the camera.

Darren walked over behind Soda and studied the pictures, too. "I'd call this proof!"

"Mys, am I seeing what I think I'm seeing?"

Before Mystery could answer, a voice came from behind them. A voice they all dreaded.

"Isn't this cute?" Trevor said.

28

Trevor and Brian and Bryan had snuck up on them. Linus came strolling up behind them, looking less like a bully than the other three, as usual. Travis and Kenny weren't with them this time.

Soda ignored them for a moment and looked at the pictures on the camera. Maybe if he ignored them they'd go away? The first picture was of a man-shaped shadow behind a curtain in the bay window at Mr. Creepy's house. It was a Creepy-shaped shadow, actually. The second was the same, but he had moved a little to the left. In the third, it looked like Creepy was bending down, maybe to pick something up? There were a few in succession as he bent down. The next picture was the kicker. The shadow was no longer a man, but a dog . . . or a wolf! A few more showed the shadow walking to the left. The last few showed the shadow at the back door. There was no longer a man-shaped shadow in the bay window or at the back door. Soda looked at Mystery, then at Darren.

"You don't think, do you, Mys?"

"It sure looks that way, doesn't it? It *looks* like Mr. Creepy is"—she lowered her voice—"a werewolf. But, he can't be, since werewolves aren't real. *Are they*?"

"Gimme that!" Trevor snapped as he grabbed the camera out of Soda's hand.

"Hey, give that back!" Soda yelled and stood up. Trevor towered over him. He only stood head-to-chest with Trevor. Soda felt fear bolt through his entire body like electricity. His breathing hastened and his pulse quickened. He wanted to say something else, something tough, but was afraid his voice would crack. The fear was strong and unwavering; Soda did his best to stomp it back down. It was embarrassing being scared and bullied in front of people. The only thing worse as a kid was probably seeing your mom or dad hurt and not knowing what to do. Maybe he shouldn't have jumped up like that; maybe it was okay. Either way, it was too late now.

Trevor held the camera up over his head, hoping that Soda would jump up and try to get it over and over, but Soda didn't. Both Bryan and Brian laughed while Linus had a blank expression on his face. Mystery stood up, too, and remained quiet. She was afraid that Trevor might throw her camera in the pond or push her or Soda into the pond. Trevor glared at both of them with his beady brown eyes that begged either of them to touch him. Not that he needed an excuse to start a fight with a boy, but he would with a girl. He figured Mystery would go tattle to her daddy if he threw the first punch.

"Come on, Trevor, what are you going to do with my camera?"

Trevor thought about it for a second, as if he didn't know what to do with a camera.

"Take pictures, dummy!"

The Brians laughed like Trevor was the funniest guy alive. Soda gave them a disgusted look. Trevor looked over at them and laughed too. Soda saw Trevor was distracted and jumped up to grab the camera back. He almost had it, but Trevor pulled it back and pushed Soda with his left hand, sending him splashing into the pond. There was a smack when he hit the water—flat on his back with his arms and legs spread out. Luckily, he landed in the water and not on the rocks. Despite the embarrassment, he was glad he didn't get crippled at the creek.

"Good one, Trev!" Brian yelled as they all laughed. Linus couldn't help it this time.

"Yeah, good one, Trev," Bryan added.

"Trevor, you jerk! Just give it back!" Mystery yelled.

Soda sat up in the pond and put his wet Braves hat back on. When he stood up, muddy green water poured off him. He shook his arms, hoping to get more water off, and trudged out of the pond with sneakers that were now weighed down with pond water. He didn't want to give Trevor any satisfaction, so he said nothing. Instead, he just stood back next to Mystery, dripping water.

"I don't *just give* things back, muffin-head! Maybe you could earn it back?"

"Earn it back? You want me to *earn* my own camera back? How?" Mystery asked.

Trevor pondered for a moment, and then looked at their bikes.

"Well, how about we settle this on The Track? We'll do a High Fiver. If either of you two can beat me, the camera is yours. If you can't," he laughed, "the camera is mine."

A High Fiver was what they called a five-lap race and was often used to settle a debate or argument.

Darren quickly hopped on his bike and zipped away as fast as he could. Trevor turned toward him and saw Bryan was going to go after him. Trevor shook his head so Bryan let him ride away.

"Deal!" Soda said, pointing at Trevor's face.

"Deal!" Mystery added.

"Deal. Let's go, boys."

Trevor handed the camera to Linus for safekeeping until after the race.

"Hang on to this for me, Linus. I don't want either of these two idiots to break my new camera."

Trevor and his gang jumped on their bikes, as did Mystery and Soda; then they all headed for The Track.

"I wish we could go get our helmets," Mystery said.

"Me, too. I'd also like to race in dry clothes instead of these stinky, wet ones. He'll keep your camera for sure if he thinks we're chickening out. He won't even give us a chance to come back."

"You're right. How are we going to beat him, Soda? He's so big."

"I'm not totally sure. I still can't believe that Darren took off like that. We're getting your camera back. We'll just have to figure out how."

"We'd better think fast," Mystery said. "Real fast."

29

They rode back through the neighborhood the opposite way they had come to Crippler's Creek and turned right toward the dead end of Nighthawk Avenue to the BMX track. All the bike traffic had worn down a dirt path amidst the weeds that led to The Track. When they got there, the Brians and Linus set their bikes down while Trevor rode up the hill to the start-finish line. Linus clutched the camera like his life depended on it.

Trevor's gang walked up next to Trevor. They wanted a good view of the race and a front-row seat if there was a photo finish. Not that they figured there'd be one. They knew Trevor would totally dust the mystery-solving duo.

"You dweebs ready?" Trevor snorted at Mystery and Soda.

They both nodded. The three racers lined up: Trevor on the inside, Soda in the middle, Mystery on the outside.

Mystery realized she was still wearing her backpack. It would surely slow her down. She turned to Linus.

"Since you're already holding *my* camera, Linus, would you mind holding *my* backpack, too?" she asked, handing it to him.

"Sure," he said, trying not to sound eager.

"Okay, then, let's do this, losers," Trevor snapped. "Brian with an *I*, you call it.

"On your mark . . ."

All three of them got their pedals ready. Trevor and Soda glared at each other, and then down the hill.

"Get set . . ."

They leaned forward. The summer air was still with anticipation. All three of their hearts were pounding.

"*Go*!"

30

The three of them zipped down the starting-line hill in a cloud of dust. It was obvious from the start that it hadn't rained in a while. It was rarely *that* dusty. They were neck and neck for the first little bit. Soda was surprised that Trevor hadn't tried to start early or to knock him over. Each of them pedaled as hard as they could—partly because they wanted to have a good start and partly because the first jump was a long jump. It was only two bumps but they were far apart. This distance seemed farther on the first lap since riders didn't have the speed built up from a previous lap. They gave it all they had to hit the jump smoothly. The Track was still nearly as wide as the start-finish line at that jump, so there was little danger of hitting another rider in the air. In this case, they all hit it at the same time and safely cleared it. That would be the last time they'd be in a tie.

Trevor hit the berm on the first left turn very high and sped ahead of Mystery and Soda. Dust flew in their faces but they hardly reacted. Soda pulled slightly ahead of Mystery just before they hit the second left turn, which pointed them to the S-curve. These curves were very sharp, and it was impossible to stay in the middle and keep a straight line. Before last summer the curves weren't as extreme and it was possible to take it pretty easily, but not anymore. Soda was good at this part and gained a little bit on Trevor. Mystery fell back a tad.

Following the S-curve was a very sharp U-turn to the left. Trevor also hit this turn very high and pressed on. Soda was about ten feet behind him at this point and tried to hit the turn high and light like Trevor did but didn't get as much momentum. Mystery stayed right behind Soda.

Then it was time for what was called the "quadrumple"—four mini-jumps in a row. This section was difficult to navigate if you weren't careful. They both took it in two jumps. Soda rode it like a snake, landing on his front wheel first on both jumps, while Mystery landed on her front wheel on the first jump and on her back wheel on the second.

Next came the only right turn on The Track. Soda gained a little on Trevor, but Mystery had to slow up some.

Trevor came to the medium jump in the straightaway called "Meaty." The tricky part about this jump wasn't the distance, since it was only about three feet long, but rather the angle of the landing—it was straight up and down, forming a right triangle with the ground, and if your back tire didn't land on top or beyond it, you'd either wreck or get left behind. Trevor hit it effortlessly. Luckily, Soda did too, and Mystery.

Trevor maintained his lead as he came up to "The Mud Pit," which was normally, like its name, muddy. Today it was almost completely dry, so there was no danger of getting stuck. It wasn't a very long jump, but it was high, and the pit was a few feet deep.

Trevor hit The Mud Pit and flew into the air, clearing the would-be mud with no problem. Soda picked up some speed to hit it as Trevor rode onto the left-turn berm; Mystery was still a few feet behind. Soda went up the dirt ramp and launched into the air as if from a slingshot, and flew through the sky. It was such a good jump that he almost cleared the landing. Trevor was coming back the other way, and Soda saw the look of surprise on his face. Mystery was next. She hit it beautifully—not too high, not too far, with a smooth, soft landing. They chased Trevor around the last left turn of the track, and they all sped up the hill toward the start-finish line.

One lap down and four to go. Mystery and Soda still wondered how they could pull off a win.

As they came to the end of the third lap, Trevor had a comfortable lead and slowed up at the top of the start-finish line, almost coming to a stop. He was beaming with confidence and turned his head to watch his alleged competition. Soda saw this and, even though he was now very tired, he managed to push a little harder, hoping to catch up some; and he did. Mystery was exhausted and had fallen back a little. They were feeling the effects from not sleeping. Trevor noticed Soda's burst of determination and speed. He turned his focus back to the track ahead of him and accidentally turned his handlebars too sharply left for a second, and it cost him. He nearly rode off the side of the hill, almost off the track. Fortunately for him, he quickly turned back to the right and pedaled toward the long jump. Soda was now right next to him. They glared at each other with hatred and determination.

31

At the long jump on the last lap, Soda had the momentum from the fourth lap while Trevor had lost speed with his mishap. Soda realized this would make it difficult for Trevor to clear the jump, so he pushed harder, hitting it first and clearing it like a pro. Trevor hit it a second later and didn't have the speed. His back wheel landed awkwardly, forcing his front wheel to slam down hard, which slowed him up some. Soda pulled farther ahead and zipped through the S-curve—right, left, right, and into the left turn.

Mystery had gained on Trevor and was now only about one bike length behind him. He could feel her close and the pressure she brought—girl pressure. He'd never live it down if he lost to a stinking girl. So, he pushed his pedals with all his might through the S-curve and around the left turn. Soda hit "quadrumple" as usual and took a middle line though the right U-turn. Trevor went up the berm a little higher and gained some ground on Soda. Mystery stayed as close to Trevor as she could.

Through the long straightaway of Meaty and The Mud Pit, Soda was in the lead with Trevor's front tire even with his back tire and Mystery still a bike length behind.

As they hit the final left turn, an evil smirk slowly crept across Trevor's face. He looked down at Soda's back tire and turned his handlebars. Their tires collided for a second, making a loud rubbing noise. Trevor turned into Soda harder, and Soda felt his bike wobbling out of control. He *knew* Trevor would do something like this. Mystery saw what was happening in front of her in slow motion. She wanted to yell at Trevor but was out of breath. She continued pedaling hard, knowing this was almost over.

"Watch this!" Bryan said and slapped Brian in the chest. "He's going down! I know it!"

Soda felt the force from Trevor's bike and he knew it, too. He *was* going down. His eyes widened and his grip tightened as he tried to keep his balance. It wasn't enough. His bike wobbled back and forth and further out of control. He turned his handlebars back and forth and back and forth, trying to resteady himself. He couldn't. Just before he fell off to the right, he had an idea. He looked over at Trevor's smiling face and returned a smile as he shifted his body as far left as he could.

Trevor looked confused. Soda's right hand came free from the handlebars, his right foot came off the pedal, and he came off his seat. This was going to hurt and Soda knew it, but it'd be worth it, too. He hoped he wouldn't break any bones in the process.

Trevor realized what was going on and was helpless to do anything about it. Soda kept his left foot on the pedal and fell into Trevor's bike, sending both bikes and boys down onto the dusty track with grunts and loud, hollow thuds. Trevor fell to his left and scraped his left elbow on the ground. Soda spilled over Trevor's bike and onto his back, and his head smacked the ground. Soda saw a bright yellowish-green flash, like lightning. Fortunately, he remained conscious. He really wished they had their helmets.

"Ooooh!" the Brians moaned as Trevor, Soda, and their bikes finally came to rest in a dusty heap.

Mystery cringed as the slow-motion crash unfolded in front of her. Things returned to normal speed as she rode past them.

"No! Stop her!" Trevor yelled to the Brians as he tried to pull his bike out from under Soda.

Brian took a step forward to block Mystery or push her over. Linus stuck his arm out, stopping him. Brian glared at Linus to ask him what he was doing, but it was too late. Mystery raced across the finish line as the winner. Soda managed a smile as he slowly staggered to his feet. He tried to brush the dust off of his damp clothes. He didn't think anything was broken and didn't see any blood.

"You cheater!" Trevor screamed at Soda.

"Me? *You're* the one that wiped *me* out! *You're* the cheater!"

The Brians ran down to Trevor while Linus walked. Mystery rode past Linus, who winked at her, and stopped next to Soda. She jumped off her bike and it fell to the ground.

"Are you okay?" she asked.

"Yeah, I think so," he replied. He put his hand up to give her a high five. She smacked it hard—a high five for the High Fiver.

"Trev, are you all right?" Bryan asked, and put a hand on his shoulder.

Trevor pushed Bryan's hand away like an annoying fly. "There's absolutely no way I'm giving you your camera back, you stinky little muffin! I don't care if you go tell your policeman daddy, either!"

They should've seen this coming. Trevor could be such a typical bully, but even if they didn't get the camera back, at least they had beaten him. He'd never forget this . . . *ever*.

"Don't be a sore loser, Trevor!" Soda said.

"Oh, shut up, Soda. I oughtta deck you!" Trevor said.

He bumped into Soda with his chest, knocking Soda back a step. Then he got in Soda's face. Soda wanted to punch him in the face and knew he'd be justified since Trevor started it. For some reason, he restrained himself.

"*You're not* getting your camera back, muffin-butt!" Trevor said, pointing at Mystery. Then he turned back to Soda and pointed in his face. "And you'd better hope you didn't mess up my bike, you little puke." His right hand closed into a fist. "But I'm going to mess up your *face* anyway." He snorted as he pulled his right arm back to load up for the punch.

Trevor smiled, and Soda grimaced in anticipation of the impact from Trevor's big hand. It was going to hurt, too.

32

"I wouldn't do that if I were you, Trevvie!"

Only one person called Trevor "Trevvie" and that was Kris McShane.

Trevor cowardly turned away from Soda and slowly lowered his fist. His rage deflated like a balloon. Kris removed his red-white-and-blue motorcycle helmet as he strode up to Trevor. Now it was Trevor's turn to be towered over. Kris was tall and lean, but under all those red-and-white motorcycle racing pads was a muscular frame, and Trevor knew it. Linus's eyes froze on Kris. He realized it would be bad if Kris saw him holding Mystery's camera.

"I'm assuming you were being a jerk and took Mystery's camera? And this race was for the camera? Am I right?" Kris asked.

Mystery and Soda nodded.

"Don't you think you should have a little honor and keep your word, Trevvie? I know you're embarrassed at losing to a girl, but don't feel bad, she is a good rider." He smiled at Mystery.

Trevor opened his mouth to protest. Mystery could see that his face was pink, partly from the race and partly from this confrontation. His breathing was faster and his bottom lip was quivering a little. Trevor opened his mouth to say something.

Kris spoke before Trevor could make a peep. "I thought so."

Linus already handed the camera over to Mystery. He didn't want Kris to turn his attention to him—better to keep it on Trevor.

"Nice job," Linus whispered to Mystery.

"Why thank you." She smiled even though she knew Soda really won the race.

Kris saw Mystery had her camera back and stepped up to Trevor again.

"Trevvie, remember, no one likes a bully. That includes your buddies, your family, and even your mommy."

Mystery and Linus smirked at this while Soda tried, unsuccessfully, to hold back a giggle. Trevor didn't take his eyes off Kris, though.

Kris continued. "And if you don't believe in karma, you'd better start, because it's going to get you . . . sooner or later. I might even be there when it does."

"Whatever, Kris."

"Okay, Trevvie, I'll see you around. Let's go," Kris said as he walked away behind Soda and Mystery on their bikes. When they got to the road, Kris stopped them. "Soda, are you okay? Really okay? Why weren't you guys wearing your helmets or pads? You're lucky you didn't get seriously hurt. I don't want to hear any excuses; just don't race again without your gear."

They both hung their heads a little, knowing he was right.

"You take care, you two. I'll see you later."

"Thanks, Kris," Mystery said. "Wait, how did you know we were out here?"

"No problem," Kris replied and put his helmet on. "A little birdie told me." He started his motorcycle and sniffed a couple of times. "Soda, you stink like Crippler's Creek." He rode off down Nighthawk Avenue, slow and safe.

Mystery and Soda both knew who the little birdie was. Soda felt a little guilty for thinking badly about Darren.

"I *have* to take a closer look at those pics, Mys. Trevor grabbed the camera before I could really get a good look. And look"—Soda pointed at Mr. Creepy's house—"his car is gone."

33

"This is perfect. We can check things out in the daylight!" Mystery thought for a moment. "Unless he pulled his car into the garage?"

"Oh, no, Mys, we're not gonna—"

"Yep, we have to be sure . . ."

"Nooooo!"

". . . so we'll have to knock and see if he answers."

Soda moaned at Mystery and his stomach moaned at him. "Don't you think we should go eat lunch first? I'd really like to get out of these wet, stinky clothes."

"No way. What if he comes home while we're eating?"

"What if he *actually* answers the door?!"

Mystery thought for a moment as they continued riding. Mr. Creepy had already refused food, or the silver platter, and they didn't have anything else to offer.

"I've got it! We'll ask him if we can take his dog for a walk. We'll see if he really has a dog or not."

"Are you crazy? What if he does? And even worse, what if he says yes? Then we'll have to walk the dog that attacked Sheena! No way! Not doing it. Case closed. Let's eat," Soda said, speeding ahead of Mystery.

"Soda, we have to take the chance. I really don't think he's home, so let's not worry about it until we have to. Come on," Mystery said as she quickly turned her bike into Mr. Creepy's driveway.

Soda reluctantly turned around and followed, muttering under his breath. They set their bikes down and crept up to the front door.

"I hope you're right, Mystery."

She started to ring the doorbell, remembered it didn't work, and then knocked on the door.

"Wait!"

"What is it?" Mystery asked as she pulled her hand down.

"What if he doesn't have a dog? What if he turns into a werewolf and expects us to walk him?"

Soda was starving!

"That's ridiculous. He won't want us to know that he's a werewolf."

"Well, what if he *does* want us to know and he turns into one to attack us?"

"Soda, stop it."

Mystery put her hand back up to the door.

"Please don't answer, please don't answer, please don't answer," Soda muttered.

Mystery knocked three times. Soda held his breath and continued muttering. They waited. They waited some more. There was no barking and no footsteps—just more waiting. Still nothing. There was no movement or sound inside or outside. Even the air seemed to be silent and still. Soda finally had to breathe. Mystery turned to him; he motioned for her to walk away, but she knocked three more times. Soda's eyes nearly popped out. There was still nothing.

"What? Don't you want to be absolutely sure he's not here?"

Soda hadn't really considered that. He just didn't want Mr. Creepy to answer the door.

"One more time," Mystery said, and knocked three more times.

An extremely loud bark frightened both of them; they jumped, actually. Soda was about to yell *Run!* But there was more barking. They realized why it was so loud. It was coming from *outside* of Mr. Creepy's house. This turned out to be an awful idea. Mr. Creepy turned into a werewolf and was going to make sure they never stepped on his property again. They cringed, ducked down with their hands over their heads, closed their eyes, and prepared to feel werewolf teeth sink into their skin and rip their flesh apart.

34

"Hey, guys," came a man's voice from behind them.

They both cautiously opened their eyes, slowly stood, and removed their arms from their heads as they turned toward the voice. Mr. Hilton waved at them from the sidewalk in front of Mr. Creepy's house; he was walking their new dog, T-Bone—the former police German shepherd.

Soda and Mystery felt their panic dissipate like a ghostly mist. They stood back up, feeling a little silly.

"Oh, hi, Mr. Hilton," Mystery said, wondering if he'd ask what they were doing or stop to talk. Fortunately, he did neither, and kept walking.

"That scared the crap outta me!" Soda said as his breathing returned to normal.

"Me, too. Now, come on."

They started around the right side of the house before Soda realized something and stopped.

"Mys, do you wanna leave our bikes in front of the house? If he comes home and sees them—"

"Good call. Let's walk them behind the house with us."

They walked along the front of the house, past the front fence gate, and to the side of the yard when Mystery dropped her bike. She saw something in the dry dirt just beyond the edge of Mr. Creepy's yard. Mystery walked over to it and stared at the ground. She blinked her eyes, trying to clear them to make sure she wasn't seeing things.

"What is it?" Soda asked as he set his bike down and stood next to Mystery.

"Look," she said.

"Holy crap." Soda looked down. "No way."

In the dried light brown dirt were footprints. Right next to the yard were a few shoe prints—human shoe prints. At first, they were close together; then they got farther apart, like the person who left them started running. Then the shoe prints were gone and replaced by other prints—paw prints. They faded away into the weeds beyond the dirt.

Mystery grabbed her camera out of her backpack and snapped a few shots. She checked them on the screen to confirm they showed up. They were crisp and clear paw prints.

Their amazement was interrupted by a car engine—the car engine of a creepy car that had just pulled into the driveway. Both were glad they had moved their bikes.

"Let's go!" Mystery exclaimed. She gently tossed her camera into her backpack, picked up her bike, and pedaled with all her might.

Soda followed behind her as they headed over the bumpy terrain toward the dead end. It wasn't a bike trail, but they managed to make it to the end of the road, near the final turn of The Track and behind a small cluster of trees. Soda looked behind them, hoping there wasn't a creepy guy after them—the coast was clear. He turned back around to Mystery and saw Mr. Hilton and T-Bone a little farther away. Mr. Hilton was struggling to control T-Bone. She wanted to get at something.

They carefully rode over to see what was going on. They smelled it before they saw it.

"Ugh, what's that smell?" Soda groaned, waving his hand in front of his nose.

"T-Bone, sit!" Mr. Hilton yelled.

Finally, she listened and sat down next to her new owner, allowing a clear view of what had her so excited. They stopped their bikes a few feet from it.

"That's disgusting," Mystery said. "What is it, Mr. Hilton?"

Mr. Hilton covered his nose and slowly bent down for a closer look. Soda dismounted his bike and stood behind him.

It appeared to be the entrails of an animal strewn about on the weeds and grass. There was a heart, a lung, some other organ, a few fragments of intestines, and maybe some skin. Flies buzzed around the carcass, enjoying their find. The contrast of the reddish-gray guts against the green weeds was surprising. It really made it stand out.

"I'm not really sure *what* it is, Mystery. It looks like what's left of an animal. Although I'm not sure what kind. It doesn't look like it's been here that long, and no other animals have messed with it . . . other than the flies."

"Wonder what happened?" Soda asked.

"Well, it's not hunting season," Mystery whispered.

Mr. Hilton stepped back from the remains. "I'm assuming something else, something bigger, killed it and ate it . . . well, most of it. I wonder what, though? I'm glad y'all are on the case though. I have no doubt you'll get to the bottom of this. The town is counting on you."

"Thanks, Mr. Hilton. We'll do our best."

Mystery pulled her eyes away from the carcass and searched the ground around it. Just to the left of it, she saw something that didn't surprise her at all. There were a few paw prints, just like the ones next to Mr. Creepy's house.

35

"It *is* an animal, right?" Soda asked, hoping this was a ridiculous question.

"It appears so. I'm not an internal organ specialist, but it doesn't look human, since it's too small and arranged a little differently than a person's."

"Well, that's good, at least," Mystery said.

Soda's head still pounded from his bike crash.

"Mys, my head's not feeling too good. I think I need to go take something."

"Okay, Soda, let's go. See you later, Mr. Hilton."

"Bye, guys."

Soda and Mystery rode their bikes up the path from The Track to the road and paused. Mr. Creepy's car was backed into his driveway. They looked around, but there was no sign of him; he must have been inside. Two houses up from the Mooneys', they saw smoke rising up.

"Hey, it's the first Saturday of summer vacation! That means barbeque at the Davidsons'!" Soda exclaimed.

In Whispering Hollow, it wasn't summer until Mr. Davidson smoked a pig. It was the unofficial kickoff of summer.

"That's right! I about forgot! We'd better eat a light lunch so we'll have room for a ton of Bob-B-Q. Let's eat and get you something for your headache."

"And I can change out of these clothes!"

They rode back to Mystery's house for a late lunch and found Mr. Mooney's police car gone. This was strange since it was his day off. When they went inside, Mystery set her backpack in the kitchen chair next to her and pulled out her ponytail. Soda went to the bathroom and washed his hands; then Mystery did the same.

"I can't believe how bad my head is aching," Soda said with a moan. He felt the bump again to see if it had gotten any bigger—luckily, it hadn't.

"Did something happen, Soda?"

Mrs. Mooney gave Soda two ibuprofen tablets from the cabinet and started making ham and cheese sandwiches. Soda explained they were racing at The Track without their helmets.

"You're lucky you didn't get a concussion, Soda. Please don't do that again, you two," Mrs. Mooney said. "Come to think of it, why were you two racing anyways . . . especially without your helmets? And what's that awful smell?"

Mystery explained what happened at Crippler's Creek, what Trevor had done, why Soda's clothes were stinky, and how the race was necessary to get her camera back. She assured her mom they wouldn't ride without their helmets again. Mystery asked her mom not to say anything to Trevor's parents about what happened, and then proudly explained what Soda had done to allow her to win the race.

"That was a very courageous thing you did, Soda. I'm very proud of you. You, too," Mrs. Mooney said, looking at her daughter. "It's very hard to stand up to a bully like Trevor."

"Thanks, Mom." Soda often called Mrs. Mooney "Mom," too.

They were both glad to hear that from Mrs. Mooney. They hadn't stopped to think about it, but it was true. So many of the kids in the neighborhood just let Trevor and his gang roll over them without a word. Mystery and Soda knew how bullying made them feel, and neither of them ever wanted to make anyone else feel that way. In a way, they felt sorry for Trevor. There had to be a reason he acted like he did. Maybe it wasn't entirely his fault? They couldn't figure out why Linus hung out with Trevor's gang. He never got in trouble in school like the other three. But it was kind of like that with friends; sometimes you stayed friends just because you'd always been friends. Mystery thought that Linus deserved a better group. She thought he could be the leader of a good gang.

Mrs. Mooney looked at the children's plates.

"Is there a reason y'all aren't eating your chips?" Mrs. Mooney asked. Mystery and Soda both smiled. "Would it have anything to do with the barbeque at the Davidsons'?"

"We love some Bob-B-Q, Mom!"

"Yes, we all do, don't we?"

"For sure!" Soda yelled.

Mrs. Mooney cleaned up the table for the children and put the dishes in the sink.

"So, what are y'all doing until the Bob-B-Q, young lady?"

"Well, Mom, I was hoping I could use the computer for a little bit. I have some pictures I'd like to look at on the monitor, ya know, to get a better look."

"Oh, really? Take some good ones, did you?"

Mystery thought about it. They weren't especially good, considering that some of them she'd taken accidentally.

"Maybe. That's what I need to see."

"Yes, you can use the computer, sweetie."

"Thanks, Mom!" She paused. "Where's Dad?"

"Oh, he ran to the office to check on someone . . . or something," Mrs. Mooney answered, trying not to sound too suspicious.

"Does it have anything to do with Mr. Creepy? I mean, Mr. Sherlock?" Mystery asked.

"What makes you think that, Mystery Muffin?"

Mystery tilted her head forward and looked at her mom with raised eyebrows.

"Oh, I don't know why I even bother." Her mother sighed. "Yes, your father went to see if he could find out anything more on Mr. Sherlock. You don't miss anything, do you?"

Mystery smiled as she and Soda hustled into the family room to the computer. The computer itself was on, but the monitor wasn't. She turned it on, hooked up her camera, and transferred the pictures from it into a file folder labeled "Mystery's mysteries." They were both excited to get a better look at the creepy shadow pictures. After making sure her mom was busy in the kitchen doing "mom stuff," Mystery opened the photos and started a slide show. On the computer monitor, the pictures appeared even creepier than on the camera. There seemed to be no disputing the fact that the man-shaped shadow was there one moment, and then a dog- or wolf-shaped shadow the next.

"I don't believe this, Mys. Could Darren actually be right this time? Haven't I already asked that? But could he?"

Mystery didn't know what to say. The pictures didn't lie. They seemed to confirm what Darren had said. It literally looked like they had caught photographic evidence of Mr. Creepy turning into a wolf—a werewolf!

"I just can't believe it, Soda. I know what I'm seeing here, but werewolves aren't real."

"Then what *do* you think?"

"There's *got* to be something we're missing."

Soda wanted to believe she was right. He didn't think werewolves were real either; nevertheless, it was hard to dispute it after seeing this. He just didn't know what to think.

Mystery closed out her folder on the computer, shut off the monitor, and disconnected her Nikon.

"Let's go, Soda. We've got more to do." They walked out of the family room, through the kitchen, and out the back door. "Mom, we'll be out back."

"Okay, sweetie."

"I need to go check on Sheena again later, too, Mys." Soda smelled himself and scrunched his face. "Yuck! I need to shower, too."

"Of course. We'll go do that in a bit."

They went out back and climbed up into the tree house. It was time to get a plan together. It was time to get to the bottom of this werewolf business.

36

The afternoon slowly drifted into the evening as the neighborhood got ready for the Bob-B-Q. Many people attended the Davidsons' barbeque, coined Bob-B-Q after Bob Davidson, who'd started it. Many folks were making side dishes and gathering paper plates, cups, plastic silverware, and whatever else they thought would be needed for the event—and it *was* an event. It was the Ninth Annual Summer Kickoff Bob-B-Q. The last few years, the Davidsons had made Bob-B-Q T-shirts for the neighbors using the previous year's donations and tips. The Pumpernickels provided fresh buns from their bakery while Riley and Madelyn Sweets, owners of Dr. Sweets Candy Store and Sweets Family Dentistry, donated an assortment of candy. The Bob-B-Q was a fine Whispering Hollow tradition that was looked forward to by all, including members of the W.H. Volunteer Fire Department and the W.H. Police Department; even Chief Andrews and Mayor Fredericks would stop by. The Davidsons always rented a giant bounce house for the backyard, and there was even a free raffle. Duke Brutal donated a free membership for the summer at Brutal's Gym, and Mike and Maureen Holden would give away twenty-five-dollar and fifty-dollar gift cards to Holden's Hardware. The food was usually ready around four o'clock in the afternoon, depending on how early Bob Davidson got the pig in the smoker—sometimes, depending on how big the pig was, he'd start on Friday night. Bob's wife, Georgia, specialized in her homemade mac and cheese, baked beans, and delicious peach cobbler. She'd also fill several large orange coolers with her homemade sweet tea; she had no use for unsweet tea. Little did they know, this year's Bob-B-Q would be unforgettable—unforgettably creepy, that is.

Mystery and Soda went over to the Slooths' house to check on Sheena. She was still fast asleep and looked like she hadn't moved an inch since lying down that morning after the vet. Soda stared at her leg with the cast and felt bad again. He rubbed her head a little, and she licked his hand and then fell back to sleep.

"It's okay, Soda, you didn't know she'd get hurt. Neither of us did."

"You're right."

"Your mom will be home soon, right? And then it's time for the Bob-B-Q! I'm totally getting a T-shirt this year! We both should!"

Mystery waited downstairs while Soda showered the smell of Crippler's Creek off of him. When he was done, she moved the curtain aside and peered out the front window to see if her dad was home yet. His police car was backed into the driveway.

"My dad is home! I wonder what he found out about Mr. Creepy!"

"Let's go find out, shall we?"

They ran across the street and into the Mooney house, where they found Mr. and Mrs. Mooney in the family room at the computer desk. Her mom quickly turned off the monitor and began playing with her necklace like she always did when she was anxious—or reading.

She didn't want the kids to know she had stumbled upon the pictures on the computer that basically showed Mr. Creepy changing into a werewolf.

"Oh, hey, y'all!" Mrs. Mooney said.

"Dad, did you find anything out? Anything good?"

"Sorry, not really. You know how police reports are—just the facts. He had no arrest history and only one speeding ticket from like twenty years ago. Oh, and his driver's license pictures were all of a human Sylvester Sherlock—no werewolf pictures."

"Really? I guess that's good . . . right?" Mystery asked.

"Of course it's good. We wouldn't want some monster—I mean, criminal—moving in a few houses down from us, would we?"

Mystery noticed her mom continued to mess with her necklace.

Mystery smiled. "No, no we wouldn't."

"So, are you guys about ready for the Bob-B-Q, or what? I could smell it out there."

"We're ready, Dad!"

"Hon, we're actually waiting for Sarah to get home from The Coffee Shop. She gets done at five o'clock, so we'll walk over together when she gets here."

"Great! Let's do this!" Mr. Mooney exclaimed with a clap.

An hour later, Mrs. Slooth got home from work and joined everyone at the Mooneys'.

"So, while I was at work, several people in the coffee shop were talking about this Mr. Sherlock guy. Everyone seems very concerned or scared. In fact, a bunch of folks asked me if Mystery and Soda found out anything yet."

The mood darkened.

"I'm sorry. It was just weird to see our town acting like that."

"Don't worry, Mom, we'll figure it out," Soda assured his mother.

37

Mrs. Mooney carried her cheesecake-stuffed strawberries on a platter, and had what Mrs. Slooth thought was a concerned smile on her face.

The two families walked past the McShanes' and up the Davidsons' driveway. There were several people already there, and it smelled wonderful!

Bob Davidson had installed a wood-framed screen over his entire garage. There was a screen door, and the actual garage door could still be closed behind the screen. A huge wooden sign that read Bob's BBQ was mounted over the garage door.

The Mooneys and the Slooths walked into the garage without knocking—the Davidsons had a no-knock policy. The inside of the garage was finished and decorated like a restaurant. There were several rectangular tables with fold-up chairs and a buffet-type area with tons of plasticware, barbeque, and Georgia's side dishes. Also at the end of the table were Bob Davidson's homemade signature barbeque sauces—hot, spicy, vinegar, and sweet and spicy. By the door going into the house was a large cooler that held a couple gallons of Georgia's sweet tea and "the tip jar." A foosball table and dartboard occupied the right side of the garage. Adding to the ambience were Whispering Hollow knickknacks, including a picture of the town center with the Moustache Monument and the giant tree. There were also other signs about family, good friends, and good food hung all over the walls. The back-wall shelf, set up by Mrs. Davidson, displayed several first-place barbeque trophies and a few contest-winning plaques. Mr. Davidson had installed fluorescent lights on the ceiling along with two ceiling fans. Now it didn't feel like a garage at all.

No one was in the garage, so the Mooneys and Slooths walked out the rear garage door into the screened-in back patio where Bob's favorite country music station was playing. A few neighbors, the Pumpernickels and the Cobblers, were sitting at one of the round tables, already enjoying heaping plates of pulled pork and brisket. Darren smiled at Mystery and Soda with a mouth full of barbeque-sauce-covered meat. Mr. Mooney waved to Mr. Davidson out at the open pit grill. Mystery swore she overheard the Pumpernickels and Cobblers saying something about "I'm not sure he'll come" and "I doubt it."

"Welcome, y'all!" Mr. Davidson greeted them. He was wearing his "#1 BBQ KING" apron and, as always, his green fisherman's hat that was really his barbeque hat. He spoke with a toothpick in the corner of his mouth, as usual, and despite not wearing a red suit, you could tell why he played Santa every Christmas. "Grab yourselves a drink and some food! Mrs. M., I see you made your famous strawberries again! I love those things!"

Mystery thought he was going to end that statement with "Ho ho ho!" Mrs. Mooney offered Mr. Davidson a strawberry, and he popped the whole thing in his mouth, leaving a little bit of graham cracker on his bottom lip.

"Mmmm, delicious!"

"Thank you, Bob. I'll take the rest of these to your lovely wife," Mrs. Mooney said and turned to go inside. "And, Bob, you got a little something on your lip there," she added with a smirk.

Mr. Davidson licked his lips and pointed his sauce-covered grilling tongs at Mr. Mooney. "That's one heck of a lady you got there, Officer!"

"Don't I know it!"

"Are y'all kids ready for summer vacation?" Mr. Davidson bellowed at Mystery and Soda.

"For sure!"

The summer feel of freedom and parties filled the Davidsons' backyard, infecting everyone with smiles and joy; it was nearly impossible to resist the feeling. Mystery thought of someone who would probably try, though—a creepy someone.

Mr. Davidson and Mr. Mooney continued their conversation. All the wood smoke made Mystery and Soda very thirsty. Soda opened a cooler and pushed the ice around, but he couldn't find what he was looking for.

"Not that cooler—the one to the right of it," Mr. Davidson said.

Soda closed that cooler and opened the red one to the right. Inside he could see the tops of several glass bottles—his all-time favorite drink, Stewart's Grape Soda.

"Jackpot!" Soda yelled, and smiled as he pulled out a frosty bottle. It reminded Mystery of a soda TV commercial.

People came and went throughout the evening, enjoying the fellowship, food, and games. Some of the younger children jumped in the bounce house while the adults played the "grown-up" games.

The Davidsons had a horseshoe pit on the back edge of the yard near the wood line. They had cornhole set up, and the bocce ball set was out. But what Mr. Davidson was most proud of was his custom-made open-pit grill and his smokers. The grill consisted of a round shallow hole about ten feet across that was filled with oak wood. It was huge! He sometimes added some pecan shells for additional smoke and flavor. To the left of the grill were three smokers—small, medium, and large. The large one held the half of a pig that had been smoking for the past fourteen hours.

Soon they were all enjoying pulled pork and having a great time. Mrs. Davidson, with her big gray hair, encouraged everyone to be sure to get some peach cobbler before they left. Her Southern accent was like no other.

The Greenes, Trevor's parents, arrived with Travis and mingled with everyone. Mr. Greene went over to where most of the men were hanging out while Mrs. Greene went inside with the women. Travis joined Mystery, Soda, and Darren. The four of them ended up playing two-on-two foosball: Mystery and Soda versus Darren and Travis. It was a very close game, but Travis ended up scoring the winning goal. There was a slightly obnoxious celebration by the winners, but it wasn't anything Mystery and Soda couldn't handle.

After they were done eating and chitchatting with everyone, Mrs. Mooney and Mrs. Slooth decided they were going to leave.

"Try not to keep them out too late, hon," Mrs. Mooney warned her husband.

"Don't worry, hon," he assured her with a kiss.

"Behave, Soda," Mrs. Slooth said to her son quietly.

"I will, Mom."

The ladies walked out, saying good-bye to everyone on their way. Mr. Davidson lit the tiki torches around the yard, and Mrs. Davidson plugged in the strings of party lights, which used to be multicolored smiley faces that Mr. Davidson had recently replaced with little lanterns. The lanterns clattered in the breeze against the neighbors' fences, making a hollow wooden noise. The darkness had set in. Then the howling began.

38

It wasn't just one howl, or even two. There were several, but it sounded like one animal. Everyone at the party stopped talking and looked toward Whispering Woods. Someone turned the country music down while everyone waited and listened. There was another howl that cut through the night like a freshly sharpened knife. It was a long one—very long.

Darren Pumpernickel snuck next to Mystery and Soda. "I betcha it's him," he whispered.

Neither of them responded. They stared out at the trees like everyone else. Sean Tarkanian and Robert Jason, from the post office, stopped their game of horseshoes and slowly backed up toward the Davidson house. There was no fence at the back of the property. Mr. Davidson had cleared out a bunch of the trees to make his backyard larger, and since both his neighbors had fences, he didn't bother with one. This was the first time it seemed like a bad idea. Luckily, the younger children had gone home with their parents, so there was no one in the bounce house out near the wood line.

"That sure sounds like a wolf," Mr. Davidson said.

"We heard some howling last night, too, Bob, did you?" Mr. Mooney asked.

"No, this is the first I've ever heard howling coming from Whispering Woods. I didn't know we had wolves around here."

"I'm not so sure we do . . . exactly," Mr. Pumpernickel said.

"What do you mean?" Mr. Davidson asked.

Mr. Mooney knew where this conversation was going. It was going to get creepy.

Mr. Pumpernickel was about to elaborate when he was cut off by another howl. This one sounded close—too close.

"We'd better get everyone inside, just in case," Mr. Mooney suggested.

At that time, Chief Andrews and Officer Antley walked into the backyard. They had been looking forward to enjoying some Bob-B-Q, but it would have to wait. Such was the life in law enforcement—it's not just coffee and donuts.

Mr. Greene leaned toward Mr. Pumpernickel and asked him what he was talking about. Mr. Pumpernickel quietly explained the werewolf rumors.

Mrs. Mooney and Mrs. Slooth had been at the end of the Davidsons' driveway when they heard the howl. Settling in for the night and relaxing would have to wait; they had to see what was going on. They went back inside the Davidsons' house, afraid to walk home.

Chief Andrews said, "Let's get everyone inside until we know what's going on." It wasn't a yell and it wasn't mean; it was firm, clear, and calm.

People didn't panic and run all over the place, but they did scurry a little.

"Bob, go inside. We'll check this out," Mr. Mooney said.

Reluctantly, Bob listened. He turned the stereo off as he entered the patio where several people had gathered. Mystery, Soda, Travis, and Darren stood at the front of the group, watching. A small group of the ladies gathered in the Davidsons' kitchen at the back window. Mrs. Mooney poked her head around the curtains to make sure that Mystery and Soda were inside the patio. During all the commotion, Mr. and Mrs. Greene called to Travis, and the three of them promptly left. Travis was sad to leave during the excitement and had wanted to hang out with his friends a little longer, but he knew there was no point saying anything to his dad.

Chief Andrews, Officer Antley, and Mr. Mooney were left alone in the Davidsons' backyard. It was very quiet now. Another breeze banged the lantern lights against the McShanes' and Ms. McCall's fences. The three cops crept toward the back of the Davidsons' property and the wood line. As they got a few feet from the horseshoe pit, Officer Antley froze. The other two saw this and stopped.

"What is it, Derek?" Chief Andrews asked Officer Antley.

"Chief, it looks like eyes out there. Yellow eyes about ten to fifteen feet into the woods. Over there." Officer Antley pointed.

The other two looked where he was pointing, but they couldn't see anything. Officer Antley slowly drew his gun and pointed it at the eyes. They reminded him of old Scooby-Doo cartoon eyes. The eyes blinked a few times, and then disappeared.

The three cops stood in a line, Chief Andrews on the left, Officer Antley on the right, and Officer Mooney in the middle.

"Chief, you want to go into the woods? Or would it be better if we just stayed here and made sure no wolves came into the yard?" Antley asked with the feeling that they needed to stay.

"Normally I'd say going into the woods is a bad idea, Derek, but I have a weird feeling about this, like we *need* to go."

Officer Antley thought about it. He wasn't one to question the chief.

"Okay, Chief, I'm with you," Officer Antley said.

Chief Andrews turned to Officer Mooney.

"Matt, I know I'm not your chief, but I think it'd be best if you stayed here while Derek and I head out there. Just in case you're needed here instead of—"

"Say no more, Chief. I'll stay here for now." Officer Mooney patted his right hip where his shirt covered his gun. Chief Andrews had no rank over Officer Mooney, but he still respected the fact he was the chief. In reality, Officer Mooney had no jurisdiction in Whispering Hollow—it was outside of Mecklenburg County—but cops helped cops in times like these, since the brotherhood goes beyond jurisdiction.

Chief nodded and turned to Officer Antley. "Let's go."

Officer Antley sighed as they walked into Whispering Woods with their flashlights lighting the way. They soon disappeared, leaving only the searching flashlight beams visible. Eventually, that light also faded into the dense trees, leaving darkness behind.

Rather than being out in the open, like a sitting duck for a wolf... or a werewolf, Officer Mooney retreated closer to the Davidsons' house.

"Guys, come here," Mystery said to Soda and Darren. She snuck to the side of the patio and sat down at a round table that had a few abandoned barbeque plates.

"What is it, Mys?" Soda whispered.

"There's something we need to do. Listen."

She spoke quietly while the boys listened intently. When she was done, they both nodded.

"Okay, good. I'll tell my dad." Mystery walked out of the screened patio and told him her plan.

"Be quick and be safe, muffin, all right? Then come right back here—no stopping. And stay together."

Mystery nodded. "Okay, Daddy."

Officer Mooney watched his daughter walk back into the patio. Soda and Darren followed her into the garage and out front.

Please be careful, he thought.

Mrs. Mooney looked at him with a bewildered look on her face and her arms out, asking what in the world he was doing.

He mouthed, *It'll be okay.*

39

"I know it's not far, but I think we should get our bikes," Soda said. "It'll be much faster."

Mystery thought about what her dad had said. She figured he meant "no stopping" on the way back, afterward. Soda was right; it *would* be faster.

"Let's go get Darren's first; then we'll get ours," Mystery stated.

They ran up to Darren's house, and he grabbed his bike from the open garage. Next, they grabbed Soda's and then Mystery's.

"Let's go," Soda said.

They rode down the road toward Mr. Creepy's house. The streetlights were out again, and it would've been extremely dark if not for the giant moon above them—the giant *full* moon. Darren pointed up to it as if it proved his point.

"So, we're just gonna see if he's there, right?" Soda asked.

"Right."

"And if he is, what are we going to say?" Soda asked.

They continued riding while Mystery thought about it. The

summer air rushed over them, blowing their hair and howling in their ears as the moon lit their way. To Soda there was something about the color of the moonlight; it was special. It created such a unique look to the darkness. It was so bright that they could see their shadows tagging along beside them on the road.

"I know. We'll invite him to the Bob-B-Q," Mystery answered.

She figured he'd rudely refuse, and they'd be on their way—simple as a Georgia Davidson pie.

Soda and Darren looked at each other.

"Good call, Mystery," Darren said. "I don't think we'll have to worry about it. I doubt he'll answer the door. I betcha he's out roamin' around in this full moonlit night."

"We'll see," Mystery muttered, hoping he was wrong but afraid he was right.

Mystery and Soda weren't quite as nervous as earlier. It sure wasn't the same as going to see if your friend could come out to play. Soda's heart raced and Mystery's stomach was full of butterflies. The anticipation of seeing Mr. Creepy up close wasn't there this time around, and they didn't have to apologize either.

As they got closer to his house, they saw four or five shadows on bikes in front of Mr. Creepy's house. One of them turned and saw Mystery, Soda, and Darren riding in their direction. Another one yelled *let's go* in a familiar voice, and they zipped through the darkness down Dark Pines Drive. The shadow riders laughed as they disappeared into the darkness. There was a smaller shadow rider at the rear of the line.

They heard him yell, "Wait up, guys. I didn't even do anything!"

For a second, the moonlight revealed he was on a bright neon-green bike. They knew who the shadow riders were, but not what they were doing in front of Mr. Creepy's house.

They pedaled up Mr. Creepy's driveway, being careful not to hit his creepy black car, and Mystery saw that Darren might be right. They may *not* have to worry about it.

"Look!" Soda said. "The door! It's open!"

They set their bikes down on the walkway to Mr. Creepy's porch. Soda was right; the storm door was open a foot or so, and the front door was wide open. They also saw what the shadow riders had been doing. There were smashed eggs all over the front of the house. A few were dripping down the storm door onto the porch.

"Like I said, I betcha he's not here," Darren boasted.

"Now what?" Soda asked.

"Nothing's changed," Mystery answered as she walked up to the door and knocked.

It was a hard knock and the door creaked open a little more.

"I'm tellin' y'all, he's not here," Darren said.

There was no answer.

Mystery knocked again, remembering how earlier he hadn't answered right away. They quietly waited, bunched together as if they were atop a pedestal and would fall off into an infinite abyss. Each of them tried looking deeper into the house from where they were, but there wasn't much to see. There was only one light on inside the house, and it was either very dim or nowhere near the creepy front hallway. All they could see was an empty hallway leading to the kitchen. There weren't any pictures or decorations on the wall, and there was only one chair at the kitchen table. Mystery found this to be kind of creepy . . . but also kind of sad.

"Wonder where the other three chairs are?" Soda whispered.

"Who knows? Guess he's not planning on having dinner guests?" Mystery wondered.

"I doubt werewolves have many folks over for dinner," Darren added.

Mystery and Soda glared at him.

"What? I just figure that werewolves eat *out* a lot! Get it? Eat *out!* Like *out*side!" Darren laughed.

Soda tried not to chuckle.

"Maybe we just can't see the other chairs? Who knows? All we know right now is he's not answering the door."

"I wonder where he is. And why would he just leave his front door open like this? It's creepy," Soda said.

"I didn't see anyone chase after Trevor and the gang, did you guys?"

Both boys answered, "Nope."

"I really wasn't looking, though," Soda said.

Mystery knocked again, then yelled, "Mr. Sherlock!"

Her voice was so loud that Soda and Darren jumped.

"Jeez, Mys! Warn me next time!" Soda gasped.

"Mr. Sherlock! Are you in here? We're having a barbeque and wanted to see if you wanted to come," she yelled with her head nearly inside the door.

"Mys, what are you doing?"

"Soda, I'm just trying to get a better look. Maybe we should go inside?"

"Are you kidding me?" Darren asked.

"Yeah, Mys, we can't just go inside his house."

"Well, my dad says you can if you think someone is hurt or something like that. What if he's inside and hurt or passed out and his dog ran out the front door? Maybe he was letting the dog out, felt funny, went to call for help, and fell out?"

"Or maybe he opened the front door, the moonlight hit him, and he violently transformed into a wolf?" Darren suggested, making contorting movements with his arms, legs, and head as if *he* were transforming.

Soda smiled.

"Darren, stop it!" Mystery snapped.

"I dunno, Mys, it doesn't feel right," Soda said.

Mystery pondered in silence for a moment.

"I guess you're right. We don't really have any reason to think he's hurt inside. I guess we'll just hurry back and tell my dad that Mr. Creepy wasn't home. He'll be starting to worry if we don't hurry back."

They stood there in silence for a moment.

"Do we shut the door?" Soda wondered.

"I'm not sure," Mystery started. "Maybe we should—"

The sound of her voice was drowned out by a loud, sharp bang that echoed all around them. They all nearly jumped out of their skin and frantically looked all around them for a source, but there was nothing. Mystery realized what the bang was—a gunshot.

40

The gunshot pierced the stillness of the night and echoed through the neighborhood and the Davidsons' backyard. There was a collective gasp from everyone at the Bob-B-Q. Officer Mooney drew his gun and commanded everyone on the patio to get down as he ducked behind a big tree. He pressed his back against the tree and then motioned for the ladies in the kitchen window to move away. They complied, with looks of worry and awe. Some were screaming while others held their hands over their open mouths. Mr. Mooney saw his wife put her arms around a few of them and escort them away from the window, leaving an empty breakfast table behind. He waited for another shot or return fire, but there was neither. Then he thought he'd hear Chief or Officer Antley say something, but it was still silent. Officer Mooney really wished he had a police radio to hear what was going on out there. Maybe they'd call headquarters for an ambulance or call for help from other officers. He felt useless just waiting, but what else could he do? The shot left behind a hollow echo in the air.

Officer Mooney's thoughts turned to Mystery. He momentarily started to panic . . . a little. It was hard to tell exactly where the shot had come from, but he was pretty sure it was fired from somewhere out in Whispering Woods. His worry about his daughter diminished; however, he was still concerned about who fired the shot and why. He'd been a member of the Charlotte Police Department for over eight years, and he'd never had to fire *his* gun in the line of duty.

He waited in the silence for another minute or so. A few crickets chirped in unison from somewhere in the backyard.

"Chief? You guys okay? Tell me you're okay," he pleaded to the wood line. "Chief?"

No answer. Despite wanting to go out there and see if everyone was okay, Officer Mooney fought off the urge and stayed put. He'd have to wait.

He wondered if there were any other Whispering Hollow officers working. Usually there were at least two working, sometimes three if you counted Chief. Maybe Sergeant Frisk or Sergeant Major was working and had heard the shot or the radio traffic, if there was any, and they'd be on their way here. Then, almost as if on cue, Officer Mooney heard a siren approaching. As the responding officer got close to the Davidsons', he cut the siren off, but the blue lights still illuminated the night. Officer Mooney could see them flashing between the houses.

Seconds later, the blue lights went off and a car door slammed shut. Sergeant Frisk hustled through the screened-in patio, past the frightened partygoers, and into the backyard.

"Sarge, over here!" Officer Mooney motioned from the tree he was using as cover from any wolves, werewolves, or gunshots. He wasn't quite sure which he was more concerned about—and this bothered him. Sergeant Frisk, a little out of breath, quickly ran up to Officer Mooney. "Sarge, tell me you know what's going on!"

"All I know is that Chief didn't fire the shot and that Antley hasn't responded since the round was fired. I've called for an ambulance to stand by until we know for sure what the deal is. We don't know who fired the shot," Sergeant Frisk explained in his strong Southern accent. He brushed his brown hair off his sweaty forehead and back into its proper place.

Despite this information, Officer Mooney felt like it only raised more questions.

The cricket chorus came to an abrupt stop midtune. Sergeant Frisk and Officer Mooney slowly turned toward Whispering Woods.

"Do you hear that, Mooney?" Cops always seemed to use each other's last names.

It sounded like leaves rustling.

"Yeah," he said as he turned to get a better view.

"Do you see anything?"

Officer Mooney looked around, all over, back and forth. "Sarge, I got nothing."

There was some more rustling; it stopped for a few seconds, and then continued. Suddenly a figure appeared at the wood line. They couldn't tell if it was a hunched-over person or an animal.

"I'll be dipped in grits! Mooney, do you see that? Is that a man? Or a dog? Or a wolf?" Sarge asked in awe. He drew his gun and took aim. *"Don't move!"*

41

Chief Andrews was glad that Officer Mooney hadn't given him a hard time about staying behind. He knew he'd keep everyone safe at the party and didn't want to risk anything happening to him out in the woods. It's not that he didn't care if anything happened to Officer Antley or himself, but it was *their* job, *their* town, and they were on the clock.

Chief and Officer Antley stayed close to each other as they crept deeper into the woods, shining their flashlights all around. Sometimes shining a flashlight around in the dark wasn't a good thing. It gave away your position and could give the bad guy, or a wolf, a target. As they went deeper into the woods, they couldn't see a thing, let alone navigate through the woods without a light.

"Derek?"

"Yeah, Chief?"

"Be careful."

The light coming from the Davidsons' backyard was completely gone, leaving only darkness behind them. After about twenty yards into the woods, they came to a small clearing that had paths going in two directions. The "path" had overgrown weeds and other growth covering it, but it was there. Chief surveyed both options and saw the path to the right had some trampled-over weeds while the other did not. He looked back at the fork in the path and motioned to the right, so they went right.

Officer Antley felt sure they were being watched and looked around for someone or the eyes he had seen before. They trudged on with only the sound of their footsteps. He was now in front of Chief and came to an abrupt stop when he heard a noise, like maybe a twig snapping, and saw something in his flashlight beam. Chief didn't say anything, but instead shone his light around Officer Antley, looking for whatever had made the noise. A dark figure moved just beyond his light. His cop instincts took over and he took off after it without thinking.

"Derek, wait!" Chief yelled.

In an instant, Officer Antley disappeared into the darkness.

This is why we don't go into the woods at night, Chief thought as he carefully chased after his officer. He wasn't running, exactly, but he was moving quickly without being reckless, unlike Officer Antley.

Officer Antley was determined to catch the shadow figure, but it was pulling away. He took fairly good care of himself; however, with the extra weight of all his police equipment, the adrenaline surging through his veins, and the effort it took to pick his way through the woods, this chase was wearing him out. He ducked under branches, jumped over tree roots, and weaved left and right around trees and bushes. Just as he was gaining on the figure, he turned to look behind him—Chief wasn't there. He looked back ahead of him and stumbled on a tree root that sent him flying through the air. He put his hands out to brace his fall, allowing his flashlight and gun to fall to the ground. The impact of crashing onto the ground stole his breath away. His flashlight rolled to a stop, shining right in his face; he felt like he was in a spotlight. His gun, luckily, didn't go far. It was in the pine needles close by. He gripped it and brought it close to him. As he tried to get his breathing under control, he jumped back to his feet and pointed his gun into the darkness, ready to pull the trigger. He waited. There was no movement. Whatever it was, was gone.

Officer Antley slid his gun back in the holster and brushed off his uniform. He bent over with his hands on his knees, trying to catch his breath, when he heard something off to his left. He didn't want to move so he only shifted his eyes, but he couldn't see anything. His own flashlight was still shining at him and robbed him of a clear view. The sound got louder. It was an awful rumbling that slowly rose up to growling. He started to panic and couldn't move. The growl got louder and closer. He could only imagine what was right next to him, ready to take a piece of him. He slowly reached for his gun and gently removed it from the holster.

The growling got louder and sounded even closer. It was impossible to tell which direction it was coming from. Officer Antley didn't want to shoot blindly into the darkness in the direction of the growl. He might hit Chief or someone else. He was afraid if he moved, whatever was growling at him would attack. Sweat ran down his forehead into his eyes as his breathing slowed a little. There was only one thing to do—run. It might draw out whatever or whoever was lurking in the darkness. He turned around and sprinted in the direction he had come from. After about ten feet, he glanced behind him and didn't see anything; he didn't stop running, though. Just because he didn't see anything didn't mean it wasn't there, or that he was safe. He was in a full sprint when his head smacked a thick, low tree limb that knocked him completely off his feet. His right pointer finger tensed and jerked, pulling the trigger. The gun fired as he hit the ground. Officer Antley raised his head up a little, but it was too heavy to hold up. His eyelids wouldn't stay open as his vision of the woods and sky darkened. He was unconscious.

42

Mystery, Soda, and Darren, being careful not to slip on egg, hopped on their bikes and sped back to the Davidsons'. They all wondered who fired the shot and if someone was hurt. Mystery's thoughts turned to her dad. She hoped he was okay, and wanting to make sure made her pedal even harder. It could also be dangerous going toward where the shot came from, but Mystery figured if things were really bad there would've been more shots. Then again, it only took one shot to take someone's life.

They saw an ambulance parked on the roadside a few houses up as they pulled into the Davidsons' driveway. A few neighbors were rushing out to their cars and hurrying up the sidewalk. They weren't in a panic but they weren't exactly calm. That was hopefully a good sign that no one at the Bob-B-Q was hurt. Each of them dropped their bikes next to the driveway and went through the garage. People were still watching the backyard, and there was excitement and concern on most of their faces. Mystery ran out to her dad despite Mr. Davidson yelling at them to wait. Soda and Darren heard him and stopped at the doorway to the backyard.

Officer Mooney watched Sergeant Frisk scurry toward the wood line and didn't see Mystery until she was right next to him. She kind of startled him, but he couldn't have been more relieved that she was safe. He tried not to show how worried he'd been. Mrs. Mooney would've killed him if something had happened to Mystery.

"What is it, Mys? Was he there?"

Mr. Mooney saw his wife look out the kitchen window. She stopped messing with her necklace and put her hand on her chest in relief. He shared the feeling.

"Dad, he wasn't there. Well, he didn't answer the door and his door was left wide open. We saw Trevor and the gang riding off after they egged his house, and we thought maybe he chased after them, but we never saw him."

"Those knuckleheads egged his house? What about his dog? Was Goliath there? Did he bark?"

"We didn't see or hear him. I thought maybe we should've gone—"

"I'll be dipped in grits! Mooney, do you see that? Is that a man? Or a dog? Or a wolf?" Sergeant Frisk asked in awe and drew his gun and took aim. *"Don't move!"*

"Mystery, get inside! Now!" Officer Mooney yelled.

Mystery saw the concern in her dad's eyes. It scared her, but she hurried to the patio.

"Everyone get down!" Officer Mooney yelled.

All the people on the patio dove on the ground with a collective panicked groan. Everyone was quiet, and some safely peeked out into the backyard.

Sergeant Frisk tried to blink his eyes clear to make sure he was seeing what he thought he was seeing. It started to look like the shadow of a man now. Whether this was a good thing or not was unclear. It was good it wasn't a dog or wolf that he may have to shoot, but it would be bad if it was someone who had just shot Chief or Antley. He looked it over, trying to see if there were police patches on the shoulders or a shiny badge or nameplate on the chest, thinking it might be a fellow officer. The last thing he wanted to do was shoot the wrong person—especially one of his coworkers. He kept his gun focused on the shadow as it moved from right to left and came closer and closer to the Davidsons' house.

Officer Mooney took aim as well from behind the cover of the tree. *Please let it be Chief please let it be Chief please let it be Chief,* he thought to himself.

The shadow rustled its way out from the woods some more. Sergeant Frisk was ready to yell at the shadow to stop and get down on the ground.

Everyone who dared watch held their breath as the shadow came closer. Mystery's eyes were wide open and she didn't blink; she *couldn't* blink.

Sergeant Frisk opened his mouth to give the order, when the shadow took one more step into the light, revealing his identity.

"You've got to be kidding me!" Officer Mooney whispered when he saw who it was.

43

Sergeant Frisk didn't hesitate. "Stop where you are and put your hands up!" He shone his flashlight in the man's face, causing him to squint and obscuring his vision.

The man stopped and put his hands up over his head. Mystery saw who it was and turned to Darren and Soda.

"I knew it! He was runnin' round in the woods, howlin' at the moon . . . in wolf form!" Darren exclaimed in a whisper that was hardly a whisper.

Officer Mooney walked out from behind the tree and approached Mr. Creepy.

"Turn around and put your hands behind you back, *now*!" Sergeant Frisk ordered. "Mooney, cover me?"

Officer Mooney nodded and kept his gun pointed at Sylvester Sherlock. They didn't know if he fired the shot or had been shot at or what was going on. Sergeant Frisk pulled out his handcuffs and slapped them on Mr. Sherlock, one wrist at a time.

"Mr. Sherlock, are you okay?" Officer Mooney asked.

"I was out looking for Goliath. He ran out my front door and into the woods. I've been looking for him for a while and kind of got lost out there. I don't suppose he came by here? Didn't you hear me yelling for him?"

"No, we didn't hear you and we haven't seen Goliath," Officer Mooney said, "but we did hear some howling out there."

"I heard the howling, too. It sounded like a wolf; that's why I came to the edge of the woods. I didn't realize where I was."

The partygoers who had taken cover slowly came out from hiding when they realized that things appeared safe. Everyone quietly muttered about what happened as they gathered around. Mystery and the boys snuck up to the tree that Officer Mooney had taken cover behind. They all stared at Mr. Creepy with suspicious eyes.

Sergeant Frisk patted Mr. Sherlock for weapons and found nothing—no gun.

"Mr. Sherlock, there was a gunshot while you were out there . . ."

"I heard it. It couldn't have been far from me. It was very loud. I didn't see anyone, though. I'm afraid someone shot Goliath. He can be pretty intimidating. I guess they still could've. I won't know until I find him."

Mr. Sherlock spoke in a tone of voice nothing like when Mr. Mooney, Mystery, and Soda had gone to his door. He wasn't being mean, rude, or put-out at all. It didn't seem to fit him one bit. Then again, no one really knew much about him other than some rumors. Besides, it took more than a few brief moments to get to know someone.

Officer Mooney was suspicious. Perhaps he was acting this way out of fear for Goliath or from the gunshot? Maybe someone shot at him, or at a wolf.

This was the first look that Mrs. Mooney got at brownie-refusing man. Now she understood why her husband and the children called him creepy. The soft glow of the Davidsons' backyard contributed to it. It exaggerated his facial features and made his skin look pale and nearly fake, like a corpse almost. She shivered.

Darren Pumpernickel and his dad were convinced that Mr. Creepy was out roaming the woods as a werewolf until he encountered the police who likely shot at him and scared him back into human form.

Mr. Pumpernickel stepped off to the side of the yard by himself, took out his cell phone, and whispered to whomever he called.

Mystery was suspicious about Mr. Creepy, too. She wasn't sure what to make of this. His front door *had* been left open and no one was there. Maybe he really was out looking for his dog—likely his only friend. He'd said it was the *howling* that made him come out of the woods, not the *gunshot*, though. She thought that was strange.

Soda, meanwhile, wasn't thinking about what to believe. He was excited, watching the police do their work.

Many of the ladies—including Mrs. Mooney and Mrs. Slooth—came outside and joined their husbands and the others. They hurried out and stood close to the children. The music was still off and it was eerily quiet. Sergeant Frisk called Chief and Antley on the radio again, but there was no response. He asked Judy, the dispatcher, to transmit an alert tone to get their attention.

"Mooney, do you mind walking him out to my car?" Sergeant Frisk asked.

"Sir, I hardly think that will be necessary. I'll answer whatever questions you have. I just really want to find Goliath. So, whatever we need to do, by all means."

Sergeant Frisk thought for a moment. He looked at Officer Mooney, then at Mr. Sherlock, and then back at Officer Mooney, who gave him a shrug.

"Okay, Mr. Sherlock, let's just have a seat over there," Sergeant Frisk said, pointing to a chair just outside the patio. "Let's see if we hear from Chief before we do anything else." Sergeant Frisk got back on his radio. "Judy, you copy?"

"Ten-four, Sarge, go ahead."

"Have you heard from Chief yet?"

"That's negative. I tried Chief and Antley. Neither has responded."

"Can you try the tone again?"

"Ten-four," Judy replied. Her voice was followed by another loud tone that went up and down, almost like a siren. "Headquarters to Chief Andrews, do you copy?" Fear and concern cracked her voice a little.

Officer Mooney; his wife, who was playing with her necklace again; Mrs. Slooth; the children; Mr. Pumpernickel and Darren; Mr. Davidson; and a few others gathered around Sergeant Frisk to listen for a reply. Someone was crossing their fingers; another was quietly whispering "Come on, Chief"; and another was thinking *Please let him be all right*. Moments passed. The radio silence was almost deafening.

Sergeant Frisk thought about calling the Charlotte Police Department to see if they could have a K-9 unit and their helicopter respond to help.

Judy was starting to lose her patience. "Chief Stanley Andrews, you answer me right now!"

There was nothing but dead air.

44

Chief Andrews heard the shot and darted toward where he thought Officer Antley had gone through the woods. He was off the path and in a thick stand of trees, which made him nervous. The trees shielded any moonlight, so the only source of light was from his flashlight. He reached down for his radio to relay the info that there had been a shot fired in Whispering Woods, but he grabbed only air. The radio must have fallen off while he was running. He'd felt his police duty belt bouncing around a little but had no idea it fell off. He couldn't tell anyone about the shot fired, and he was also unable to communicate at all, other than by yelling, which is what he did.

"Antley, can you hear me?" he shouted to the trees.

He stopped to listen . . . no response. He continued. As he searched, he remembered his cell phone. He could call Antley and tell him to stay put and shine his flashlight until he found him. He reached into his uniform pocket to get his phone, but he found only his notebook. Where was his phone? Then he remembered—he had left it charging in his police car. Things were not going well.

There was some rustling up ahead of him. He crouched down a little and scanned the area. The rustling stopped, and then continued again. It sounded like it was moving away from him so he followed it, gun out, just in case. Chief went another twenty-five feet, when the rustling was right next to him. He spun around and shone his flashlight all around. A startled squirrel jumped from one tree to another, causing his heart to skip a beat. After he caught his breath, he saw some light up ahead that looked like it was on the ground. A second later, he heard a loud tone that sounded like a siren. It was a noise he recognized, and he sprinted toward it.

"Antley?" he called out again.

Officer Antley didn't respond, but he did hear a familiar voice. "Chief Stanley Andrews, you answer me right now." It was Judy.

When he came to the light source, he froze in his tracks. What he saw was the last thing he wanted to see. Officer Antley was flat on his back, not moving, with his flashlight next to him lighting up the left side of his body. Chief hurried over to him and checked for a pulse; he was alive. He grabbed Antley's radio.

"Judy, it's Chief; I copy you. We've had a shot fired and Antley is down! Stand by." Chief checked Antley for injuries and, to his relief, discovered he wasn't shot. He did see a nasty abrasion on his forehead, though. Antley's gun wasn't in his holster. He shone his flashlight around and saw it in Antley's right hand—his finger was on the trigger. He safely removed the gun from his hand and secured it back in Antley's holster. "Antley is ten-four, but he's unconscious. He has not been shot. I repeat, he has *not* been shot!"

"Oh, thank God!" Judy replied over the radio. "Units, do you copy? Chief and Antley are ten-four."

Chief Andrews patted Officer Antley on his chest and gently spoke his name. At first, Antley didn't respond. A few seconds later he moaned a little and put his hand up to his forehead. He rubbed the abrasion, which was swelling into a goose egg.

"What . . . what happened?" Antley muttered, looking around as if he didn't know where he was.

"I'm not sure, but you're okay," Chief assured him. Officer Antley started to move the rest of his body. "It looks like you're not broken. Can you get to your feet?"

Antley moaned a little more, bent his knees, and turned on his side. With the Chief's help, he made it to his feet. Chief helped him brush off.

"Oh, my head," Antley said, and groaned.

"You sure took off. What were you after? Or could you even tell out here?" Chief asked him.

"Well, Chief, that's the thing. I couldn't say for sure. At first, the shadow looked like a man. But as I got closer, it started to look like a dog . . . or a wolf—but I did take my eyes off it for a second or two."

45

Back at the Davidsons', there was cheering and clapping when they heard Chief on the radio say that he and Officer Antley were okay. Sergeant Frisk raised his arms and motioned for everyone to quiet down.

"Chief, do you guys need assistance out there?"

"That's negative. We're going to make our way out now . . . hopefully."

"What about the shot, sir?"

"It was an accident. I'll have Antley explain when we get there," Chief said as they picked their way through the woods.

"Ten-four, Chief." Sergeant Frisk turned his attention to Mr. Sherlock now. "Well, that's good news for you, Mr. Sherlock. I suppose I can take those cuffs off you."

Officer Mooney assisted Mr. Sherlock to his feet and turned him around so Sergeant Frisk could remove the handcuffs. Mr. Sherlock rubbed his wrists where the cuffs had left marks on his skin.

"Thank you, sir," Mr. Sherlock said.

"Let's get back to it, y'all!" Mr. Davidson announced and went back to manning the last of the burgers on the fire pit. He had to trash a few that got burned during the commotion.

People drifted back to the barbeque they had left at their tables while others resumed the games they were playing. Some of the ladies went back inside the house, and Mrs. Davidson turned the radio back on.

"Mr. Sherlock, care for a burger or some barbeque before you continue the search for your dog?"

"Thank you for the offer, but I already ate dinner. But I truly like the setup you've got here," he said, pointing all around the backyard. "I think I'll just get back to searching, if you don't mind."

Before Sergeant Frisk could tell Mr. Sherlock he could go on his way, Chief and Officer Antley came trudging out of the woods. Several people went over to greet them, including Officer Mooney and Sergeant Frisk; they crowded around the two policemen like they were the heroes who just won the big game. Sergeant Frisk asked everyone to give them some space. Officer Antley was holding his forehead, which had swollen even more.

The two policemen explained what had happened to them out in Whispering Woods, from Chief losing his radio, to Officer Antley seeing the shadow figure and banging his head, to the fired shot. Mr. Sherlock was among those listening intently.

When they were finished telling their tale, Mr. Sherlock again expressed his desire to search for Goliath.

"Of course, Mr. Sherlock," Sergeant Frisk started. "We appreciate your cooperation in all this. I hope you understand our need to detain you until we could figure out what was going on."

"I understand completely, Sergeant." Mr. Sherlock turned to Mr. Davidson. "Thanks again for the offer." Mr. Davidson nodded at him. "Now, if you don't mind, I'll be on my way." Mr. Sherlock started toward the woods.

"*Sylvester Sherlock*!" a man yelled.

Mr. Sherlock stopped in his tracks, and everyone turned to the person who had yelled. Instead of just one person, there were four people standing by the patio door. The person who called to Mr. Sherlock was Fred Fredericks, the mayor. His smile beamed and his thick wavy blond hair had every strand just where it was supposed to be. The Moustaches were with him: Byron the IV and his wife, Artemia. Escorting them was their butler, Franklin Butler, a gigantic specimen of a man. They were all liked and respected members of the community.

"Hello, everyone!" Mr. Moustache exclaimed. "Mr. Davidson, I hope we're not too late to enjoy some Bob-B-Q." He tugged on the left side of his long, thick black handlebar mustache. He let go of his wife's hand and removed his white fedora. As was typical, he was wearing a snow-white three-piece suit with a white shirt and a black bowtie, which he tied himself, of course. Although there were generations between them, Byron Moustache looked like a human replica of the historic Moustache Monument.

"Not too late at all, Mr. Moustache. You and Mrs. Moustache please enjoy some," Mr. Davidson responded with the giddy grin of someone meeting a movie star in person. His wife gave him a hard time about this quite frequently.

"Why thank you, Mr. Davidson," Mrs. Moustache said, offering her hand. Her evening gown was a beautiful white-and-black print and flowed over her as elegantly as the full black hair cascading down to her shoulders; most anyone else would've looked out of place.

"She's never *under*dressed, is she?" Mrs. Slooth muttered quietly to Mrs. Mooney. Mrs. Mooney smiled and shook her head back and forth.

Franklin Butler stared straight ahead without saying a word. He did manage a slight wave to everyone. He didn't seem himself outside of Moustache Manor. Mystery looked up at the 280-pound man in awe, all six feet and ten inches of him. She thought he resembled Frankenstein a little. And his name was Frank. It cracked her up that his last name was Butler and he actually was a butler. His black suit reminded the children of Dracula. So, he earned the nickname of Frank-ula—not that any of them would call him that to his face.

"Thanks for coming, Mayor Fredericks," Mr. Pumpernickel said as he shook the mayor's hand. Darren walked away from Mystery and Soda and stood by his dad.

"How many times have I asked you to call me Fred? Anyhow, my pleasure, Paul. Thanks for the phone call. Not that I'd miss the Bob-B-Q but this is a perfect place to finally meet the infamous Sylvester Sherlock. Might I have the pleasure, sir, hmm?" the mayor said, rubbing his hands together almost like he was washing them in invisible water.

Mr. Sherlock inched toward them like someone who'd been asked to solve a math problem on the board.

Mr. Pumpernickel leaned in close to the mayor, put a hand up to his ear, and whispered something.

"A wolf?" Mayor Fredericks said a little louder than either he or Mr. Pumpernickel expected.

Mr. Sherlock stopped when he heard it. He was just a few feet from the mayor.

Darren thought this was the perfect opportunity, and he took it.

He pointed at Mr. Sherlock and took a step back. "That's right, y'all! Mr. Creep—I mean Mr. Sherlock—is a werewolf!" Darren said, just as sure as the sky was blue and the grass was green.

46

Mystery and Soda looked at each other in confused amazement. *How could he?* they thought. The crowd gasped and muttered, and a few chuckled a little at this accusation. Darren felt like he had just revealed the biggest secret the world had ever heard. He glared at Mr. Sherlock, as anxious as a kid on Christmas morning, to see the look of shock and dismay on his face. That wasn't the look he saw, though. The smile on Darren's face slowly diminished with each passing second like a breath on glass.

"Now Darren," Chief Andrews said as he came forward. His voice was firm but comforting. He was afraid that people may start to panic and wanted to keep things calm and under control. The last thing he needed now was a riot at the Bob-B-Q over a man being accused of being a monster. "You have quite the imagination, and we all know that. But—"

"No, it's true! Just ask Mystery! She has proof!"

Everyone's head snapped around to stare at Mystery, who was standing between her parents. Like it or not, her opinion mattered.

It held a lot of weight in the neighborhood, and confirming what Darren said would turn the gigglers into gaspers. She was surprised Darren had put her on the spot and was not prepared to respond. Not that that mattered much.

"What's he talking about, young Mystery?" the mayor asked.

The spotlight was on her now. She didn't want to say that it wasn't true, but she did have some evidence. She didn't want to call Darren a liar in front of everyone. She didn't want to agree with him and declare Mr. Creepy a werewolf in public like this. Last, but not least, she didn't like being forced to make a conclusion before her investigation was complete. She looked up at her mom, who looked back with the same awe. She turned to her dad. He looked down at her with a look that said *your investigation isn't over, my little muffin*. She searched her insides for her voice, but it was on a temporary vacation. She felt a small lump in her throat.

"Do tell," Mr. Moustache said. He seemed intrigued.

Mystery knew that if anyone in the neighborhood had an answer to something like this, it would be her; and *she* knew *they* all knew it. Darren stared at her, waiting for her to shock them all with the news. He got concerned when she didn't confirm his claim right away and got more nervous as seconds ticked by and she was still silent. She saw out of the corner of her eye how he was nodding at her with wide eyes that said *come on, spit it out.* She could feel her heart pumping blood through her body now, and the small lump in her throat that had appeared moments ago seemed to grow to the size of a baseball. There was no swallowing it back down, but she did manage to find her voice.

"Well, um, you see, Darren has—"

"Is this about my dog? Goliath?" Mr. Sherlock interrupted. "Yes, he howls like a wolf. He can't help it. He was abandoned as a puppy, and a mama wolf found him and raised him. He still has a few of those old habits."

The crowd seemed to relax a little after this explanation, crazy as it was. It seemed that Mr. Creepy had gotten Mystery off the hook, for now at least. People knew this wasn't the first time Darren Pumpernickel had let his imagination get the best of him. Just last summer he swore he saw a UFO land just beyond Crippler's Creek and told everyone the town had been invaded by aliens. That, of course, was not the case.

"Now, if you don't mind, I really need to find Goliath!" Mr. Sherlock said in frustration, sounding more like the Mr. Creepy they had first encountered. Then he stormed off toward the woods.

Mr. Pumpernickel turned to Chief Andrews. "Can't you stop him, Chief? He's getting away!"

"I can't very well hold a man for being accused of being a werewolf, Mr. Pumpernickel, especially without proof," Chief Andrews replied with a smile that didn't quite call Mr. Pumpernickel a fool.

A few people, including Robert Jason and Sean Tarkanian, chuckled at this. Paul Pumpernickel knew Chief Andrews was right as he watched Mr. Sherlock run into the woods.

"Mr. Sherlock!" Chief called out before he got too far away.

"Yes, sir?"

"Be careful out there. There could still be a wolf on the prowl."

Mr. Sylvester nodded, and a few moments later they heard him calling out to Goliath.

"Well, then, let's eat!" the mayor said, licking his lips.

Mr. Davidson escorted him and the Moustaches to a table in the garage; Franklin Butler followed with a smile, ducking as he went inside.

The Mooneys and the Slooths all looked at each other, wondering if Goliath had been the one doing all the howling. Was it really

Goliath that fought with Sheena? What about the photos that looked like Mr. Creepy had transformed? Mystery and Soda didn't know what to believe.

Mr. Davidson announced it was time for the gift-certificate drawings. He grabbed a plastic fish bowl filled with the names of people who'd entered the one-dollar drawing. Then he and his wife stood in front of everyone.

"First we'll draw the winner of the one-year membership to Brutal's Gym. We'd like to thank Duke Brutal for this generous donation."

Duke Brutal, and all his muscles, stood up from the table he was eating at and waved. This brought on some light applause.

"The winner is . . . Robert Jason!"

"Yes!" Mr. Jason exclaimed and walked up to Mr. Davidson, who handed him the certificate.

Next were the gift certificates to Holden's Hardware. Steve May, Bryan's dad, won the twenty-five-dollar certificate. Now it was time for the fifty-dollar one.

"And the winner is . . . Matt Mooney!"

Mrs. Mooney started clapping right away, and then others joined in. Mr. Mooney walked up to collect the certificate and thanked the Holdens for their donation. He walked back to his wife.

"How about that? And you say you never win anything!" She smiled.

At ten o'clock, Mr. Mooney felt it was time to go. They walked through the patio into the garage and thanked the Davidsons, who were sitting with the mayor and the Moustaches, for their hospitality and the best barbeque in North Carolina. Mr. Moustache gave Mystery a wink as her father spoke. Mr. Mooney stuffed some cash in the tip jar, and they started to walk out the front of the garage when Mr. Moustache called to him. Mr. Mooney walked back over to the table. The rest of them waited outside the door.

"Yes, sir?"

"Officer Mooney, I continue to hear great things about your daughter and her friend there. I hope it wouldn't be too much trouble if I had to call upon her services one day. I'm afraid we've had an antique musket go missing."

Mr. Mooney smiled with fatherly pride. "A musket? I'm sure she'd be willing to assist you, Mr. Moustache."

"Great! I thank you," he said as he wiped some barbeque sauce off his lips and then shook Mr. Mooney's hand.

"Good evening to you all," Mr. Mooney said to the table, trying to sound formal, and he walked out the door.

"Hey, y'all, don't forget to grab a T-shirt before ya head on home," Mr. Davidson said, pointing over at the stack of shirts by the wall.

"Thanks, Bob," Mr. Mooney said.

They all went to the stack of shirts, picked one that fit, and thanked Mr. Davidson. Then they walked out of the garage and stood in the driveway.

"Oh, I almost forgot. I need to get a doggie bag for Sheena. I'll be right back," Soda said.

They waited in the Davidsons' driveway for Soda.

"What was that about?" Mrs. Mooney asked her husband.

"Yeah, Dad, what did Mr. Moustache want?"

Soda returned with Sheena's dinner, and they strolled down the sidewalk toward their house.

"Well, he said he might need some assistance from Mystery and Soda. Something about a missing musket."

"Really?" Mrs. Slooth asked.

"Yep. These two have quite a little reputation around here." He smiled.

"Not like Darren Pumpernickel, though." Mrs. Mooney chuckled. "I'm sorry—I shouldn't laugh." After all, she had seen the pictures Mystery had taken.

Mr. Mooney had seen them, too. Neither of them had said anything about it. They knew Mystery and Soda would get to the bottom of this mystery.

The group stopped in front of their houses. Mystery wondered if her parents were going to ask her about what Darren had said and if she really did have some kind of evidence. She didn't really want to get into all that tonight, though. Her plan was to go straight up to bed and hopefully avoid the chance of that conversation even getting started.

"Another exciting Bob-B-Q, I'd say, wouldn't you?" Mr. Mooney asked them.

"Well, you did win the fifty-dollar gift certificate to Holden's Hardware!" Mrs. Mooney said.

They all laughed and said good night to each other.

"Well, it can't get much weirder than that, huh?" Mr. Mooney laughed as they walked up their driveway.

He was wrong about that—*dead* wrong.

47

Mystery stuck to her plan when they got inside the house. She quickly kissed her mom and dad good night on the way to her room. They had church in the morning, and the day had worn her out. She slipped into her pajamas, brushed her teeth, and crawled into bed. Her body hadn't quite calmed down enough to fall asleep yet, so she decided to read for a few minutes. She turned off her ceiling light, turned on the lamp on her nightstand, and took her book out of the drawer. After a few minutes, there was a knock on her door. It wasn't closed all the way, but her parents still knocked if they wanted to talk or come in.

"Mys, can I come in?" It was her dad.

"Sure, Dad."

He opened the door and sat next to her on the bed. She set her book down and sat up a little more.

"I just wanted to see if you were okay after all the commotion tonight. Ya know, with the gunshot and all that." His voice was quiet and calm.

"Oh, yeah, Dad, I'm fine. I'm just glad no one got shot or hurt." She wondered if he was going to bring up the wolf thing now.

"Are you sure? I'm here to talk about anything you're feeling or wondering . . . or whatever."

"I know you are, but really, I'm fine. I do think it was a weird night, though." She smiled.

"It sure was." He stood up. "Well, don't forget to say your prayers. And get some good sleep. It's been a long day."

"Okay, Daddy. G'night."

"G'night, my little muffin." He kissed her on the forehead and then left her door the way she had it. A second later he poked his head back in. "I love you, Megan."

"I love you, too."

When he was gone, she shut off her light, said her prayers, and was asleep within two minutes.

Mrs. Mooney was already in bed and reading a book herself. When her husband walked in, she flipped it closed and set it on her lap.

"Well, did you ask her?"

"It never came up," he said, not looking at her.

She laughed. "I knew it! You couldn't do it. Don't you want to know what Darren was talking about? Aren't you curious at all?"

"Of course I am. We saw the pictures, but I have a feeling they're only part of the story. She's looking into it. She'll let us know when she's done."

"Darren Pumpernickel seemed pretty convinced, didn't he? I wonder why?"

Mr. Mooney went into the bathroom to brush his teeth.

"No one's going to believe him anyways," he mumbled with a toothbrush in his mouth. "Good kid, but he's like the little boy who cried wolf." He stopped brushing and stuck his head out the door to look at his wife. They laughed.

Not long after, the Mooneys' house was dark and they were all asleep.

* * *

Over at the Slooths' house, Soda walked inside and immediately checked on Sheena. She was asleep, but her food and most of her water was gone. This was a good sign that she was feeling better. Soda pulled the bag of barbeque from behind his back and shook it. Sheena perked up. Soda dumped the meat in her food bowl and brought it over to her bed. She stepped her front paws out of her bed and devoured the barbeque. She licked the bowl until it was completely clean. She crawled back in her bed and curled up. It didn't look like she'd be sleeping with him tonight, though. His mom assured him it would take a few days before Sheena could jump up in his bed. He knew just how to solve this problem. He went upstairs to his room, grabbed a pillow and blanket, and lay down next to Sheena on the floor.

"I'm sure she'll appreciate that," Mrs. Slooth said, looking at her son with a loving smile. "Make sure you brush your teeth, okay?"

"Okay, Mom, I will." He knew she had something on her mind.

"Tonight was scary, huh? I mean, with the gunshot and no one knowing what was going on? Anything you'd like to talk about?"

"Not really. I knew I was safe. Mr. Mooney was there the whole time. I know he'd never let anything happen to me and Mystery," he replied with a shrug. Then he pulled his covers back and jumped up to brush his teeth in the upstairs bathroom.

"All right then," Mrs. Slooth said to Sheena, who was nearly snoring.

Soda ran back down the stairs and slipped under his blanket; he was almost in Sheena's bed with her.

"Good night, Scott," Mrs. Slooth said as she kissed him. She walked into the downstairs bathroom, turned on the nightlight, and went up the stairs for bed.

After a while, all was quiet. The moon lit Whispering Hollow like a giant night-light. The Bob-B-Q was over, and fun had been had by all, except maybe Mr. Creepy. His night would've been better if he hadn't lost Goliath. In fact, it was possible he was still out searching in the woods.

There was rustling at the edge of the woods behind Mr. Creepy's house. It was just after midnight when the shadow, or shadows, emerged from the trees and stumbled into Mr. Creepy's backyard. No one was there to see it, though.

48

The bluish-purple night passed without any further incidents. The sun rose slowly, bringing a bright yellowish-orange morning. A short time later, dark clouds painted the sky different shades of dreary gray. Whispering Hollow as a whole seemed tired and worn out, but most of the residents managed to make it to church. The church was on the north side of the town on Deadwood Lane, which dead-ended near the old graveyard. They didn't use the graveyard anymore, so it was no longer manicured. The obvious abandonment made the creepy graveyard even creepier.

The Mooneys and Slooths were able to get up in time for the 9 a.m. service—they rode together. Other than the weather being overcast, Sunday had been a very nice day so far. It was warm, but not hot, and there was a pleasant breeze.

Mr. Mooney pulled Silverstreak out of the church parking lot, turned right onto Moonlight Avenue, and then swung right onto October Drive. Before he could turn left onto Main Street, the doors at the Whispering Hollow Fire Department flew open and

Chief Jerry Kiker pulled the emergency van out with its red lights flashing. The engine, probably driven by Dallas Carter, pulled out behind Mr. Mooney. The engine's red lights came on, too; then the sirens pierced the still morning air.

"I wonder what's going on?" Mrs. Mooney asked.

"Haven't we had enough drama lately?" Mrs. Slooth added from the backseat.

Soda leaned his head forward to get a better look. He loved fire trucks.

Mr. Mooney pulled over to allow the firetruck and van to pass and noticed that the pump truck stayed put.

"It doesn't look like a fire, at least."

The fire van and the engine sped down Main Street. Mr. Mooney followed behind the engine with its American flag waving in the pleasant breeze. When they turned left onto Weeping Willow Lane, the Mooneys gave each other a concerned look. Were the vehicles heading down to Mr. Creepy's house for some emergency? Instead of turning right on Nighthawk Avenue, the fire trucks turned left behind The Main Street Shoppes onto the gravel road that led to ball fields, the pool, and the playground and picnic area.

Mr. Mooney turned on his right-turn signal to head home.

"Hon, aren't you going to see what's going on?" asked Mrs. Mooney.

"I was just going to mind my own business. It looks like it's probably a medical call. They won't need me for that. You know how annoying an audience can be when you're trying to work. I deal with that all the time, so I don't want to be 'that guy' standing around getting in the way."

Before he turned, Mr. Mooney stopped and watched the van and the engine rumble up the gravel road and skid to a stop at the playground and picnic area. Sirens blared from behind them as an ambulance sped onto the street and swerved around them to follow the fire trucks.

Mrs. Mooney gave her husband a look; he knew what it meant. He looked back at Mrs. Slooth and she gave him the same look.

"Okay, let's go see what the deal is," he said, somewhat defeated. "But we'll stay out of the way!"

Reluctantly, but wisely, Mr. Mooney turned off his right-turn signal and turned left. The gravel crunched under the tires, making a soothing sound as they passed behind Mimi's and Pumpernickel's Bakery; then they pulled up to the scene just before Deb's Diner. Instead of stopping behind the ambulance, Mr. Mooney pulled off to the side, next to the pavilion that covered several picnic tables. The crunching sound stopped as they pulled off the gravel onto the worn-down grassy area, and Mr. Mooney turned off Silverstreak.

The firemen, Jerry Kiker and Dallas Carter, as well as the two county medics, were all huddled together. Randy Nelson and Donnie Nichols were standing near the engine; they must have come with Dallas. One of the medics had rolled the stretcher out with them. Mr. Mooney opened the door and stepped out onto the ground with his eyes on the first responders. They were positioned in a way that shielded what they were doing and who they were working on. Mrs. Mooney, Mystery, Mrs. Slooth, and Soda got out of Silverstreak. When they gently closed the doors, Jerry looked over and saw the Mooneys; he subtly shook his head from side to side at Mr. Mooney, who took the hint and asked everyone to stay at the truck. Normally, Mrs. Mooney would've thought her husband was being overprotective, but she saw the look in his eyes so she stayed put without any resistance.

Mr. Mooney walked over by the stretcher but still couldn't see what was going on. What he could see was a trail of blood in the dirt that went from Whispering Woods to the picnic area. Mr. Mooney looked around for anyone else in the picnic area, but there was no one—and no cars. Most people were at church or getting ready for church or lunch. There was nothing and no one at the pool and clubhouse. A little farther up the gravel road, at the first baseball field, he saw a baseball sitting atop a tee and a bat lying on the ground nearby. There was also a bright neon-green bicycle leaning against the fence behind home plate.

Mr. Mooney walked up behind one of the medics, finally saw what he and Dallas Carter were doing, and realized why Jerry had shaken his head at him. There was no reason for Mystery or Soda to see this. They were wrapping bandages around Travis Greene. Blood was all over his face and everywhere else, for that matter. Medics had cut off Travis's shirt and pants to be sure they'd located all his wounds, and Dallas was taking his blood pressure. To keep Travis warm and prevent trauma, Randy Nelson used a blanket to cover where they had already bandaged the boy.

"Does anyone know his name?" the male medic asked.

"It's Travis Greene," Dallas answered.

"Travis, I'm Stephen. Linda and I are going to take care of you. Can you hear me?" There was no response. "Squeeze my hand if you can hear me."

Travis didn't react.

The red blood was so bright against his pale white skin. His body was limp with his head tilted back to one side and resting on Deb McCall's lap. He was barely conscious and wasn't making a sound. Despite being a police officer, this was still hard for Mr. Mooney to watch—a hurt child always was.

"Now, Deb, tell me what you saw," Chief Jerry said.

"I couldn't be sure exactly, but when I pulled up to go in the back door of the diner, I saw him playing at the ball field, ya know, hitting off the tee. I went inside, grabbed my purse, and came out. I looked over and saw he wasn't at the field anymore. I got in my car and started to leave when I saw him lying there. I ran over to him and saw something going into the woods just beyond the picnic area. I couldn't tell what it was exactly, but it looked like a big dog . . . or a wolf, if you can believe it. I looked away for a second or two, and when I looked back, it was gone. Then a little way farther down the woods, I saw what I thought was a man. It looked like the new guy, Mr. Sherlock, kind of. He ate at the diner the night he moved into the neighborhood—creepy fella, that one. After that I called 9-1-1."

Mr. Mooney didn't mean to get involved in the conversation, but he couldn't help it. "Deb, did you say 'wolf'?"

Deb McCall looked up at Mr. Mooney as if she just realized he was there. She nodded with wide eyes, seemingly on the verge of shock herself. There was blood on her church dress, but she didn't seem to notice, or maybe she didn't care. She tried to wipe some blood off Travis's forehead. It smeared it more than anything, but it seemed to make Deb feel like she was helping.

"It was so weird. It looked back at me as it disappeared into the woods."

Mr. Mooney looked over Travis's body and realized his injuries were bite marks and scratches. It was a good thing Mystery and Soda stayed at the truck; they *really* didn't need to see this.

Mystery looked around at the picnic and playground area, and then up at the pool and clubhouse. She looked past the pool, up to the ball fields, and saw a bright neon-green bicycle at the first baseball field. She turned to Soda.

"Isn't that Travis's bike?" she asked.

It was hard to miss such a brightly colored thing. She looked around a little more to see if Kenny's bike was there, too, but it wasn't.

"It sure is. I guess he was practicing his baseball swing again. He really wants to be a big-league player."

"Uh, oh, he shouldn't have been out here alone, with all the howling. I guess it would be too much to hope for that it's Trevor over there instead of Travis."

"Scott! Stop it!" his mom snapped.

"Mys, you don't think Mr. Creepy went after him for egging his house, do you?" Soda whispered.

"I don't know. That's an extreme reaction to a house egging, don't you think? And I doubt Travis did anything other than tag along."

Dallas Carter, who looked like he never missed a day in the gym, removed the blood-pressure cuff and told the medics that Travis's blood pressure was dropping. After they had Travis pretty well bandaged up, they carefully lifted him onto the stretcher and then hurried to the back of the ambulance.

"Randy, can you drive the engine back to the station? I want Dallas to ride with the kid to the hospital. And get Ms. McCall something to wipe off that blood." Jerry was only about five feet four, but you couldn't tell that by his voice. It was a deep, authoritative voice that commanded respect. No one could believe that big voice came out of such a short man.

"Sure thing, Chief."

Jerry turned to Dallas. "Are you good with that?"

"Yes, sir," Dallas responded without hesitation and jumped in the back of the ambulance with Linda. Stephen thanked everyone for the assistance, slid into the driver's seat, and drove off with the lights flashing and sirens blaring. Travis had no idea how bad off he was.

49

Mr. Mooney walked over to Silverstreak, trying to conceal the concerned look on his face —it did no good.

The ambulance flew past them and turned onto Weeping Willow Lane. Soon it was out of sight, but the sirens lingered in the air like a heavy fog. The fire van and engine left moments later. Chief Kiker and Randy Nelson waved as they went by.

"What's going on, hon? Who was in the ambulance? What happened?" Mrs. Mooney asked.

"Was it Travis, Dad?"

Mr. Mooney shot his daughter a look of surprise; then he realized who he was dealing with here. *She must have seen the bike,* he thought.

"Yes, it was Travis, and he didn't look good."

"What happened to him?" Soda asked.

Before Mr. Mooney could answer, Deb McCall walked over to them, covered in Travis's blood.

"Oh, my goodness," Mrs. Slooth said.

"Deb, are you okay?" Mrs. Mooney asked, wanting to put her arm around her without getting blood on her church dress.

"Me? Oh, I'm fine. It's Travis I'm worried about. It was awful. All the blood. And what was Mr. Sherlock doing out there in the woods? Someone needs to tell Travis's parents." Ms. McCall looked down at her hands and saw they were blood red.

"Deb, I'm sure that's what Jerry went to do," Mr. Mooney assured her. "You need to get cleaned up."

Mrs. Mooney walked Deb McCall over to her car.

"Are you okay to drive?" Mrs. Mooney asked. She saw Ms. McCall was shaking a little.

"I think so." Ms. McCall saw her hands were trembling. "I'm good. I just need something to eat. My blood sugar must be a little low. I'm going to head home and eat lunch. Thanks, guys. Matt, are you going to check on Travis?"

"Yes, I'll let you know how he is or have Jerry or someone let you know. Don't worry."

"Okay, thanks."

Deb McCall got in her white Ford Focus and slowly drove off. Mrs. Mooney watched her go with a worried eye.

"Don't worry, hon. She'll be fine. She's just a little shaken up. Let's head home ourselves."

"But what happened, Matthew? And what did she mean about Mr. Sherlock being in the woods?"

Mr. Mooney didn't want to answer that question, but he knew they needed to know. They gathered around him and stared at him with anxiety and fear. There was no way to sugarcoat it. He just had to come out and say it. Knowing that didn't make it easy, though.

"Deb said it looked like he got attacked . . . by a big dog . . . or a wolf. She couldn't be sure since she only saw it briefly before it ran into the woods. She also said she looked away for a moment, and when she looked back, it was gone—but Mr. Sherlock was there walking along the wood line."

"Oh, that's awful," Mrs. Mooney said. "I don't want y'all wandering around near the woods, okay? It's just not safe right now. Hon, they need to do something about this. We can't have a wolf or a dog running wild out there and attacking kids! This is Whispering Hollow! If it's a wolf, they need to catch it. If it's Mr. Creepy's dog, they need to take it from him and put it to sleep. It's attacking children, for God's sake!" Her voice got louder, higher, and more upset as she spoke. She should've been done ranting, but she was too emotional. It just slipped out. "If this Mr. Sherlock truly is a werewolf, then we need to do something! We saw the pictures that Mystery took!" Tears rolled down her cheeks.

Mystery and Soda realized they must not have closed out all the pictures on the computer. No wonder they didn't ask her anything more about her evidence—they already knew!

This is what Mr. Mooney had been afraid of—the panic. Once word of what happened to Travis got out, it would infect the whole town. Then things would get bad. A few people in a panic were bad enough, but a bunch of them were downright dangerous. There was reason for concern, and the last few days had proven that. If Travis was worse than hurt, God forbid, then there'd be a crazed wolf hunt or a mob attack on Mr. Sherlock and his dog. Then there was the possibility, however slim, that Sherlock really was a werewolf. How would they handle that?

"Let's go. There's things to do," Mr. Mooney said, and opened the door for Mrs. Mooney.

"Wait," Soda said, "I'm gonna go get Travis's bike and baseball stuff. Can I put it in the back of the truck so we can bring it to him later, Mr. M.?"

"Absolutely," Mr. Mooney replied.

"I'll help," Mystery added.

Soda ran up to the ball field to get the bike while Mystery gathered Travis's glove and a few baseballs. Soda rode into the outfield, picked up a few more balls, and threw them toward Mystery at home plate. Mystery grabbed the tee, and they loaded everything into the back of the truck.

They all got back into Silverstreak and drove home, wondering if their friend would be okay.

50

Mystery wanted to see if Mr. Creepy was home, but she realized if he *had* attacked Travis as a werewolf, there had been plenty of time for him to make it back, so it wouldn't prove anything either way. She wondered if werewolves actually came out in the daylight. After all, there was a full moon hiding behind the clouds.

Mr. Mooney pulled into their driveway and everyone got out.

"We should go check on Travis. I'm assuming he went to Union County General. Do you two want to come with me?" he asked Mystery and Soda.

Everyone changed out of their church clothes and met in the Mooneys' kitchen. Soda walked Sheena over; she appeared happy to get out of her bed, and the house, but wasn't up for a full walk just yet. She immediately went for her favorite spot at the Mooneys'—the rug by the patio door. Mrs. Mooney quickly threw together some more ham-and-cheese sandwiches with Doritos for everyone.

The parents were quiet during the meal. Mrs. Mooney was playing with her necklace again. When everyone's food was gone and the table cleared, they found out why. As they all sat at the table, it looked like tears might leak out of her eyes. She'd wanted to say something ever since the ambulance pulled away with a seriously injured boy in the back.

"Mystery, Soda, listen. I don't think you guys should be hanging around outside right now." It seemed that finally speaking released the pressure, and her tears subsided for the moment. She turned to Mrs. Slooth. "Sarah, I'm sorry. I'm not trying to interfere, but—"

"Melissa, it's okay. I understand." Soda's mom put her hand on Mrs. Mooney's for a quick moment of reassurance.

"Okay, thank you for understanding."

"You're his second mother anyway. Now continue with what you were saying."

Mrs. Mooney turned back to the children. "I just don't want to risk you guys getting attacked by a dog or wolf or werewolf, or whatever in this crazy world is out there! You'll just have to stay in the backyard or right out front if you want to play outside. I want you to stay away from Mr. Sherlock until we know what's going on! I just couldn't bear to see . . ."

She couldn't finish. Tears silently streamed from her eyes.

"It's okay, Mom. We understand, don't we, Soda?" said Mystery. He nodded. "We'll be careful and stay around the house."

Mrs. Mooney leaned in between Mystery and Soda and hugged them both. "I love you guys." She kissed them both on top of the head.

Then Mrs. Slooth took her place and did the same thing.

"I guess it's my turn now?" Mr. Mooney said with a smile. Then he also hugged them and kissed their heads.

Mrs. Slooth chuckled while Mrs. Mooney tried to hold hers back—it didn't work.

"All right, are you two about ready to go now that your mothers have expressed their worry?" Mr. Mooney said.

Before they could answer, the doorbell rang. They looked at each other, wondering who it could be. Mr. Mooney went to answer it. As he walked down the hallway, he could see who it was through the glass door. It was likely the visitor didn't have good news. Mr. Mooney opened the door and motioned for him to come inside.

"Chief, come on in." The chief wasn't alone. "Mayor Fredericks, please."

Mrs. Mooney peered down the hallway from the kitchen.

The mayor and the police chief, who had to duck his head, stepped inside and lingered in the foyer. Chief Andrews nearly blocked all the light coming in from the doorway.

"First of all, Matt," the mayor said with a sigh, "let me express my thanks for you being there on the gravel road for the . . . uh . . . medical call, shall we say, earlier."

"Oh, Mayor, I didn't do anything. I just stood by in case there was anything I *could* do," Mr. Mooney said.

"I know, I know, but you stopped by and, like you said, were there in case they needed you." The mayor was sincere in what he said. Chief Andrews cleared his throat. The mayor recognized this as a hint to cut to the chase. "Listen, we have some . . . news . . . bad news."

51

The ambulance pulled off Main Street onto Shadow Drive, and then turned out of Whispering Hollow for Union County General Hospital—Dallas Carter and Travis Greene were in the back. Travis had lost a lot of blood, and the ambulance sped off with lights flashing and sirens blaring.

Jerry was behind them, but instead of following them out of the neighborhood, he elected to turn down Deadwood Lane and stopped in front of the Greenes' house to break the news. It was the first house on the corner of Shadow Drive and Deadwood Lane. He quickly walked up to the front door and rang the doorbell. Mr. Greene answered the door. The smile on his face faded when he saw the look on Chief Kiker's face.

"What happened?"

Chief Kiker didn't hesitate. "Tony, Travis was attacked and is on the way to UCGH. He's lost a lot of blood and—"

"What do you mean attacked? By who?" Anger and fear competed for their dominance over Mr. Greene's voice—neither would back down.

Again, no hesitation from the chief. "It looks like a dog, or maybe a wolf. We're not sure at this point."

"A wolf?! How can that—" Mr. Greene stopped and grabbed his keys out of a bowl on a small table by the front door. "Dawn! Trevor! Come on! We're going to the hospital. *Now*!"

Dawn Greene came running down the stairs to the front door and saw Chief Jerry. "Oh my God! What happened?" She knew Travis had gone to the ball field to practice before church.

Mr. Greene walked out of the front door. Trevor, almost expressionless, followed. Mrs. Greene trailed behind, with confusion and worry.

"I'll tell you on the way, Dawn. Thanks, Chief."

Mr. Greene backed his white Chevy Silverado out of the driveway and sped off. The engine roared like an angry lion and the tires screeched. They caught up to the ambulance before it pulled into the emergency-room entrance. Chief Kiker was behind them.

As Mr. Greene parked his truck, not caring that he took up two spaces, the medics unloaded his son from the ambulance and rushed him inside the medic entrance of the ER. The ER staff was waiting for them—luckily it was a slow Sunday. Travis Greene was no stranger to the ER. Last summer, he'd been racing on The Track when his wheel went too high over a berm and got caught. He had tried to pull it back down onto the track, slipped, and when he'd put his arm out to break the fall, broke his left wrist. Nearly all summer he was stuck in a cast, which hampered his baseball playing. He still managed to squeeze his glove on, but mostly worked on his pitching. This summer was *supposed* to have been a different story.

Mrs. Greene ran up next to her son, yelling his name, and collapsed to the ground when she saw all the bloody bandages. Trevor looked a little afraid when he saw his mom's reaction. He was a bully; however, he was still a son and a big brother. In fact, his mom and dad had hardly a clue he was a bully. Travis knew, though, since he had firsthand experience. This could've been what sparked the sudden fear and remorse in Trevor.

Mr. Greene pulled his wife up off the ground while the medics wheeled their son into a room. He tried to go inside, but was unable to since several other ER personnel forced their way in front of him. One of them muttered something about a dog or wolf bite.

"Hey! That's my son, for God's sake!" Mr. Greene said as he tried to force his way through everyone and into the room.

"Sir, please go to the waiting room, and we'll update you as soon as possible," a plump nurse with a hypnotic voice and smile told him.

"Is he gonna die?" Mr. Greene asked, afraid the answer would be yes.

The nurse shut the door without answering. Mr. Greene pounded on the door with his fist. The lady with Patient Registration watched and called security, just in case.

"Let's go!" Mr. Greene barked at his wife and oldest son, and then stormed down the hall to the waiting room. Several other members of the ER staff saw how angry he was. Unfortunately, this sort of thing sometimes happened.

Mrs. Greene and Trevor sat down in chairs that were supposed to be comfortable but did not do their job. Mr. Greene paced back and forth in the nearly empty room. The security guard walked into the waiting room and kept a concerned eye on Mr. Greene—who glared at him.

After what felt like hours, during which Mr. Greene had paced nearly a mile, the nurse who had told him to go to the waiting room came busting through the door.

"Mr. and Mrs. Greene?"

Mrs. Greene jumped up and hurried over to her.

"How is he?" Mrs. Greene asked in a voice saturated in desperation.

"Well . . ."

52

The mayor glanced at Mystery and Soda with a serious look. "Listen, for the next little while, until all this wolf stuff is straightened out, we're instituting a town curfew. We'll need everyone inside by nine p.m. That goes for everyone, not just the kids. After what happened to Travis Greene, we just can't take any chances. And this wasn't just my decision. The chief and I both agree it's best for the town's safety."

"We were just talking about something similar, Mayor," Mrs. Mooney said.

"We're having a town meeting at the school gymnasium tonight at six o'clock," Chief Andrews said. "I'm sure people will want to weigh in on the rumors and concerns about Mr. Sherlock. Sorry, you kids, but it's just for your safety. Try to understand, okay?" Chief said softly.

"Well, thanks for coming by. I appreciate you guys taking the time to let us know about the meeting tonight."

Mr. Mooney shook hands with the mayor, and then with Chief. They both waved at the kids and the moms.

"Y'all have a good one now," Mayor Fredericks said with a smile.

The chief and the mayor walked out of the Mooney household and got into Chief Andrews's patrol car. The five of them watched them drive off.

"You see, it's not just a crazy, overbearing, worry-for-nothing mother. It's the police chief and the mayor, too!" Mrs. Mooney said.

"At least you recognize you're crazy and overbearing and you worry for nothing," Mr. Mooney said with a smirk.

This earned him a playful smack on the arm from his wife, along with an eye roll. The rest of them chuckled.

"All right, let's head to the hospital," Mr. Mooney said and gave Mrs. Mooney a kiss.

Mrs. Mooney and Mrs. Slooth returned to the kitchen and found Sheena still lying on the rug by the patio door, while Mr. Mooney and the kids went out and climbed into Silverstreak. On the way, they stopped at the Greenes' house and unloaded Travis's bike and baseball gear onto the front porch. His baseball mitt was shredded from the attack and no longer usable.

"Mys, Travis is gonna need a new glove, don't you think?"

"I've got an idea! Maybe we could do what we did last summer for the school fundraiser. We'll buy and sell candy, but this time we'll use the profit to buy him a glove!"

"That's perfect," Mr. Mooney said. "After this trip, we'll head to Charlotte and buy some bulk candy from Faye's Famous Candy. I'll talk to Chief Andrews and Mayor Fredericks and get you guys set up at the meeting tonight. All you'll need is a little table or stand strategically placed at the entrance to the gym."

"Great, Dad! We'll have to make a sign, too, so everyone knows our cause!"

Normally they'd just buy the candy from Dr. Sweets in Whispering Hollow, but it was Sunday and the whole town shut down.

The rest of the drive to the hospital was quiet. There wasn't much to talk about when going to the hospital to see a friend who was possibly in critical condition. Mystery broke the uncomfortable silence.

"Dad, Travis asked Soda to help him with his swing this summer," Mystery said, beaming with pride.

"Is that so?"

"Yep, he said he'd seen Soda hit before and thought he could help. Travis is playing in the summer league this year, and his bully of a big brother won't help him out."

"Well, that's a shame. But, Soda will be perfect for helping him out. You'd make a great big brother, you know?"

Soda's face turned two shades of pink, and he couldn't say a word about it. Instead, he thought of Travis.

"I hope he's okay. I'd be sad if I didn't at least *try* to help him."

Mr. Mooney thought of how bad Travis looked before they wheeled him away on the stretcher, and tried to keep from looking worried. "I'm sure he'll be fine."

A few minutes later they pulled into the parking lot and saw Mr. Greene's truck parked crooked across two spaces. Mr. Mooney parked in the next space over. The three of them walked, filled with hope and fear, into the ER waiting room.

A nurse had just come out and called for the Greenes to give them the news about their youngest son. Mystery thought she saw concern on Trevor's face. Maybe he wasn't a bully all the time. Maybe he felt bad for bullying his little brother.

The nurse spoke. "Well . . . Mr. and Mrs. Greene. Your son . . ."

53

Principal Dean unlocked the school gymnasium for the meeting. The basketball hoops were down for the summer, and they left them down for the meeting. Several teachers and a few other folks—including Mayor Fredericks and his secretary, Nancy Nichols—were setting up chairs. On the stage, they set up a row of chairs and the microphone. They were expecting a couple hundred people. It seemed that the word about all the howling, werewolf rumors, and the attack on Travis Greene had made its rounds throughout the neighborhood. Nearly anyone with children knew the Greene family, either because of how friendly Travis was or because of how *un*friendly Trevor was. Most people, ashamed or not, would've agreed with Soda when they heard about the alleged wolf attack—Trevor was the one who deserved it, not Travis.

Chief Andrews called in all the officers of the Whispering Hollow Police Department for the meeting. He didn't expect the town to lose control, but he didn't want to take a chance.

Chief Andrews made his way to the police station to meet his officers. It was a small station with an old-time feel to it. Out front, on both sides of the stairs leading up to the front door, hung classic globe lights with *POLICE* written on them in black letters. There was a double set of doors with the Whispering Hollow badge on them that opened into the main lobby, where Judy sat. She usually did double duty as the dispatcher and the secretary. When she was off, one of the officers would answer the phones and dispatch the calls. There was the sergeant's office, the chief's office, a holding cell, an interview room, and a small waiting area with a bench. Down the hall was a conference room, as well as a break room with a small round table and four chairs. That might sound like a lot to outsiders, but once inside, they'd see it wasn't very big at all. But, it served its purpose.

When the chief arrived, all his troops were there and waiting in the conference room. They'd completed all the neighborhood notifications. Those who were on duty were in uniform, and those who were off duty were in their civilian attire. The chief stood at the front of the room at the small podium.

The chief's team was seated in order of rank and seniority. Up front were the two sergeants, Mark Frisk and Jack Major, and then Orville Kent, who'd been a cop for over twenty years. Behind them were Glenn Sears, Eric Erickson, and Derek Antley—still with a bruised forehead.

"Thanks for coming in, guys; I really appreciate it. For those of you who were called in, feel free to go home just as soon as this meeting at the school is over. I'm going to need everyone in uniform for this one. You'll have plenty of time to gear up after this briefing. Again, guys, sincerely, I appreciate this. I know when you're off you don't expect to be called in to work. Please pass along my apologies to your wives, kids, girlfriends, or other family members this has affected. This was not something I *wanted* to do, but rather something I *had* to do for the safety of Whispering Hollow."

The chief explained the curfew, gave them the plans for the night, and then walked away from the podium. Neither he nor any of his troops had any idea they might have to shoot a man.

54

Mr. and Mrs. Greene unknowingly held their breath as they waited for the nurse to deliver the news. It was an awful feeling—much worse than being called to the principal's office for some unknown reason. Mrs. Greene felt like her heart was going to beat its way up and out of her throat. Mr. Greene tried to stay calm, but his clenched fists and angry eyes gave him away. His brown eyes were big and white, and his pupils were hardly visible.

Mr. Mooney, Mystery, and Soda also felt the anticipation. It was almost like waiting for a bomb to explode after the fuse had burned away.

"Travis lost a lot of blood, and one of the lacerations was quite deep . . ."

"And?" Mr. Greene blurted out. "Spit it out, for crying out loud! Please tell me—"

"Fortunately, it looked much worse than it is. He's in stable condition following some stitches on a few of the deeper cuts. He did pass out and may have an issue remembering what happened at first."

"Oh, thank God!" Mrs. Greene said as she collapsed to the floor again.

Mr. Greene was relieved but didn't react much. "When can we see him?"

"It'll be a little while, but I assure you someone will come get you as soon as it's time."

"Thank you," Mr. and Mrs. Greene said together.

The nurse walked back through the door, leaving the Greenes with some relief.

"Tony, I'm so glad to hear that," Mr. Mooney said, extending his hand.

Mr. Greene took it and shook it quick and hard. "Thanks, Matt, I appreciate it. What are you guys going here?"

"We came to check on Travis. I followed the ambulance down the gravel road to see what was going on. I was there when they loaded him up. I saw the condition he was in, and Mystery and Soda wanted to check on him, too."

"That was very nice of you," Mrs. Greene said. "We're just going to wait until we can go back and see him."

"I'd be interested in what he has to say about all this," Mr. Mooney said, echoing what Mystery was thinking.

"We'll let you know . . . if he remembers anything at all," Mrs. Greene said, being her normal sweet self.

Mr. Greene finally plopped into a seat. His adrenaline had worn off and he looked like he had just run a marathon. Trevor was still sitting in a chair, watching the TV, and had hardly moved, even when he saw Mystery and Soda.

"We'll leave you guys alone, then. Do you need anything before we go? A drink or something to eat?" Mr. Mooney offered.

He could tell Mr. Greene wasn't going to answer, so he turned to

Mrs. Greene.

"Thank you for the offer, but we'll be fine." She sat down next to her husband and rested her head on his shoulder.

"Okay, then, let me know if anything changes or if you end up needing something. Let's go, you two."

Mystery waved at Travis's parents. Mrs. Greene smiled while Mr. Greene didn't seem to see her. Mystery and Soda followed Mr. Mooney to the exit, when he suddenly turned around.

"I almost forgot. You guys might not be home for a while, but I wanted to tell you about the meeting at the school gym tonight at six. The mayor and chief have organized a forum to discuss what's been going on in the neighborhood recently. They're going to enact a curfew to help keep the kids safe. Anyway, we'll be there; I just thought you should know."

Mr. Greene didn't verbally respond. Deep inside him something changed. His son had been attacked and could've *died* if Ms. McCall hadn't found him. It had to be someone's fault. He knew of the rumors about Mr. Sherlock and his dog, and he knew he couldn't let it go. His fear and panic slowly became rage.

55

"We're back," Mr. Mooney yelled as they walked in the front door.

"How is he?" Mrs. Mooney asked.

"He's alive and stable. He needed over fifty stitches and a blood transfusion, but it looks like he'll be okay." Mr. Mooney turned to Mystery and Soda. "Before you guys go, I talked to Madelyn Sweets, and she agreed to meet you at their candy store after you guys got home."

"That's great!" Soda exclaimed.

"You guys let me know when you're ready to head up to the candy store," Mr. Mooney said.

"Let's go out to the tree house, Soda."

Soda detected something in Mystery's voice and knew there was something going on in her head. Chances were that it was more than sitting in the tree house.

"Okay."

"Keep the back gate secured, Mystery," her mom ordered.

They stopped to give Sheena some love before going out the patio door. Soda walked straight out to the back gate to make sure it was shut tight and secure.

"All right, Mys, let's hear it. What's going on in your head? I know you don't just want to hang out in the tree house until the meeting tonight."

They climbed up into the tree house and sat at the tree-stump table.

"I really feel like we need to investigate a little more *before* the meeting tonight. I'm not sure why, but I just have a feeling. Maybe it's a hunch . . . like the police get sometimes."

"That's great, but how do you think we're going to do that after what happened to Travis and what your mom said earlier? There's no way they're going to let us go roaming around by ourselves! She definitely won't let us anywhere near Mr. Creepy!"

"I know that. That's why I'm going to ask my dad to follow us in his police car. We'll have him keep an eye on us while we do it. We'll go on the way to Sweets Candy store."

Soda thought about it for a moment. "Sounds good, but how do you know your dad will do it? And where are you planning to go? Mr. Creepy's house?"

Mystery smiled. "I'll just ask him very nicely. He'll do it. He's worried about all this, too. And of *course* we need to go to Mr. Creepy's house. And I'll need to go over the pictures we have again, too."

"We'd better hurry, then. Six o'clock is coming fast."

"You're right! It's already one o'clock! C'mon!" They slid down the fire pole and started running. "Let's see if Mr. Creepy is home first. I'll need to tell Dad if he is or not."

They went out the gate to the front yard and walked down to the bottom of the driveway. The sky had become more overcast and there was a breeze in the humid air. Clouds upon clouds filled the sky, most of them dark and moving fast. Mystery and Soda looked down the road—Mr. Creepy's driveway was empty.

"Looking like a storm's coming out there," Mr. Mooney said as he walked down the driveway.

"Dad?"

"Yes?" he said as if he expected something.

"Can you do us a favor? We have some things to check out, but don't want to go it alone. Mom would worry. We don't really want to get attacked or anything, so can you keep an eye on us? Maybe from your police car? It won't take long, and we'll do it on the way to Sweets Candy Store."

"Would this have anything to do with Mr. Sherlock?" Mr. Mooney smirked.

Soda smiled; then Mystery grinned, too.

"Maybe," she said, drawing out *maybe* so that it sounded like two words. "Will you? I feel like there's something else, like maybe a clue or something."

"Sure. Let me get my keys. Wait here. I'll have to tell your mom we're heading out," Mr. Mooney said and went inside. They waited on the porch for a couple of minutes.

"It's not gonna work. She's gonna know something is up, I'm tellin' ya," Soda said.

"Stop. It'll be fine. Just wait and see. She knows we're going to get candy. I'd better go grab my camera. I'll be right back, too."

Mystery ran out back to the tree house, grabbed her camera and the walkie-talkies, and came out front. She leaned her head against the storm door. She could hear her dad talking to her mom but couldn't tell what he was saying. A few minutes later, her dad returned.

"Let's go. You guys walking or do you want a ride?"

Mystery gave Soda an I-told-you-so smile. He stuck his tongue out at her.

"We'll walk, Dad. Here," she said and handed him one of the walkie-talkies. Make sure we're both on channel three," she commanded as she handed hers to Soda.

"Okay," Mr. Mooney said, "I'll drive down to the intersection and stand by there."

"All right."

The two friends walked down the sidewalk past Ms. Sims's and the Cobblers', and arrived at Mr. Creepy's. The wind had picked up some more and was blowing Mystery's hair around; she pulled it back into a ponytail. Mr. Mooney had set up across the street, facing Mr. Creepy's house. They went around to the right side of the house and found the front fence gate open. Mystery didn't want to go in his backyard but felt like she had to. She didn't think her dad would approve either.

Soda saw what she meant to do. "I dunno, Mys. Probably not a good idea."

"We'll be quick!" she said. She took a few steps into his backyard and saw something she didn't expect at all.

56

They were leaning against the side of the house by the back door. It looked like two poles, or handles, with a place to put your feet—kind of like some weird stilts that didn't make you taller at all.

"What are they, Mys?"

"I have no idea whatsoever. What would you do with stilts like this?"

Mystery reached for one of the poles.

"Mys! What are you doing?" Soda yelled just as her hand touched it. She jumped and pulled her hand back like she'd touched something very hot.

"I was just going to get a closer look, jeez!"

"Well, get a closer *look*; don't touch it."

"Would you stop? It's not going to bite me," Mystery said, exasperated.

She reached out for the pole again. As she touched it, a flash of lightning and a roar of thunder made her jump again! Soda giggled a little, and Mystery gave him a look that said to *knock it off.* It was accompanied by a smile she couldn't hold back.

"Maybe you're not meant to touch it?" Soda shrugged.

Mystery let out a heavy, irritated sigh and grabbed it.

* * *

Mr. Mooney sat in his patrol car at the corner of Nighthawk Avenue and Dark Pines Drive. It wasn't directly across from Mr. Sherlock's house, but it was in front of and across the street from the Hiltons' house. He watched the skies turn from gray to dark blue while his daughter and her best friend went into the backyard of the alleged werewolf. Mr. Sherlock wasn't home, and Mr. Mooney had the front covered. Mr. Sherlock's backyard had the fence, so Mr. Mooney felt the kids would be safe from Whispering Woods.

"What am I doing?" he asked aloud. "I'll tell you what I'm doing—I'm aiding my daughter in trespassing and making sure she doesn't get caught! Now all I need is for Jeff or Rochelle to come out here and ask me what I'm doing, and why I'm doing it in my police car. I'll tell you what else I'm doing. I'm talking to myself and answering my own questions! Come on, Mys. I don't know what you're looking for, and I don't know if *you* know what you're looking for, but hurry up and find it. *Please.*"

* * *

Mystery held the pole in her hand. It was relatively light and made of wood. She grabbed the other one, too, and held one in each hand. They almost seemed like canes or some other walking sticks or tools. There was a neatly carved-out area shaped like a foot at the bottom of each one—she put her feet in them. Soda looked at her with raised eyebrows and wide eyes. At the top of the poles were basically little grooves, almost like a wooden handlebar grip, where she put her hands. Then she lifted her right foot in unison with her right hand, and took a step. She repeated this with her left, and then her right again. It made her walk almost like a robot, a wobbly robot, and didn't reveal its purpose. The bottoms weren't touching the ground evenly and could've been contributing to her lack of balance, so she stepped out of them and turned the right one over. The bottoms were like a rubber stamp that left an impression or shape on the ground. At first, she couldn't tell what the shape was, so she turned it around. She was stunned, absolutely stunned. This was *definitely* what they were looking for.

"Soda, look at this." Mystery was now whispering for some reason.

"No way! You don't think?"

"I sure do. That's exactly what I think. I have to snap some pics and then we're out of here!"

"I wonder why?"

"Me, too. I guess we'll just have to find out."

Mystery set the pole things back against the house where she found them and took a few pictures. She turned one over and took a few more.

Mystery checked the backyard some more, just to be sure they weren't missing anything else, but there was nothing. The back patio was still empty—just a concrete slab with a chair. Mystery couldn't help but think again of how different it had looked when the Johnsons lived there. It had been so full of life, but now it was like a skeleton—especially with the playground gone. It was just a plain, empty, lonely backyard.

The wind picked up some more and blew some leaves in a rustling sound that caught their attention. They half expected to see a wolf or a person sneaking up on them from the back of the yard. They held their gaze on the back fence, and then let out a sigh of relief when they realized it was nothing more than the leaves.

Out front, a creepy black car drove down Nighthawk Avenue. Mr. Mooney grabbed his walkie-talkie.

"The eagle is heading for the nest," he said.

Mystery looked at Soda as her dad's voice crackled over the radio. "Let's get out of here!"

They were able to get out the front gate but knew they couldn't just walk straight out to the sidewalk—it would be too obvious. They had to decide if it was worth being seen by Mr. Creepy or take a chance of being out in the open and unprotected. Mystery made a snap decision, and they went toward the backyard, near Whispering Woods, past the human footprints that turned to wolf footprints, and toward The Track. Soda looked around, hoping not to see a wolf.

Mr. Mooney watched Mr. Sherlock drive by with his severely tinted windows—he couldn't see inside at all. He was unable to tell if Mr. Sherlock had looked at him or not.

"Come on, you two, get out of there," Mr. Mooney murmured.

Mr. Sherlock slowly backed into his driveway.

Soda's voice came across his walkie-talkie. "Rendezvous at The Track."

Mr. Mooney put his patrol car in drive and turned down to The Track. When he got to the dead end, Mystery and Soda emerged and got into the backseat.

"Did you guys find what you were looking for?" he asked them through the shield that separated the front seats from the back.

"I think so, Dad; I think so."

"Good! Now, let's go."

Mr. Mooney drove toward Main Street and called the Sweetses' house on the way. Mrs. Sweets said she'd meet them at the store in a few minutes. Mr. Mooney drove as inconspicuously as possible and peered over at Mr. Sherlock and waved. Mr. Sherlock saw this and might have returned a head nod; it was too hard to tell. What Mr. Mooney could tell was that Mr. Sherlock had an unpleasant look on his face. Just like in the movies and TV, a bright lightning bolt flashed its way across the sky, followed by a loud crash of thunder. Then the rain joined the party and brought some more wind with it. The storm was finally here, physically and figuratively—although no one knew the second part . . . yet.

57

Back at the hospital, the Greenes were now in Travis's room. He still hadn't woken up, but was moving and moaning a little. Mr. Greene asked the doctor if he thought Travis would remember what happened. There was a slight chance, but it was doubtful.

Trevor's eyes were glued to the TV in the room. Mrs. Greene sat next to Travis and held his right hand, resting her head on top of her forearm. Mr. Greene wasn't looking at Travis or his wife, and he wasn't watching the TV. He was staring at the wall with a blank expression on his face. His mind was miles away—so far away that he didn't hear his wife shout Travis's name when he momentarily opened his eyes.

"Tony! He's waking up!"

Mr. Greene did not react, whether he heard his wife or not. He was still staring off into space and wasn't blinking his eyes.

"Tony!" Mrs. Greene repeated and snapped a finger in front of her husband's face. He blinked, shook his head like he'd been in some sort of trance, and looked at his wife.

Mr. Greene turned to look at Travis, who was letting out some quiet moans and slowly blinking his eyes. Travis turned his head a little back and forth as his eyes focused. He opened his mouth to speak, but nothing came out but a warm breath.

"Get him some water," Mr. Greene told his wife, even though he was closest to the sink.

Mrs. Greene grabbed a paper cup out of the cup dispenser next to the sink, filled it up, and handed it to Travis. He took it with an unsteady hand and carefully brought the cup up to his lips. Instead of drinking it in a few giant swallows, he slowly sipped it—almost like someone who was afraid it would taste horrible or that it was too hot.

Mr. Greene was really hoping he'd be able to ask Travis about what happened and get an answer, while Mrs. Greene just hoped he'd be okay.

Travis finished the water. "Where am I?" he whispered, and then cleared his throat. "What happened?" he asked a little louder.

"Travis, just relax for now. I'll go get the doctor," Mrs. Greene said and dashed out of the room.

Trevor managed to yank his attention from the TV and stood next to his dad beside Travis's bed. He looked at his little brother with some relief. Moments later, Dr. Garner walked in, wearing light blue scrubs; Mrs. Greene followed.

"Hey, Travis," the doctor said softly through his salt-and-pepper goatee. "How are you feeling?" He looked at Travis over the top of his glasses.

"I'm . . . I'm not sure . . ."

"Are you in any pain?" he asked as he washed his hands.

Travis looked himself over, holding his arms out. He saw the IV and the rows of stitches on both arms. He pulled the bed sheets back and saw his clothes were gone and he was wearing a hospital gown. There were a few bandages on his upper body and more stitches here and there. Despite the medication he'd been given, the sight of the injuries made them burn and pulse with pain as his heart pushed blood through his veins. Dr. Garner saw panic starting to set in on the young boy.

"Travis, you're okay. You were attacked this morning. Attacked by what we believe was a dog or a wolf. You needed stitches to close up a couple of bite marks, but you're going to be fine. Do you remember any of this?"

Travis closed his eyes, partly in pain and partly in thought. Dr. Garner checked Travis's clipboard and then his blood pressure and heart rate; he seemed pleased.

"Travis, on a scale of zero to ten, with zero being no pain and ten being the worst pain you've ever felt, what's your pain number?"

Travis thought about it for a moment. "I'd say a four."

"That's pretty good. I'd like to get it down to three or lower before you get out of here. How is your stomach feeling?"

"It's okay. Maybe a little empty is all."

It had been awhile since Travis received his medication and was due for the next dose. Dr. Garner handed Travis two pills and another cup of water. Travis hardly hesitated and popped the pills in his mouth and drank the water. The pills felt like bricks as they slid down his barren throat. To prevent them from getting stuck, he drank the rest of the water.

"Travis, we should be able to get you out of here shortly. Just need to get that last bag of IV fluid in you and then you'll be free to go," the doctor said with a wink. "Mom and Dad, do you have any questions?"

Mr. Greene didn't answer. He just stared at Travis.

"No, I don't think so, Doctor. Thank you for taking such good care of him."

"It's my pleasure, ma'am. Please let me know if you need anything. Someone with Patient Registration should be in soon with the discharge paperwork. The nurse will remove the IV; then you'll be able to enjoy the rest of your Sunday *outside* of the ER. You guys take care now." Dr. Garner walked out of the room.

"You don't remember what happened, son?" Mr. Greene asked.

"I don't think so, Dad. Lemme think a little."

"I'd really like to know," he said, trying not to sound too demanding.

Travis put his head back onto his pillow and closed his eyes. He tried to remember, but it wasn't working.

"Maybe if you just thought a little harder . . ."

"Tony, I think if you just give him a little more time maybe he could—"

"Dawn, don't tell me what to say to my son!" Mr. Greene roared.

Mrs. Greene was taken aback. His words felt like a smack across her face. She closed her mouth, hung her head, and slunk back down next to Travis.

The ER room suddenly became a fish bowl, filled with tension rather than water, and it was nearly overflowing. No one said anything or even moved.

After twenty-five long, silent minutes, the nurse came in to check on Travis. This pulled the plug and drained some of the tension from the room.

"How's it going, Travis?" she asked, checking his hospital wristband and then his vitals. His blood pressure was normal and his pupils were reactive.

The tension was nearly gone now but had left behind its sticky moisture. The nurse felt it, too.

A few minutes later, someone with Patient Registration came into the room. The Greenes completed all the paperwork, and Travis was discharged. The nurse assisted in getting Travis out of the bed and into a wheelchair.

She wheeled him over to the ER exit while making motor noises and steering him like a stock car in a race; Travis smiled and would've laughed if he hadn't been so out of it. They loaded Travis into the truck.

"Good luck," the nurse said with a wave and went back into the ER.

The ride home was quiet and uncomfortable for everyone except the source of the discomfort: Mr. Greene. His rage was growing. Travis felt some relief when they pulled into their driveway. Home was a much more comfortable place to recover than the hospital. He got out and slowly shuffled to the front door. The relief quickly dissipated.

"You're going to remember what happened, like it or not!" Mr. Greene yelled, grabbing Travis by the back of the neck.

Travis jumped and cringed at the squeeze. All his stitches screamed out in pain at the same time. He didn't—couldn't—respond. Mrs. Greene wanted to intervene, but her courage was absent; a few tears slowly tumbled down her cheeks. Some were the result of fear, while others were from shame. Mr. Greene let go of Travis as suddenly as he'd grabbed him.

Just before his mom opened the front door for him, Travis saw his chewed-up baseball mitt. Now *his* eyes started to tear up. He knew his dad wouldn't buy him a new one even though it wasn't his fault. That sorrow triggered something in his brain: it flashed back to the baseball field. The memory came rushing back in large waves as they walked inside the house. Travis delicately sank in the recliner in the living room like an old man. He shut his eyes and tried to remember for a little while.

"Dad, I'm remembering!"

58

Sergeant Major purchased animal traps and fox urine from Union County Camping and Hunting Supply House and brought everything to the station.

"Sarge, what's with the fox urine?" Officer Erickson asked, holding the bottle up like a strange alien artifact.

"It'll attract the wolves. Wolves are very territorial, and they'll be very upset if they smell a fox that has moved in on their turf. It should draw them to the traps."

"If you say so," Officer Erickson said with all of his twenty-two years of life experience; he didn't seem convinced.

"Don't you worry about it, Rookie," Sergeant Major scoffed.

Eric Erickson had been a police officer for just under a year, but he'd be a rookie to Sergeant Major for years to come.

They put one of the traps in the police pickup truck that Sergeant Major drove rather than a patrol car. It was the only truck they had. They also put a trap in the back of Erickson's patrol car and one in the back of Sergeant Frisk's patrol car.

"Antley will ride with me, Kent with Sergeant Frisk, and Sears with Erickson. We'll head out to the ball fields, Sergeant Frisk will go out behind Mr. Sherlock's home, and Erickson, you guys find a spot somewhere between Sherlock's and the ball fields. Spread the fox urine like I showed you and put the trap right next to it. It would be best if the traps were at least ten to fifteen feet inside Whispering Woods. Everyone, keep your head on a swivel. I don't want anyone getting hurt out there."

"I wonder if werewolves feel the same way about fox urine as regular wolves," Erickson inquired.

"We may just find out, kid," Sears said.

"Meet back here when you're finished, fellas. Let's get this done," Sergeant Major ordered and jumped into the driver's seat of his truck.

Within thirty minutes, all the traps were set. The only issue they had was when Ms. Sims saw them and ran out to warn Sergeant Frisk and Officer Kent that they'd be in big trouble if one of her cats got caught in the trap. Sergeant Frisk told her he understood her concern and that her cats likely wouldn't go near the fox urine.

When they were all back at the station, Sergeant Frisk called Chief Andrews over the radio to inform him the traps were set.

Chief Andrews checked on Travis's condition and then headed to the school gym to relay the good news to Mayor Fredericks, who expressed his pleasure.

"The only issue now is whether or not you're going to notify Mr. Sherlock about this meeting."

"Good point. I'll have to decide that very soon since the meeting starts in an hour."

Chief Andrews stepped away from the mayor and walked out a side gymnasium door, away from all the activity inside.

"Has anyone notified Mr. Sherlock about the meeting?" he asked into his radio, not knowing if he hoped they had or hadn't.

Sergeant Frisk spoke up after a few moments of silence. "Chief, we haven't at this point. We didn't know how you wanted to handle that."

"Ten-four. I'll have to figure that out. I'd like to get all units to respond to the school."

Everyone acknowledged, and within a couple of minutes all the officers arrived. Neighbors would be showing up soon, and Chief hoped the police presence would stop any trouble before it started. Chief's motto was "the best way to clean a mess was to not make a mess." He could always ask for help from the Union County Sheriff's Office, if needed. Now that he thought about it, having this meeting at the church might have been better, but there was no time for second guessing. The meeting was about keeping people safe, especially the children, until they could catch the wolf or wolves that invaded Whispering Hollow.

Chief Andrews came to a decision and walked out to his patrol car. He drove to Mr. Sherlock's, a.k.a. Mr. Creepy's, house to inform him of the meeting. It was the right thing to do, and he was going to do it. What he *didn't* do was tell someone where he was going. That was a decision he'd soon regret.

59

After choosing from all sorts and types and flavors, Mystery and Soda had all the candy they needed from Sweets Candy Store. The Sweets owned both the dentist's office across the street and the candy store, ironically. Mrs. Sweets came in, opened the store for them, and gave them a discount since they were raising money for Travis.

Mystery and Soda finished making the signs indicating all the profits from the candy sale went toward buying Travis Greene a new baseball mitt. Of course, Mrs. Mooney had poster board and markers ready for them to use. She told them they did a magnificent job. The top read CANDY SALE and underneath it ALL PROCEEDS TO BENEFIT TRAVIS GREENE. The second one read NEW BASEBALL GLOVE FOR TRAVIS. The letters were all big and easy to read, and Soda drew a very detailed picture of a baseball mitt. Mystery was very proud, and they both really hoped they'd raise enough money.

Now all they needed was a price list. They went to the computer, thought about how much each item would cost with a little help from Mr. Mooney, typed it up, and printed it out.

Mrs. Slooth took Sheena home, so she could get ready for the meeting. Mystery and Soda reviewed the pictures Mystery had taken last night at Mr. Creepy's. Mystery hooked up her camera to the computer and pulled them up. At first, there wasn't anything different. They still saw pictures of a shadow-man and then of a shadow-wolf or shadow-dog. There was no denying that.

"I dunno, Mys, this is weird. These pictures seem to say a lot. I don't know what to believe."

Mystery kept scrolling through the pictures of the "transformation." They watched it over and over until Mystery thought of something.

"Wait a minute—let me check something." She looked at the time/date stamp showing for each of the pictures and saw something that might just be a clue. "That's it!"

Soda didn't realize what she was talking about until she pointed to the screen. His eyes opened wide.

"I don't believe it. Seeing isn't always believing!" Soda exclaimed.

"I guess not. This puzzle is starting to make sense. Now we just need to find out why."

"For sure!"

It was almost time for the meeting, and Mystery and Soda wanted to get set up before people arrived. Before they left, Soda went into the bathroom and took his Braves hat off. He had a bad case of hat head. He ran his hands through his hair, hoping to organize it a little, but it hardly did anything. He tried fluffing it up all over the place—that didn't help much either. Wearing a Braves hat wasn't exactly the look he wanted when he was trying to sell candy for a hurt friend on a Sunday; however, hat head was worse than actually wearing the hat, so he just left it on. When he came out, Mystery went in. Her hair was back in a ponytail, so she took it down. She did nearly the same thing Soda did, and she just couldn't get her hair to look how she wanted it. She walked out with it back in a ponytail.

"Tried to fix your hair, too, huh?" Soda said to Mystery.

She laughed. "Yeah. I guess you tried to do without the hat?"

"Yep . . . it didn't work. I guess we were meant to stick with our signature looks!"

They both laughed.

A few minutes later, Mr. Mooney came downstairs. He grabbed a folding table from the garage, loaded it into Silverstreak, and then went back inside to see if the kids were ready to go.

"Sure, Dad. Is Mom going now?"

"No, she and Soda's mom will meet us there when the meeting starts."

Mystery and Soda grabbed the candy out of the refrigerator, which kept it from melting, and got into Silverstreak. Mystery brought her camera in hopes of taking a few pictures after they succeeded in making enough money. Just before they pulled out of the driveway, Mystery yelled for her dad to wait a minute. She jumped out of the truck, went inside, and came back with an old lunch box.

"What's that for?" Soda asked.

"To keep the money in. Dad, do you have any cash we can use to give change back?"

"I actually set aside a little for that very reason," he said as he backed out of the driveway and headed for the school.

They got a fairly close parking space, which was good since they had a lot to carry. They walked into the gym and found the setup was nearly done. It always felt weird being at school after school was out. All sorts of school staff were there to make sure some doors were unlocked while others remained locked, and some were still bringing out extra chairs. Principal Dean set up a computer and projector for a small presentation he and the mayor had prepared regarding the proposed curfew. He saw Mystery and Soda walk in with the signs and Mr. Mooney with the folding table behind them.

"Well, well, well, what do we have here, Mystery Muffin and Soda Pop Slooth?" Even the principal called them by their nicknames.

"Hi, Mr. Dean. Soda and I were just hoping we'd be able to set up a table near the front over there. We're selling candy to raise money to buy Travis Greene a new baseball glove. His got chewed up today when he got attacked."

"That's very considerate of you two. That would be just fine. You can set up over there." He pointed to a doorway they designated as the entrance. On the other side of the gym was where they wanted people to exit after the meeting. "We'll try to keep this very organized so everyone attending this meeting will walk past you."

"Thank you, Principal Dean," Soda said.

"Yes, thank you," Mr. Mooney said as he set the table down and shook Principal Dean's hand.

"My pleasure. Now, if you'll excuse me, I've got a few more things to do before this kicks off." Principal Dean walked over to Mayor Fredericks, said something, and then walked away.

Mr. Mooney pulled the table legs out and stood it up. It was just big enough for two chairs, which Soda said he'd get. Before he could, Mayor Fredericks walked over to them with a folding chair in each hand.

"I heard there was some fundraisin' for a noble cause goin' on over here," the mayor said with a smile.

"Yes, sir, we're trying to help Travis Greene," Mystery said proudly.

"I'll make an announcement at the beginning of the meeting to make sure everyone knows. But, they should have no problem seeing you with those wonderful signs you've made."

"Thank you, sir," Mystery and Soda said together.

"You've got yourself some good kids there, Officer Mooney," the mayor said and gave Mr. Mooney a pat on the shoulder. "I'd like to be your first customer if that's okay with you." He looked over the candy they were setting out and picked out a few candy bars. "I'll take these."

"Gee, thanks, Mr. Mayor!" Soda said.

They were off to a good start.

Whispering Hollow residents started arriving for the meeting. The way it looked, there were going to be more people than they expected. This wasn't necessarily a bad thing—it was good to see the community involved in what was happening—but it could be more than they were prepared to handle, especially if things got out of control. Mr. Mooney stood close to the candy table just in case there was an issue. Not that he expected one, but they did have cash on hand and you never knew what could happen.

Nearly everyone saw Mystery and Soda, including Darren Pumpernickel who had come in with his parents and the smell of their bakery.

"Hey, y'all, need some help? Is that okay?" he asked his parents.

"Sure, Darren, see if you can find a chair if you want," Mystery said.

"Fine with me, Darren," Mrs. Pumpernickel said.

Darren looked around and saw a few folded-up chairs against the wall. He grabbed one and sat behind Soda and Mystery.

For the next forty-five minutes, people filed into the gym and many bought candy. It *was* easy to see the table and *impossible* to miss the brightly colored signs. It helped that most parents brought their children and that Travis was well-liked in the neighborhood. One couldn't help but wonder if things would be different if Trevor had been the one who got hurt.

Before the meeting officially started, the mayor got on the microphone to ask for everyone's attention. He told them about the fundraising event going on for Travis. Despite the attempts to get everyone in through the main doors, some had still slipped in other doors and hadn't seen the candy table. The mayor's announcement stirred a few people to stand and walk over to the table, resulting in more sales.

Mrs. Mooney and Mrs. Slooth arrived together and each bought a little something.

"This looks great, y'all!" Mrs. Mooney said.

"Yes, I'm very impressed with your signs," Mrs. Slooth added.

Mrs. Mooney leaned over to kiss her husband; then she and Mrs. Slooth found their seats. Mr. Mooney saw that several Whispering Hollow police had arrived over the last few minutes. Sergeant Frisk and Officer Kent were up on the stage with the mayor, Principal Dean, Vice Principal Phyllis Blacksmith, and Mayor Fredericks's secretary, Nancy Nichols. He looked around the gym and saw Sergeant Frisk and Officer Antley standing in the back; he was sure he'd seen Officer Sears and Officer Erickson come and go within the last little bit. The one member of the Whispering Hollow Police Department that he didn't see was Chief Andrews.

60

Just as Travis had started telling the recollection of his wolf attack, Chief Andrews eased his patrol car to a squeaking stop in front of Mr. Sherlock's house. There was an old black car in the driveway. He popped the gearshift into park and let out a long sigh.

"Here goes nothing," he said to himself in a grunt as he got out. It wasn't easy getting that large body out of a passenger car.

He knew the meeting was about to start—but felt like he'd regret it if he didn't tell Mr. Sherlock about it and he ended up hearing about it elsewhere. Chief Andrews did not want that. He was a professional, and pushed aside any rumors about Mr. Sherlock—no matter how crazy they were. It wouldn't look good on the police department if they purposely left someone out of the loop regarding an emergency neighborhood-safety meeting. Mostly it just didn't *sit* right with him. That is what ultimately had him walking up the driveway.

He pushed the doorbell and then knocked when it didn't ring. There was no answer. He knocked again and waited a few moments. There was a chance Mr. Sherlock had gone somewhere in the house to look out a window to see who was at his door. It was weird how people answered the door when they saw a cop car out front. Some people answered right away, while others acted confused—like they didn't know if they should answer or not.

Chief checked the windows for any movement, but didn't see any. The garage door was closed, and he didn't hear anything inside the house. He walked around the right side of the house and saw the front fence gate was open. He poked his head in and called out, "Hello?"

There was no answer. Hesitantly, he walked into the backyard and knocked on the back door. Maybe Mr. Sherlock hadn't heard the knock at the front? Either way, there was no answer at the back. He checked the back windows, too, but didn't see anything. The feeling that something was wrong overwhelmed him. He'd had a similar feeling when he and Officer Antley had gone out into Whispering Woods in the darkness. He paused momentarily, interrupted by a strange sound on the other side of Mr. Sherlock's back fence—from Whispering Woods. The noise wasn't a snarl or a bark or even a howl; it was more like a pathetic whine or cry. Chief Andrews had to decide if he was going to open Mr. Sherlock's gate or walk out the front and around. Like most cops, he only took a second to make a decision that could change a life forever; he went out the front gate and around to the woods with his hand on his gun. He had no idea what to expect, especially the way things had been going lately. It felt like he was sneaking up on an unsuspecting criminal. Mr. Sherlock's privacy fence seemed to go on forever. He slowed down as he got closer to the edge of the woods. A few more whining sounds made Chief Andrews draw his gun. He was prepared for whatever threat awaited him around the corner.

He came to the edge of the fence line, paused, and quickly poked his head around the fence. There was nothing, but he did it once more to be sure and then crept around the corner. After a few more steps, he heard it again. It sounded like it was directly to his right, about ten feet or so into the woods. His replacement radio remained on his hip, but curiosity and concern derailed any ideas about him telling Judy or the others where he was or what he was doing. The whining was getting louder, and there was some rustling along with it. His gun was aimed directly in front of him. His finger slowly and carefully slid to the trigger. A few more steps . . . then a few more, and he discovered the source of the whining. Chief Andrews's eyes widened. The wolf trap his officers deployed had done its job and done it well.

61

Mystery and Soda were very excited about all the candy they sold, but they didn't want to count the money until the meeting was over. There was a very large stack of bills and a pile of change in the lunch box. Some people gave a donation while others told them to keep the change.

On the stage, Mayor Fredericks walked over to Sergeant Frisk and whispered in his ear to ask if he knew where Chief Andrews was.

"I'm not sure. He'll no doubt be here soon. I know he wants us to get started on time."

"You're probably right," the mayor said and looked out at everyone. "There's a lot more folks than I was expecting."

A few people were still looking for seats while some were buying candy and others were finding places to stand along the gym walls. A quiet chatter filled the air as people said hello to each other or discussed what rumors they'd heard about the meeting and the curfew. The mayor stepped to the microphone and turned on the computer projector. It displayed a picture of the Whispering Hollow sign at the entrance to the town on the white screen behind him.

With perfect timing, Mr. and Mrs. Moustache strolled in with Franklin Butler. They sat in the three empty seats right up front. This was customary since the Moustaches were very involved in what was happening in Whispering Hollow. At every event, meeting, or get-together, three seats were reserved for them in the front row.

"Good evening, Whispering Hollow residents," the mayor said with a polite smile. The chatter promptly ceased. "First, I'd like to thank y'all for being here. I don't want to take up too much of your time, but I'd like to thank Principal Dean and the rest of the school staff for allowing us to have this meetin' here tonight." There was some sporadic applause. "I'd also like to thank the Whispering Hollow Police Department for assisting with this, and especially Chief Andrews for collaborating with me to help keep this community safe." He looked around for the chief but there was still no sign of him. "I'm sure Chief Andrews will be along shortly."

The mayor clicked to the next slide, which showed the front of the Whispering Hollow Police Department. "I'll just get right to it, folks; then, when I'm done, I'll open it up for any questions you might have." He sighed, took a breath, and then continued. "There has been a clear danger that's moved into the area. It may be a single wolf or a pack of wolves; at this point, we're just not sure. Either way, we'd like everyone to stay inside as much as possible." The chatter resumed and grew louder. "Chief Andrews and I are instating a nine o'clock curfew to be in effect until we can get this handled. Your police force has taken measures to capture the wolf or wolves, and I believe—correct me if I'm wrong, Sergeant Frisk—that the Union County Sheriff's Office will be on standby, and we'll be dealing directly with their Animal Control Division. For those who are wondering, Travis Greene *was* hurt pretty bad; however, it appears he's going to be fine, according to Chief Andrews."

The next slide was a picture of the traps they had set up along the edge of Whispering Woods. "We've placed several of these traps near the edge of the woods to capture the animal or animals. They've been strategically placed where there've been sightings, reported howlin', or other occurrences that will give us the best chance of catching these deadly animals. So, we're also asking that you stay clear of the woods, especially along the edge where the traps were set up. We don't want anyone to get attacked, accidentally set the traps off, or, more importantly, get caught in one."

The chatter got louder again, and this time Steve May, Bryan's dad, stood up. He couldn't wait until the mayor was ready for questions.

"What good is a curfew going to do, Mr. Mayor? The Greene boy got attacked in broad daylight! How are we supposed to even let the kids out of the house? How can *any* of us leave the house?" Mr. May snapped and then sat down, confident he had made his point.

Most of the people seated around him had heard him fine, but many people behind him had not. Many people clapped while others were quiet and looked to the mayor for an answer.

"I understand your concern, Mr. May, and we've thought about that. Based on the research conducted by our very own Nancy Nichols"—the mayor nodded at his secretary, who beamed at the acknowledgement—"the incident with Travis Greene was extremely rare. We feel it was sparked simply by the fact that the boy was out near the woods, alone, and a pack of wolves can be very territorial. Folks, if you could please hold your questions until the end. We've set up a microphone out there so everyone can hear you. Thank you."

"Are you blaming Travis?" someone yelled.

It was apparent that some people weren't going to listen. The mayor maintained his professional patience, though.

"Of course not. We're just tryin' to do what we can to prevent any future attacks until we can catch these animals."

There was a moment or two of silence; then what Mr. Mooney was afraid was going to happen, happened. Mr. Pumpernickel slowly rose to his feet and strutted to the microphone.

"Mr. Mayor," he started. He spoke a little too loudly and close to the microphone, so there was some high-pitched feedback.

"Uh, oh," Mr. Mooney said to himself, but loudly enough that Mystery, Soda, and Darren heard it.

"What is it, Dad?"

"This could get ugly."

"Yes, Mr. Pumpernickel?" Mayor Fredericks answered.

"Don't you think the community has the right to know about the *other* possibility of what's going on around here lately?"

There was more clamoring from the crowd. The mayor found himself wishing he hadn't set the microphone up—or that he had at least waited until he was done speaking to point the microphone out.

"What do you mean, Paul?"

Now Mystery understood where this was heading and she saw the concerned look on her dad's face. He had explained to her how a single person could incite a riot—how people who are normally calm and would never act out in violence could suddenly explode. It could become a very dangerous situation when a crowd that felt passionately about something was encouraged to take action. Mystery did not want to see that happen in Whispering Hollow.

"Mr. Mayor, I'm speaking about our new resident, Mr. Sherlock," Mr. Pumpernickel continued. He moved away from the microphone so his voice was loud and clear.

Mystery and Soda turned back to Darren with raised eyebrows. Darren shrugged,

"Yes, what about him?"

"I'm talking about him being . . ."The crowd was silent and waited to hear what he'd say. Some had already heard the rumors, while others had absolutely no idea. "Well, I'm talking about him being . . . a werewolf!"

With the exception of the Moustaches, who hardly had any reaction whatsoever, the crowd nearly went into hysterics. The clamoring was now yelling and screaming.

Sergeant Frisk stood up from his seat on stage and walked over to the microphone. Mayor Fredericks stepped away.

"People, people, let's settle down," the sergeant said in a firm but calm voice.

"There's a werewolf in this neighborhood, and you've done nothing about it?!" someone screamed.

Someone else yelled, "Werewolf! That's ridiculous!"

It was a good thing everyone didn't believe it right away, but sometimes that didn't matter. It's very hard to make someone stop believing something without solid proof. Even then, it can still be difficult, and sometimes impossible.

"He's a werewolf! I've heard all about it! And Mystery Muffin has proof!" Mr. Pumpernickel exclaimed, pointing at her.

There it was, another of Mr. Mooney's fears. All eyes turned toward his daughter in a collective gasp. Without even thinking about it, she took her ponytail down for a moment and made it even tighter.

Sergeant Frisk also looked to Mystery. "What's he talking about, Mystery?"

Mystery's blood ran cold. It was just like at the Bob-B-Q, but this time it wasn't the boy who cried wolf; it was his father. Mr.

Pumpernickel didn't have the same reputation as his son, though. This time there was no getting out of it. She'd *have* to say something. She hoped she was ready.

It was a good thing she had her camera. That wasn't why she had brought it, but it didn't matter now. She stood up, smoothed out her shirt and shorts, and walked up onto the stage with her dad behind her. Soda already knew what he had to do: plug her camera into the computer that was running the projector.

Sergeant Frisk motioned for Mystery to continue over to him, and he lowered the microphone for her. She stepped up to it and gazed at everyone in the crowd. It was hard not to feel nervous, but she did her best to fight it off. Mr. Pumpernickel sat down with a satisfied look on his face. It appeared he was ready for everyone else to hear what he already knew. A monster had moved into Whispering Hollow, and something had to be done about it.

Mr. Mooney wondered if Mr. Pumpernickel felt bad at all for bringing Mystery in on this and making her the center of attention—for making her the one who'd convince the neighborhood of the rumors. Mystery's father also wondered what other evidence, if any, she and Soda had come up with. He was proud that the town relied so heavily on his daughter's word, but he was still nervous for her.

Mystery cleared her throat and prepared to speak. Before she could, Sergeant Frisk leaned down into the microphone.

"I'd like to ask that everyone remain seated and quiet until Mystery is done speaking, please."

Mrs. Moustache smiled at her husband and then up at Mystery. She seemed very anxious to hear what Mystery had to say. It was deathly quiet in the gymnasium.

"Thank you," Mystery said to Sergeant Frisk, and then turned to the audience again. *Here goes nothing,* she thought.

62

"Travis, tell me. Tell me what happened," Mr. Greene said as he took his son by the hands and sat down like he hadn't just treated him horribly.

Mrs. Greene wanted to settle her husband down, but she knew it was still too soon. She was afraid he'd hurt Travis again. Of course, she wanted to hear about what happened, too, and sat next to Travis, hoping to provide a little comfort and support.

Travis closed his eyes, and pictured himself back at the field. "I got up early and got my baseball stuff together and then rode out to the field. I was just practicing my swing on the tee. I was the only one out there, so I had to fetch my own balls. Kenny was still sleeping. At first, it was no big deal. I'd just run out there, gather 'em up, then hit 'em again. I was in a nice groove," he explained with a sparkle in his eye. He just loved talking about baseball—it relieved his pain almost as much as the medicine. "I hit another round, and a few balls rolled out to the edge of the wood line. I was crushing some of 'em! I went to get them and saw a ball on the other side of the fence. So, I opened the gate and went out to grab it. That's when I heard it."

"Heard what?" asked Trevor, who had also gathered around Travis.

"The growling. It sounded like a dog . . . but worse—meaner somehow. I looked all around but didn't see anything. There was some movement off to my right, and I looked and saw a man. It looked like that creepy guy, Mr. Sherlock. He didn't say anything and I didn't say anything, so I grabbed the ball and ran back through the gate opening. I tried to close the gate, but before it shut all the way, a huge wolf jumped toward me. I fell backward, got to my feet as fast as I could, and sprinted for home plate. But the wolf followed me! I turned around for just a second and threw the baseball at it. I hit it right on the head, but it didn't slow down for even half a second. I didn't see Mr. Sherlock anymore. I kept on running, but it was too fast. I felt it breathing down my neck and yelled for help, but there was no one around." Travis's closed eyes leaked some tears. He paused for a moment to calm down a little.

With each passing second, Mr. Greene seemed to get angrier and angrier. When Travis mentioned Mr. Sherlock, his face became a dark shade of red. Mr. Greene remembered all that Mr. Pumpernickel had told him about the werewolf rumors. He was having trouble wrapping his head around a legend like that, but his rage didn't care.

Mrs. Greene wiped a few tears that dribbled down her cheeks despite her best efforts to contain them. Sometimes tears had a mind of their own, it seemed. She wanted to tell Travis he'd said enough for now, that he could finish later, but that would be pointless. She didn't want Travis to see her tears and make him more upset. It was difficult, but she got herself under control and let Travis continue.

"Then there was a howling snarl or a snarling howl—I'm not sure which—but it was right behind me when I felt paws on my back. I was running as fast as I could when my feet flew out from under me. I fell flat on my back. It chomped onto my left foot, but I managed to kick it with my right and I scrambled to my feet. I ran to home plate for my baseball glove just as it jumped on me again. I hit it over and over with my glove. The wolf ripped the glove out of my hands and chewed it up! It lunged at me and hit me right in the face. I saw a bright flash and everything went dark. I guess I got knocked out. I kind of remember Ms. McCall standing over me and a fireman or someone . . . Then I woke up in the hospital." More tears spilled out when he opened his eyes.

Mr. Greene sat there in silence, along with his wife and Trevor, listening to Travis sniffle and wipe his tears. Travis developed a cold sweat. The anxiety of retelling the attack really got his blood pumping, and his wounds throbbed with each heartbeat.

"These stitches hurt. Is it time for more pain medicine?" Travis said. His voice quivered.

"It'll be a little longer, sweetheart, but as soon as it's time—"

"That son of a—" Mr. Greene yelled as he punched his right fist into his open left hand. "I'll kill him!" He jumped up, stormed into the garage, grabbed a baseball bat, and walked out the front door. "You coming, Trev?"

Trevor looked at his dad in surprise coated with a smirk, and followed him to the truck. One thing Trevor enjoyed was inflicting pain on those who couldn't defend themselves. Mrs. Greene ran to the front door and found some courage that could possibly get her hurt. She decided that would be better than what her husband would do to Mr. Sherlock.

"Tony, please don't do this. We'll call the police and let them handle it."

"Shut up, Dawn, I'll handle this *myself!*" Mr. Greene screamed and slammed the driver's door. Then he sped off.

63

Everyone was staring at Mystery while on the edge of their seats. Mystery's eyes found her mom and Mrs. Slooth out in the crowd. Her mom was playing with her necklace, but she managed to smile and give her a quick wave. Mystery tried not to, but she smiled back. To help remain calm, she pretended she was merely talking to her "moms."

Soda got the camera hooked up and gave Mystery a thumbs-up. He was a little nervous for Mystery but was very relieved it wasn't him up there in front of everybody. It was bad enough he'd had to hook up the camera with everyone wondering what he was doing. Thankfully, the hookup went smoothly. He might have completely frozen with all those eyes on him if something had gone wrong.

Last year in English class, he had been called up to read a poem he wrote that Mrs. Albright really liked. It had totally caught him off guard, but luckily he hadn't had to sit there drowning in the anticipation. So, there he had been, standing in front of the entire class, nearly hyperventilating, and who was up front? Trevor Greene.

He'd been moved to the front after he was scolded several times for talking during class—lucky Soda. He'd read the whole poem, with all his heart poured into it, looking down at his paper and never looking up at the class once. When he was done, he'd quickly folded his paper up and nearly sprinted back to his seat. The entire class was in shock at what he'd written—it was a beautiful poem about a lone flower in a field. It was really about his mom, but of course he wouldn't tell anyone except Mystery that. As he had hurried past Trevor, Trevor stuck his foot out and tripped him. Soda's hands had been busy folding his poem so he fell flat on his face. His nose had started spewing blood immediately. The heartfelt feeling that had hung in the air like a pleasant spring aroma was quickly displaced by screeching, yelling, and blood. Yes, Soda was glad it wasn't him up on the stage all right.

"Okay, so when Mr. Creepy moved in—" Mystery started as the crowd let out some stifled laughter. "Excuse me, when *Mr. Sherlock* moved in, Soda and I wanted to know who our new neighbor was. It started when we got off the school bus and walked down the road toward his house to get a closer look. We saw him at the front door; we looked away for a moment and heard howling. When I looked back, Mr. Sherlock was gone, and there was a dark figure at the front door that appeared to be a large dog or maybe a wolf. It howled and barked, and we ran off.

"Later that night, we heard more howling coming from Mr. Sherlock's house. We decided to investigate. We brought Soda's dog, Sheena, with us to help out. There was nothing suspicious at first, but shortly after, Sheena got nervous and upset. I saw a shadowy figure shaped like a person initially, but then it looked more like a dog or a wolf. I saw what looked like a tail inside of Mr. Sherlock's fence. I snapped a few pictures just as Sheena became very upset and protective of us. The next thing we knew, Sheena was fighting something, and we ran off, leaving her behind. A few minutes later she came home and was hurt bad. The next day we saw the pictures I took. Soda?"

Soda clicked a button on the computer, and the pictures were projected for the whole gym to see. He scrolled through the pictures in sequence, showing the shadow-man turning into the shadow-wolf. People murmured and gasped as they saw the evidence with their own eyes.

As this was going on, Sergeant Frisk stepped backstage and called Chief Andrews over the radio. He paused and waited for an answer, but there wasn't one.

"Frisk to Chief Andrews, do you copy?"

No answer.

"Judy, have you heard from him or seen him at the station?"

"Negative, Sarge, neither. Not again!"

Judy tried several times to get a hold of Chief, but he didn't answer.

"Frisk to Erickson."

"Go ahead, sir."

"Head over to the Sherlock place and see if the chief is there. Maybe he stopped over to tell him about the meeting. Tell him the meeting has started. Sears, you may want to ride that way, too."

"Roger that, Sarge."

Mystery continued her speech.

"The next morning, we met Mr. Sherlock face-to-face and saw his hand was bandaged and bloody. He said it happened the night before when his dog, Goliath, bit him during the fight with Sheena. It seemed awfully coincidental and led us to consider it *was* actually Mr. Sherlock who had attacked Sheena while he was in wolf form and that Sheena had bit *him* during the fight. Then another strange thing happened. We offered him some brownies on a silver platter, and he rudely refused them. We also saw that he was wearing a gold wedding band. We figured he was afraid of silver—just like werewolves.

"We also have some pictures of a dead animal we discovered down by The Track. It had been killed and mostly eaten." She nodded at Soda, who went to the next photos. "These show human footprints changing into what appear to be wolf tracks."

There were a few more groans and someone said, "I can't believe it."

"During the time he's been here, we have never seen Mr. Sherlock and his dog together at the same time." The crowd quieted down again. "My dad found some reports filed by his old neighbors in Virginia, where they suspected he was a werewolf." Mr. Mooney gave her a cross glare for eavesdropping. "At the Bob-B-Q, we heard more howling just behind Mr. Davidson's house. We saw what looked like a wolf or dog shadow in the woods, but when it came out of the woods, it looked like a human shadow. When the shadow stepped into the light, it was Mr. Sherlock."

"Son of a gun," someone said.

"A werewolf? In Whispering Hollow?" another questioned.

"Mr. Sherlock said that Goliath ran out of the house and he was out searching for him. To explain the howling, he said that his dog was raised by wolves when he was a puppy.

"According to a witness, Mr. Sherlock was also seen nearby when Travis Greene was attacked by a wolf this morning. I haven't spoken to Travis yet, but we went to check on him at the hospital today. He got a bunch of stitches and was unconscious when we were there."

"We can't allow a werewolf in this community!" someone yelled. "Mayor, this is outrageous!" Many people in the crowd agreed and yelled out as well.

Sergeant Frisk strolled back to center stage and stood with the mayor, who had stepped in front of Mystery. The tension level in the room had significantly risen in the last few minutes, and they were concerned things would get out of hand. Many people were standing and yelling and demanding answers and pointing their fingers and pumping their fists.

"Folks, let's settle down. Mystery isn't finished yet and we asked that you—"

"What are you going to do about this?!" another angry voice yelled out.

The crowd was losing control. Mr. Mooney knew people would either rush the stage or rush over to Mr. Sherlock's house to take care of business their own way.

64

Officer Erickson rolled up to Mr. Sherlock's house and found Chief Andrew's patrol car parked out front. Empty.

"He must be inside, talking with Mr. Sherlock," Officer Erickson said to himself. "Yeah, things must be fine. Chief must have his radio turned down and just can't hear us. Or maybe his replacement radio isn't working right?"

A dense fog had slowly moved in, as if to contradict Officer Erickson's positive thoughts. The post-rain humidity still lingered and left an uncomfortable stickiness in the air. He took another look inside the chief's car, to make sure he really wasn't in there, and walked to the front door. He rang the doorbell but nothing happened. Officer Erickson rang it repeatedly but still nothing. He tried pushing it very hard and then a bunch of times in a row, but it still didn't ring. He realized he could knock on the door before he started yelling out for Chief Andrews. Nervously, he pounded on the door so hard that it hurt his knuckles. This did no good, though. Neither Chief Andrews nor Mr. Sherlock answered the door. He looked around in disbelief, and then did what most officers do when no one answers the front door—he checked the side and the back. Before walking through the open fence gate, Officer Erickson heard whining coming from behind the fence in the woods. He crept along the side fence in the same manner as his chief, but with his gun still in the holster. When he turned the corner, there wasn't time to wish he had his gun out and ready. What he saw seemed surreal or fake. It was like a dream, but there was no waking up from this.

Chief Andrews was on the ground. Blood covered his hands and arms, and some was smeared on his face, too. Officer Erickson's eyes tried to focus while his brain tried to process the scene. The chief was moaning in apparent agony, or maybe he was grunting. Either way, the scene scared the heck out of Officer Erickson. He tried to see where the blood was coming from, and why the chief was on the ground. It would've been easier to simply open his mouth and ask, but he couldn't do it—his whole body was frozen in awe. Chief Andrews didn't see Officer Erickson and was still struggling around on the ground. Next to the chief was a four-legged animal that appeared to be a dog or a wolf—the source of the whining. Before he could tell what the animal was doing, something out of the corner of his eye caught his attention. He finally broke his trance when he saw Mr. Sherlock stalking toward Chief Andrews. He had a crowbar in his hand with the curved portion of it resting on his right shoulder. His face displayed determination and fear, which was enough to get Officer Erickson's hand and arm moving. He pulled out his gun quickly and smoothly, pointed it at Mr. Sherlock, and yelled in his deepest, darkest cop voice:

"*Stop right there and drop it! Drop it! Drop it or I'll shoot!*"

65

"Dad, what are we going to do?" Trevor asked over the roar of his father's truck engine.

"We're going to make him pay—that's what we're going to do."

Mr. Greene didn't take his eyes off the road—and certainly wasn't obeying the speed limit. If any Whispering Hollow officer had seen him driving like that, they would have pulled him over in a heartbeat for reckless driving. However, that consequence didn't deter Mr. Greene in the least. He wouldn't have stopped even if they turned on the blue lights and sirens and ordered him to pull over. Nothing was going to stop him now, least of all some cop. He was a madman on a mission, no matter who or what got in his way.

Fortunately, the streets were empty as Mr. Greene skidded around the turn toward Main Street while almost riding on two wheels. Believe it or not, Trevor looked scared, and with good reason.

66

Sergeant Frisk had the same feeling as Mr. Mooney—things were breaking bad.

"*People*!" he uncharacteristically yelled with some squealing feedback from the microphone. This snapped the gym into silence. "Let her finish, please."

Sergeant Frisk and Mr. Mooney cautiously felt relieved for the moment as Mystery stepped back to the microphone. People sat back down in their seats and returned their attention to Mystery. It was a miracle.

"Everyone, Soda and I thought what you guys do. We were convinced Mr. Sherlock was a werewolf." The silence got louder throughout the gym. "Soda, if you could show the shadow pictures again. I looked further at the picture data and realized something. There was a slight delay in the picture of Mr. Sherlock bending over and the one of the shadow-dog. This made me realize there was enough time for Mr. Sherlock to step out of the frame and the dog to take his place."

The crowd was silent.

Mr. Pumpernickel stood up and shouted without using the microphone, "But that doesn't really disprove anything, Mystery."

"No, not by itself, but it does allow for some doubt. Plus, there's more. Mr. Sherlock being seen near encounters doesn't prove he's a werewolf. After all, his dog, Goliath, does resemble a wolf and was apparently raised by wolves. This could explain the howling at least."

"But we've never had wolves here before he moved in!" came a voice with its owner concealed within the crowd.

"And what about the attack on the Greene boy?" someone else yelled.

Mystery looked a little flustered. Mr. Mooney almost stepped in, but she shook her head, gathered herself, looked out at her mom, and continued.

"No, we've never had wolves around here before, but Soda and I have researched how hurricanes in North Carolina have pushed wildlife farther inland, and this includes wolves. It's likely that Goliath's howling caught their attention and caused them to move in.

"As far as the attack on Trevor goes, there's no proof that it was a werewolf that attacked him.

"There's one other thing that makes me think Mr. Sherlock is not a werewolf. We found something quite interesting in his backyard."

Soda flashed the pictures Mystery had taken of the stilt-like poles on the big screen. It took people a few moments to realize what they were looking at as Soda scrolled through them.

"As you can see here, it appears that Mr. Sherlock made these things to make it appear that his footprints became wolf footprints.

They're basically footprint stamps. I was able to put my feet into them and walk around. So, it's likely that he went to an area he knew would leave his footprints and was carrying these things with him. As you can see, the bottom of each one has a wolf footprint, so after he made a few of his footprints, he slid his feet into these and continued walking, leading us to believe the transformation."

People couldn't believe it. Moments ago they had been *absolutely* convinced that Mr. Sherlock was a werewolf. Mystery's evidence had helped them reach that conclusion along with the rumors. Then, a child who had just finished the fifth grade overturned their view. She and Soda had debunked The Legend of Mr. Creepy.

Mr. and Mrs. Moustache smiled proudly. They couldn't have been prouder if it had been their own daughter up on stage. Mystery saw their smiles and looked over at her dad, who was also smiling proudly at her.

Mystery was happy, but now she needed to know why Mr. Sherlock wanted people to think he was a werewolf—and she meant to find out.

67

Officer Erickson kept his gun pointed at Mr. Sherlock, who slowly lowered the crowbar to the ground. Chief Andrews finally realized Erickson was there.

"Erickson, help me!"

"Chief, do you need a medic? You've got blood all over you." He turned back to Mr. Sherlock. "Turn around and get down on your knees," he ordered.

"Erickson," Chief said.

"Don't worry, Chief. I've got this guy."

"Erickson, I know what it must look like, but you're wrong. Put your gun away and help Mr. Sherlock get up." Officer Erickson was flabbergasted. He scowled and cocked his head to the side. "Now!" Chief barked.

This snapped Officer Erickson into motion, and he helped up the so-called werewolf. Mr. Sherlock picked up the crowbar again, and Chief Andrews saw the look on Officer Erickson's face.

"Relax, Eric," Chief said.

Mr. Sherlock walked over to Chief Andrews, squatted down, and jammed the crowbar into the animal trap, trying to force it open. Chief helped and they were able to free the giant dog. Mr. Sherlock fell to the ground with his pet and best friend, Goliath, who rolled around and licked his master's face. Goliath was injured and bleeding, but he'd survive. Officer Erickson realized the blood all over Chief had been from the dog and not from Mr. Sherlock beating him with a crowbar.

"Thank you so much for your help, Chief Andrews," Mr. Sherlock said with all the sincerity he could muster.

Chief Andrews reached out his bloody hand, and Mr. Sherlock shook it. "Glad I could help."

Mr. Sherlock held the grip and pulled himself up to his feet. Despite the pain in his back leg, Goliath did the same. The four of them walked out of the woods and around the side of Mr. Sherlock's house.

"Chief, Mr. Sherlock . . . I'm so sorry. I didn't realize . . ."

"It's okay, Officer; I'm just glad you didn't shoot me," Mr. Sherlock said, putting a comforting hand on Officer Erickson's right shoulder.

"Chief . . . I didn't know."

"It's fine, son. It worked out. You may have learned something, too."

They walked to the front porch.

"I guess I did learn something," Officer Erickson said with his head hung low. "Things aren't always what they seem."

He didn't know his lesson wasn't over.

Chief Andrews saw a white pickup truck parked crookedly in front of his patrol car. It looked like Tony Greene's truck. *But what would he be doing down here?* he thought. Then Mr. Greene answered that question.

"You've got a lot of nerve attacking my boy! Now you're going to pay, you animal!" Mr. Greene screamed. He had the bat in his hands and pulled back, ready to knock Mr. Sherlock's head out of the park.

68

Some people in the crowd were murmuring, wondering why Mr. Sherlock had the wolf-print stamps. Why would he want them to think he was a werewolf?

Sergeant Frisk, still up on stage, heard his radio click like someone was trying to say something, but nothing came . . . at first. No one *said* anything, and then Officer Erickson *screamed* something.

"Put it down! Don't make me shoot you!"

Sergeant Frisk looked over at Mr. Mooney. He could tell he heard it, too—it wasn't his imagination.

"Erickson, are you okay?" Sergeant Frisk asked, trying not to sound rattled.

"Mr. Greene is here, trying to kill Sherlock with a baseball bat," Chief Andrews shouted over the radio. In the background, they could hear Officer Erickson yelling at Mr. Greene—apparently, he wasn't obeying Erickson's commands.

Mystery and her dad heard all this and knew that Mr. Greene

was doing this because he thought Mr. Sherlock was a werewolf and had attacked Travis.

Sergeants Frisk and Major, and Officers Kent and Antley, all sprinted out of the gym to their patrol cars. Mr. Mooney almost instinctively did the same thing but caught himself before he did. Most of the crowd merely stared at the policemen with curiosity and concern as they ran out. They'd rarely seen this kind of thing in Whispering Hollow. A few people followed the officers out to their cars to see where the police were going and why.

"Folks, let's stay out of the way and let the police do their job. I have no doubt they'll be able to handle whatever it is, so let's just stay calm," the mayor said into the microphone.

"We need to go help!" Mr. Mooney said to Mystery. "C'mon!"

"To Mr. Sherlock's house?"

"Yeah, let's go!"

"Dad," Mystery started and put her hand on his. He froze and looked her in the eyes. "We need to go somewhere else first," she said. She was calm and determined as she told him her plan.

69

Mr. Mooney, Mystery, and Soda jumped into Silverstreak and tore out of the school parking lot, being careful not to hit anyone.

"Are you sure about this, Mys?" Soda asked her.

"Yep," she said, hoping she sounded surer than she actually felt.

Mr. Mooney turned right out of the school parking lot onto Ravenwood Drive and stopped at the stop sign. He turned right onto Weeping Willow Lane and then left onto Main Street, heading to where his daughter thought would help this deadly situation taking place at the suspected werewolf's house. It felt strange to Mr. Mooney to be driving away from that scene, but he trusted his daughter and pushed the strangeness aside.

70

Sirens filled the air as the rest of the Whispering Hollow Police Department drove to Mr. Sherlock's house as fast as they could. Mr. Greene either didn't hear them or didn't care, because he still stood there, filled with rage, holding the baseball bat. Mr. Sherlock was still with Goliath's leash in his hand. Goliath was barking and lunging at the man who was threatening his master. Mr. Sherlock thought about letting go of the leash, but as fast as Goliath was, he was hurt, and he thought Mr. Greene would crack his skull open before Goliath could get to him.

"Don't make me do this!" Officer Erickson yelled.

"Erickson, watch your background," Chief warned.

Officer Erickson's tunnel vision subsided and he did see a blurry figure behind Mr. Greene. He momentarily focused on it and was able to see it was Trevor.

"Okay, Chief, I see him," he said, and then shifted his focus back to Mr. Greene.

Officer Erickson had Mr. Greene very clearly in his gunsights.

Behind him and off to the left stood Trevor in awe and fear. The boy was only about fifteen feet away from Mr. Greene, and if Officer Erickson's shot wasn't perfect, he would risk hitting Trevor.

"Trevor! Move!" Officer Erickson screamed.

Trevor was in shock. He couldn't move. He had thought this was going to be exciting, but he didn't realize this would happen. Now there was a chance the cops would have to shoot his dad.

"Tony . . . Tony . . . *Tony*!" Chief Andrews tried to get his attention.

Mr. Greene stood there in an angry trance. He didn't, however, progress in his attack on Mr. Sherlock. Chief yelled his name again. Mr. Greene snapped out of the trance for a moment and looked at Chief Andrews.

"Tony, please don't make us shoot you . . . or worse," Chief pleaded.

The sirens got louder as backup arrived. The police cars skidded to a stop in front of them. The sirens faded away, but the blue lights still flickered. The smell of hot engines and hot brakes wafted through the air. Even though it was daylight, the hanging fog reflected the blue lights, creating a weird light show with the bright strobe lights.

"Chief, he attacked my boy . . . and for what? Because he was there when some eggs were thrown at his house? That's ridiculous! And he's not gonna get away with it!" Mr. Greene's voice was fierce, and he was breathing so heavily his whole body moved with each breath.

It looked like Mr. Sherlock wanted to say something, maybe defend himself or confirm he didn't change into a werewolf and attack Travis. He couldn't open his mouth, though. He couldn't do anything other than stand there and hope this enraged father didn't smash a bat across his face. He hoped and prayed the police could diffuse this situation quickly.

The rest of the police force secured the scene and directed the gathering crowd away from the area and across the street—luckily for them, they could still hear and see everything going on.

Sergeant Frisk motioned for Trevor to come to him, and surprisingly, he listened. Officer Kent pulled out his baton, which was almost like a bat, and held it ready with his eyes locked on Mr. Greene. Since his partners had their guns on him, he wanted to have an option where no one got shot. He'd have to move quickly before Mr. Greene could strike Mr. Sherlock—it seemed almost impossible. Sears, Antley, and Major kept the arriving Whispering Hollow residents from getting too close. Among those people were Mrs. Mooney and Mrs. Slooth. They were trying to drive home, but the street had been blocked by onlookers, cars, and trucks. The two mothers stayed back at a safe distance where they still could see the commotion. It seemed like half the town was there now.

Just down the road, Mr. Butler drove up in a black Lincoln Town Car. He pulled over to the side, stepped out, and opened the door for the Moustaches. They strolled toward the scene, with Mrs. Moustache hanging on her husband's left arm, in no particular hurry, and made their way to the front of the curious crowd.

"Tony, whether or not this man turned into a werewolf and attacked your boy or whether he didn't, this *isn't* the way to handle it," Chief explained as he put his gun back in the holster. The chief's voice was calm and quiet, which somehow demanded more attention than if he were yelling.

Mr. Greene stood there with the bat now resting on his shoulder—an improvement from having it ready to strike. It looked like the chief might be getting through to him; however, Officer Erickson kept his gun pointed at him.

"Are you really gonna shoot me with a bat in my hands? I'm not holding a gun, Chief," Mr. Greene explained as his breathing slowed a little.

"No, you're not holding a gun, but that bat is a deadly weapon. If you get a good hit on Mr. Sherlock, you could seriously hurt him or even kill him. And I wouldn't want you striking one of my officers while trying to get at Sherlock. Either way, we can't allow this. It's our job to protect people."

"Well, you didn't protect Travis from this . . . from this . . . this *animal*!" Mr. Greene said and pointed at Mr. Sherlock. His breathing picked back up again.

"Tony, we don't know that."

"It was a man taking revenge on a young boy! My boy!" His voice was shaky and scary.

The situation remained unpredictable. Nearly everyone from the meeting was now an audience to a possible deadly situation.

"Tony, we can work through this with no one else getting hurt. All I need you to do is—"

"Chief, someone *is* going to get hurt! *That's* why I came down here!"

Silverstreak came rolling down Nighthawk Avenue with Mr. Mooney behind the wheel, Mystery in the front seat, Soda behind her, and one other person in the back. Mr. Mooney maneuvered around the vehicles that were scattered in the road. Officer Erickson saw this movement beyond Mr. Greene, but he remained focused on his target. Mr. Greene didn't seem to realize Mr. Mooney's truck was approaching. Chief Andrews wondered what Mr. Mooney was doing.

"Tony, if you could just—"

"Stop saying my name, Chief! He's gonna pay for what he did!"

All the progress they had made calming down Mr. Greene was now gone. He was as riled up as when he first got there. Maybe it was Chief saying his name over and over; maybe it was the foggy, dreary weather; or maybe there was just too much rage in the first place for it to go away without some sort of release.

Mr. Greene slowly raised the bat off his shoulder and reared back with his eyes targeted and locked on Mr. Sherlock's head.

Officer Kent tightened his grip on his baton. Officer Erickson slid his finger onto the trigger, ready to squeeze it. One of them was going to have to do something.

71

The crowd watched and held their breath. Before Mr. Greene could swing the bat and before Officer Kent or Erickson could retaliate, a voice behind them stopped everything.

"Dad, please stop," said the young and strangely calm voice.

Mr. Greene felt all his rage and anger slip away like a spirit leaving a dead body. He recognized the voice immediately and fell to his knees dropping the bat. It landed on the sidewalk and rolled into the grass.

Officer Erickson moved his finger off the trigger. He knew it'd only take a second for Mr. Greene to pick the bat up and swing, so he kept the gun pointed at him. *Better safe than sorry,* he thought.

Mr. Greene turned around and saw Travis standing there all bandaged up. He looked like an exhausted mummy. His legs were unsteady, and his pain medicine made him lightheaded as well. Mystery and Soda were nearly holding him up. All three of them were out of the line of fire but close enough that Travis didn't have to yell—Mr. Mooney made sure they were safe.

"It wasn't him. Mystery and Soda told me about what they found out, and they told everyone at the meeting. Mr. Sherlock is not a werewolf," Travis explained with a sandpaper voice.

Mr. Greene got back on his feet, walked over and gave him a delicate hug. "I'm sorry, son. You shouldn't be out here. You should be home, resting," he said as he cupped his son's chin.

"Thanks for sticking up for me, Dad, but I'll be okay," Travis said.

Embarrassment, coupled with sadness, set in on Mr. Greene. He was ashamed that it took his hurt son to snap him out of a fit of rage. His son, who was the *victim* of the attack, showed him how to be a man.

"Good idea, my little muffin," Mr. Mooney said to Mystery. "Very good indeed."

"Well, I just know what a sucker Mr. Greene is for his little boy. I'm just glad you got us here in time," she said back to her dad.

Officer Erickson holstered his gun as the sweat finally poured down his forehead. Mr. Sherlock collapsed to the ground in relief, and Chief Andrews joined him; Goliath licked both their faces. There was a collective sigh of relief from the crowd and the officers. Mrs. Mooney and Mrs. Slooth walked up to their family members and hugged them all.

"Next time, you let me know where you guys are going!" Mrs. Mooney ordered. "I knew you were going to help, but still, I was scared!"

"Same goes for you, mister," Mrs. Slooth said to Soda.

Officer Erickson walked over to Mr. Greene. "I'm sorry, sir, but I still have to place you under arrest. I hope you understand. Sorry, kid."

Everyone, including Officer Erickson, was afraid this might reignite the situation, but Mr. Greene immediately turned around and put his hands behind his back.

"I understand," Mr. Green replied with his head hung low.

Officer Erickson handcuffed him and walked him through the crowd to his patrol car. Mr. Greene apologized several times to his neighbors during the walk. Officer Erickson put him in the back of his car and gently shut the door.

The Mooneys and Slooths walked over to Chief Andrews, Mr. Sherlock, and Goliath. Some of the rest of the crowd, including the Moustaches, nearly encircled them.

"That was some sharp thinking, Miss Mystery," Chief Andrews said.

"Thanks, Chief. I'm just glad everyone is okay."

"Well, anyways, Mr. Sherlock, I came here to tell you about a meeting we were having tonight at the school, but it looks like that meeting is over," the chief said.

"What was the meeting about?" Mr. Sherlock asked.

"Well, it was about the nine p.m. curfew we were instating and telling folks not to leave their kids unsupervised due to the recent wolf attack." Chief hesitated for a moment.

"Is that so? Is that all?" Mr. Sherlock asked with a grin.

"Well, now that you mention it," Chief Andrews said, chuckling under his breath, "there was some talk about you possibly being a werewolf and responsible for the attack."

Everyone wondered how Mr. Sherlock was going to react to this news, and all eyes went to him.

Sergeant Frisk walked over to them. "That's right. For a bit there, I think everyone was convinced you *were* a werewolf. Mystery and Soda here showed everyone the results of their investigation. At first, it appeared you really were, then logic prevailed, and I think the footprint-maker-stamp-thingy sealed the deal."

"Oh, you found that, did you?" Mr. Sherlock asked, looking at Mystery and Soda.

"Yes, sir," Soda said.

"Sorry, we were snooping around . . . again," Mystery added.

Mr. Sherlock no longer seemed like a monster or a mean old man. He looked like a nice man who had been misunderstood.

"It's okay. I understand."

"You mean you're not mad?"

"Not at all. Unbelievably, I was once young, too. It's an old toy. I only wish I had been at the meeting to see how your investigation played out."

"Mr. Sherlock, why did you want everyone to think you were a werewolf?"

Mr. Sherlock sighed and slowly stood up along with Chief Andrews.

"Well, it's complicated, but to summarize, I've recently been through some rough times. My parents, who own this house, recently passed away; then, shortly after that, my wife did, too. When the Johnsons moved out, I wanted to move back in, hoping the nostalgia would help me feel better."

"Back in? Nostalgia?" Mr. Mooney asked.

"Yes, I grew up here back in the day. I wanted the comfort and memories of this house, but I didn't want to get to know people or get close to them. I needed some time to mourn and was just a grumpy old man who wasn't sleeping well. When I took Goliath out for walks, I went along the wood line or into the woods so I wouldn't have to talk to anyone. I figured if there was a creepy rumor about a werewolf, people would leave me alone. It's silly, I know, but I wasn't thinking straight. I just knew if they asked how I was, I'd either be a total jerk or I might break down and cry. No one wants to see a crusty old fella's eyes watering."

Mr. Sherlock looked more human than ever. What had once

been fear and intrigue was now care and concern, maybe even pity, for the gloomy old man.

"So, you really did get bitten between the fight with Sheena and Goliath?" Soda asked.

"Yep, it hurt, too. I'm not *exactly* sure who bit me. I'm not even sure it wasn't a wolf. It was dark, and I couldn't see very well. I had just let Goliath out to go to the bathroom before bed when it all happened."

"What about when you came out of the woods at the barbeque?" Mystery asked.

"Well, some kids were throwing eggs at my house, and when I opened the front door to yell at them, Goliath bolted after them. Before he got out of my yard, he heard something from out in the woods and immediately forgot about the kids. I only saw one of them riding a bright neon-green bike."

"That was me, sorry to say," Travis admitted. "I didn't throw any eggs, sir; I was just there."

"I appreciate your honesty, young sir. So, I went into the woods after Goliath, since he didn't have a leash. While we were out there, I heard more howling and the gunshot, got scared, and fell forward and was walking on all fours when I came out from the woods behind the barbeque. I can imagine how it looked."

"I can tell you how it looked! It looked like you were a wolf," Mr. Mooney said. "That, combined with the legend of you being one, was quite compelling. I even had the local police department in Virginia look into you. Mind if I ask about what happened up there?"

"I'm not really sure all you've heard, but it was pretty simple. I was gardening in the backyard and cut my hand with a razor blade while opening a bag of potting soil. Goliath came running over to check on me, then ran off, like he was going to get help or something. My neighbor came over, and I guess he called for help, but I had already gone inside. I called a friend to drive me to the hospital since my wife was at work."

"He seemed to think you'd been bitten—said he checked your pulse and you didn't have one. He said you somehow walked into the woods and came back a week later."

"Hmm, well, I assure you I've always had a pulse, and I *was* gone for about a week. My wife and I went to her parents' house for a quick vacation. Her mother was having a difficult time so we went to help. Old people helping older people—it was quite a sight."

"Your neighbor thought you walked back out of the woods behind your house after the week."

Mr. Sherlock thought for a moment. "I'm not sure where that came from. Sounds like maybe he was looking for attention or something. Tom Murphy was always sort of a strange guy and a weird neighbor. We never really got along, he and I."

Mystery and Soda looked at each other, feeling the irony in that statement.

"I surely didn't spend a week in the woods healing from a dog bite. I guess that's how legends get started. You can't believe everything you hear, obviously."

"No, no you can't," Mr. Mooney agreed.

"For sure!" Soda added.

"Mr. Sherlock, there is one other thing I wanted to ask you about, if you don't mind."

"Shoot. Or should I say, go ahead."

"Why didn't you take the brownies my wife made for you?"

"Oh, yeah, I'm sorry about that. I really appreciate the gesture, but I'm allergic to chocolate. I should've accepted them and not eaten them, I guess. It wouldn't have been as rude."

Mr. Mooney, Mystery, and Soda laughed.

"Well, that makes sense. We thought it was *silver* causing the issue; we noticed you had a gold wedding band, not that that's strange."

"No, I assure you. It's the chocolate."

After another chuckle, Mr. Pumpernickel walked up to them dragging Darren behind him.

"Mr. Sherlock, my son and I just wanted to apologize for adding to all of this craziness. I thought my source was reliable."

"Yeah," Darren added.

"No apology necessary. After all, I contributed," Mr. Sherlock said and shook Mr. Pumpernickel's hand.

"I'd also like to apologize to you, Mystery. I should never have put you on the spot like that in front of everyone. Please forgive me."

"No problem, Mr. Pumpernickel," Mystery said, also shaking his hand.

The mood lifted along with most of the fog. It looked as though things were clearing up. The excitement made everyone forget about something.

72

"Thanks again for helping me get Goliath out of that trap, Chief Andrews," Mr. Sherlock said. "I've got to get him to the vet."

"My pleasure. But that reminds me—we need to reset that trap and check the other ones. We still have a wolf issue at hand that needs to be dealt with."

This realization turned everyone's attention back to why they had the meeting in the first place.

Chief Andrews turned to the crowd, wishing he had a megaphone. "People, we need to head out and keep the curfew in effect until we figure this out. We'll check the traps after we clear this scene, so your cooperation will help us out significantly."

Most people listened and walked back to their cars or to their homes muttering about what had just happened, and not wanting to be the next wolf-attack victim. The Mooneys returned an exhausted Travis to his home.

"Thanks, you guys. If it hadn't been for you, my dad might have been killed tonight."

"You're the one who stopped him, buddy," Soda said.

"Only because of you guys," he moaned. "I should go lie down. I'm worn out."

Mrs. Greene had stayed home, waiting at the front door the entire time—too scared to see what her husband was going to do.

Mr. Mooney helped Travis to the front door, where he handed him off to his mom.

"Hey, Dawn. I'm sorry to tell you this but they arrested Tony. Luckily, they didn't shoot him."

"Thank you for telling me, Matt." Mrs. Greene was grateful everyone was okay and a little glad her husband had been arrested. She hoped it was a wake-up call for him. "I'd better get Travis situated. Good night." She went inside and closed the door.

Mr. Mooney, Mystery, and Soda got back into Silverstreak and headed home, where they joined the moms in the kitchen.

Over the next several hours, the members of the Whispering Hollow Police Department were assisted by the Union County Sheriff's Animal Control Unit and removed two wolves from the traps they'd set. They were confident the rest of the pack, if any were left, would move on. The chief wanted the traps set out again, a little deeper this time into Whispering Woods. He hoped this would prevent anyone from stumbling upon them, like Goliath did.

It seemed the crazy wolf weekend was coming to a close. Travis Greene was home and recovering from his injuries, while his dad was in jail, but alive. Mystery and Soda sat down on the living room floor to count the candy-sale money. They hadn't told Travis about the fundraiser since they didn't know if they'd made enough and didn't want to disappoint him if not.

"Well, I guess we can file this case away as 'closed' on The Legend of Mr. Creepy, huh, Mys?" Soda said.

"I guess so," Mystery said with a look in her eye.

"What? What is it?"

"I've been thinking about everything Mr. Sherlock said. It all seemed very deliberate, almost rehearsed."

"You think he's lying?"

"It just seems too much of a coincidence that he shows up at the same time a pack of wolves moves in. I think we'd better keep an eye on him . . . especially during full moons."

"For sure."

"I wonder if his last name was Surewolf rather than Sherlock?"

Soda smiled. They finished counting the money.

"This is awesome!" Soda jumped up and yelled.

"Did you guys raise enough?" Mrs. Slooth asked from the kitchen.

"We sure did!" Mystery exclaimed.

"More than enough, actually!" Soda said. "We'll be able to get him an awesome new mitt and batting gloves, too!"

"I'm very proud of y'all. Now, how about some dinner?" Mrs. Mooney asked.

"Yeah!" Mystery and Soda said together.

They cleared the table, and the moms starting getting things together for dinner when the doorbell rang; they all looked at each other. Now what?!

"I'll get it," Mr. Mooney said.

Mystery and Soda curiously followed. Mr. Mooney opened the door and saw the giant, Franklin Butler, standing on the porch.

"Sir, Mr. Moustache would like to speak to Miss Mystery and Master Soda, if that's possible."

"Sure, they're both right here."

Mystery and Soda walked in front of Mr. Mooney as Mr. Moustache stepped up to the door.

"Mystery and Soda, we've had an incident at Moustache Manor, and my lovely wife and I wondered if you could help?"

They looked at each other, smiled, and then looked at Mr. Moustache.

"Mystery and Soda are on the case," Mystery said.

73

Mr. Sherlock sat at his dining room table, petting Goliath, as his clock rang out twelve times. He had a relieved smile on his face.

"Well, boy, it's been a crazy few days here at our old, new home. I think we're going to like it here, though. I know you're still hurt, but do you want to go for a midnight walk?"

Goliath slowly got up and hobbled to the front door. Mr. Sherlock followed, put Goliath's leash on, and walked outside. Rather than walking up the sidewalk, Goliath smelled, or sensed something, and pulled his master out to Whispering Woods.

"What is it, boy?"

Goliath, despite his injury and bandage, pulled Mr. Sherlock about twenty yards into the woods and let out one of his wolflike howls. Clouds blocked the full moon above. There was some slow rustling from a little deeper in the woods, and it sounded like it was coming from all around them. Mr. Sherlock carefully tied Goliath's leash around a tree as the rustling got closer. Goliath was now growling and snapping his jaws.

"I just knew those kids would find the stilts in the backyard. I suspected it would seal the deal. It's good to see they don't just believe what they hear and figured out my ruse. The wolf that attacked the boy almost got me beat with a baseball bat."

Several shadows appeared within the trees, and each one had two glowing eyes. They had surrounded Mr. Sherlock and Goliath. Goliath went wild, howling and barking. The shadows were now visible and they joined Goliath in howling. This did not look good. How fitting would it be that the man thought to be a werewolf was going to be attacked by a pack of wolves near his own house?

"It appears they're looking for someone, Goliath. Maybe their alpha?" Mr. Sherlock's voice was quiet and calm. He should've been more scared than he was.

The clouds moved on, and the full moon beamed as bright as ever. Some light managed to find its way through the trees and shone on Mr. Sherlock. He smiled and embraced it.

The pack of wolves encircled them, ready to swarm.

"Stay here, boy. I'll be back."

Mr. Sherlock turned away from his beloved pet, absorbed the moonlight, and let it happen. He put his arms out to his sides and leaned his head back. His pale white skin became tough and covered with grayish-brown fur. He fell forward onto his hands, and his feet became paws. His fingernails became claws. His mouth became a snout and his teeth sharpened. A tail formed on his back end. He barely made a sound. It looked like a violent change; however, Mr. Sherlock didn't groan at all.

The pack of wolves stopped their advance to watch. They were silent, along with Goliath, and tilted their heads slightly.

When the transformation was complete, Mr. Sherlock let out an alpha howl that filled Whispering Woods. The pack joined in with fierce approval and excitement. Mr. Sherlock turned his wolf-head back at Goliath. Their eyes met for a moment; then the werewolf darted into the woods. The pack followed as the howls slowly faded deep into the dark woods beyond Whispering Hollow.

THE END

About the Author

Chad Webster grew up in New York and began his love of writing in grade school. After moving to Charlotte, NC, he began his police career, which inspired his work on the Mystery Muffin & Soda Pop Slooth series. He loves people and admires how they strive for the best even in the worst situations while on the job. Chad is a husband, son, brother, and father of four.

He is currently working on another installment of the Mystery Muffin & Soda Pop Slooth series, among ther writing projects.

Learn more about Chad on his website and follow him on Twitter @authorwebster and Instagram @Chadawebsterauthor.

CPSIA information can be obtained
at www.ICGtesting.com
Printed in the USA
BVOW06s0221170817
492329BV00006B/37/P

9 780998 165912